RAVENA GURON is a British Indian biochemist turned lawyer turned MG author, a superb new voice who brings her own captivating brand of energy, wild adventures and joy to the genre. *The Thief of Farrowfell* is the first in the series following Jude Ripon, and was shortlisted for Penguin's WriteNow scheme, as well as being highly commended in the FAB Prize. Ravena also writes YA, including the acclaimed *This Book Kills*. Ravena is a Londoner through and through: born, raised and educated in London, she lives there still.

ALESSIA TRUNFIO was born in southern Italy but grew up in Rome, where she still lives. After graduating with an Animation Degree from the International School of Comics in Rome, Alessia has worked as background artist for some of the most important animation studios in Italy. Fundamentally passionate about cinema, anime, literature, indie music and fried food, Alessia is an eclectic, energetic and inexhaustible illustrator.

To Matt and Alice, Farrowfell's first readers.

First published in the UK in 2023
by Faber & Faber Limited
The Bindery, 51 Hatton Garden
London, EC1N 8HN
faber.co.uk

Typeset in Garamond by MRules
Printed by CPI Group (UK) Ltd, Croydon CR0 4YY

A CIP record for this book is available from the British Library

ISBN 978–0–571–37117–4

MIX
Paper | Supporting
responsible forestry
FSC® C171272

Printed and bound in the UK on FSC paper in line with our continuing
commitment to ethical business practices, sustainability and the environment.
For further information see faber.co.uk/environmental–policy

2 4 6 8 10 9 7 5 3 1

THE THIEF OF FARROWFELL

RAVENA GURON
ILLUSTRATED BY ALESSIA TRUNFIO

THE THIEF OF FARROWFELL

faber

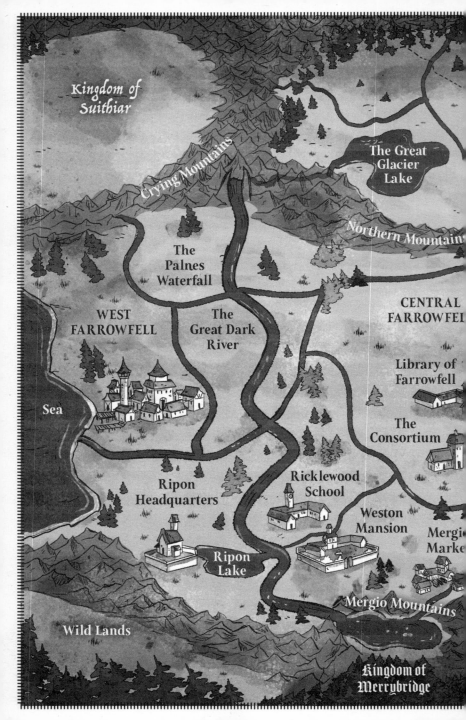

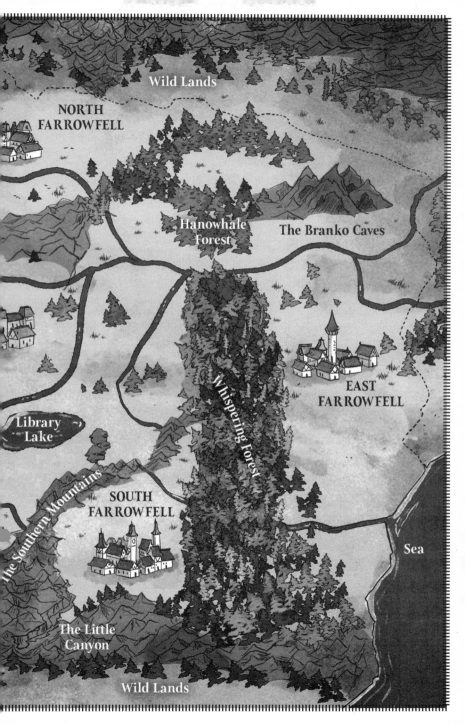

Chapter One

The Weston Mansion

Jude Ripon loved stealing.

Not just magic, or money, or diamonds and gold, though they were all fun things to pinch. She liked the quiet moments when she snuck through mansions of the rich, her footsteps muffled by thick, plush carpets. The stolen seconds of living someone else's life.

She'd never been allowed to steal on her own, and on the rare occasions her family took her on business she was normally given a lookout role, miles away from the action. Only in the lowest priority houses was she ever allowed the thrill of slipping along and swiping treasures, supervised by her snappy old aunts. Real, important jobs were given to the adults of her family who had proven themselves to the Ripon criminal empire many times. The only exception was Jude's sister Moorley, who was just three years older than Jude but got to go on all kinds of adventures. She didn't even *want* to. It was completely unfair.

No one took Jude seriously – at twelve years old she was apparently too young to do anything important. But that would change once she returned home from the Weston mansion with rare magic stolen from one of the most powerful families in Farrowfell. Rare magic the Ripons could sell on the black market.

They would *have* to take her seriously then.

The thick stone walls that marked the boundaries of the Westons' grounds towered over her. A lesser thief might have tried scaling the walls, or else wrestled with the cast-iron gate. Jude, however, was prepared. She reached into her pocket, feeling for the squelchy ghost magic she had stolen from Moorley. It was shaped like a raindrop of emerald crystal. She popped it in her mouth and tried not to gag; it tasted like feet.

The moment she swallowed, her body forgot it was supposed to be solid. As she passed through the stone wall the world went dark. All the breath was squeezed out of her lungs and an icy feeling spread through her.

Her senses returned to normal once she made it to the other side and she grinned, hurrying across the muddy lawn towards the enormous glowing white mansion.

She pulled out a second piece of magic, pinched from her father; a gritty, sand-like mixture, which would turn her invisible. Ghost and invisibility magic, though illegal, were two tools any decent thief needed, and she had got used to helping herself to her father's stash. If he didn't want anyone to snaffle little bits here and there he should have hidden it somewhere more secure than a safe with his own birthday as the passcode.

Jude crammed the invisibility magic into her mouth, wishing she had some orange juice to wash away the bitter taste. She tried to gag quietly – the magic had been made cheaply so she could still be heard. She could also be smelled, an issue because the water at home wasn't working properly. Aunt Victi kept telling everyone that *real* homeowners fixed their own pipes, so the problem wouldn't be sorted until Spry, Jude's cousin, who had a knack for practical work, turned his attention from building flying carriages to figuring out the plumbing.

Now that Jude was a proper (noisy and smelly) ghost, she strode confidently through the front door. No one would see the skinny kid with frizzy black hair and golden-brown skin entering their home.

She found herself standing in an entrance hall with a shiny white marble floor. Pillars reached up to the dome-like ceiling, painted with fluffy clouds tinged pink to resemble a morning sky. Before her was a wide staircase, which she began to climb.

There were numerous hallways, all with plump couches every few metres, as if the Westons couldn't walk ten seconds without needing to sit down. Jude kept pausing, unable to stop gawking at all the treasures: the expensive artwork, the gold candlestick holders, the precious silver. Her family, under Aunt Morgol's beady eye, didn't waste money on shiny things.

As she went, Jude could already imagine Grandleader's proud face, her mother's smile – and Moorley's envy – when they saw what she'd stolen. The last image especially spurred her on.

Moorley was the reason she'd never been allowed on a real heist before.

Around two years ago, Jude had taken to listening at doors in Ripon Headquarters, because she'd started to realise that her family's most interesting conversations happened when she wasn't around. One day, she'd heard Grandleader telling Moorley how marvellously she had done after *her* first proper heist. He was thinking of giving Jude a proper role on the next one.

Jude's heart had swelled with excitement. This was it – she was finally going to be one of the family rather than the youngest who couldn't do anything.

Moorley's reply still stung to this day. 'No,' she said. 'Jude will just mess things up. She'll never be a true Ripon.'

And Grandleader had listened. Jude wasn't invited

on the important heist and she continued to exist on the fringes of family conversations, never properly let in. Her already lukewarm relationship with her too-serious, too-perfect sister got so cold it turned to ice.

Now, in a few short hours, she would prove Moorley wrong when she burst through the doors of Ripon Headquarters with the rare magic she had come here to steal: decision-making magic.

A low-level criminal called Farlow Higgins had told her of a rumour that the Westons were keeping the magic in their home. Jude knew at once her family would make a huge profit on selling it. Just a small bite of decision-making magic could help someone plot all the possible outcomes from their choices, ensuring they picked the best one. To make it, a person needed to mix large amounts of raw magic with ingredients like the milk from a three-eyed goat, or a perfectly square rock – things almost impossible to find.

A door slammed somewhere in the depths of the house and she jumped, her focus breaking for a second. Was there someone around?

Her arm started to drift apart, disappearing like wisps of smoke as the ghost magic took advantage of her lapse in concentration. Taking a few deep breaths to calm herself she curled her fingers into fists, forcing her arm back together. She continued on her way, cursing herself. Moorley probably never almost floated away when *she* used ghost magic.

Jude made good progress until she came to a fork in the corridor. Was it left or right?

Stepping inside an alcove, she took out the map of the Weston mansion given to her by Farlow Higgins. He wouldn't say how he'd got it, but he had a knack for stealing all sorts of items. Once she was certain of the right direction, she set off again.

A floorboard squeaked underneath her boot and a door nearby opened by itself, like the house was responding to the sound. Now every other floorboard she stepped on groaned, the noise getting louder each time. The house seemed to come alive; the curtains fluttered at the windows and drawers rattled in their tables.

Jude quickened her pace, almost jogging as she rounded a corner and reached a large vaulted door with a cast-iron knob in the centre. She had arrived at her destination.

She grinned as the ghost magic allowed her to glide through.

The room on the other side was half lit with a faded golden glow and empty of furniture, apart from a raised platform in the centre. On the platform a set of display cabinets stood. Much of the space was in shadows.

Jude's heartbeat quickened. She was metres away from items of magic more valuable than anything she'd ever seen. Her breath caught. In the middle cabinet, on a plump violet cushion resting on a small stand, was a butter-yellow stone. It was barely the size of her fist.

'Yes!' she whispered as she reached out, expecting her fingers to pass straight through the glass of the cabinet. Instead there was a low buzzing, like an angry bee, and a force pushed her hand back. No matter what angle she came at the cabinet, something in the glass battled her. She tried climbing on to it, elbowing it and even kicking it. Nothing worked.

As a last option she tried a running leap to take the glass by surprise. But the force from the cabinet pushed her upwards and she sailed through the air, landing with a thump on the other side of the room. A shooting pain spread through her backside.

'Ow,' she said, wincing as she got to her feet.

The cabinet was warding her off. All tamed magic needed to be activated by something – was her ghost magic reacting with magic in the cabinet? If so, maybe all she needed to do was turn her magic off.

She squeezed her eyes shut, focusing on her fingers and toes, and imagined her body coming together again. A tingling feeling spread across her chest, and pins and needles pricked across her legs. With a soft *pop* she was solid and visible once more.

Jude ran her fingers over the glass, its temperature at least ten degrees cooler than the rest of the room. Her guess about removing her magic had been right.

As she examined the cabinet, a shiver ran down her back.

She was being watched.

Quickly, she spun around—

Nothing.

She was alone in the darkened room. Of *course* she was alone. She wouldn't get caught. Thieving was in her blood.

A floorboard creaked behind her.

At once she dug into her pocket and whipped out her magic yo-yo, squinting into the shadows. Could there be someone else here, using invisibility magic? Surely not – only well-connected criminals had access to it, and it would be too much of a coincidence for someone else to decide to make a steal at the same time she had. No, this was an old house – most likely the floorboard had creaked on its own.

She turned back to the cabinet, thinking. Grandleader had managed to start the Ripon empire with nothing but his wits. Solving this problem would show she was a Ripon through and through.

With a huff she rested against the cabinet – and found herself falling. She knocked into the stand, which fell in a crash that seemed to ring on and on. As she regained her balance, she twisted around to see what had happened.

The glass of the cabinet had disappeared.

'What in the stars?' Jude muttered. What was going on? Was this a trap?

The decision-making magic had rolled away and now lay on its side.

It shouldn't be this easy. Something was wrong.

But the magic was right there in front of her – and she had come all this way. Desperate longing clawed through her, for Grandleader to smile with goodwill, for her mother to tell her she was as good as Moorley. It pushed away all other fears and doubts.

Without a second's more hesitation, Jude picked up the magic. It was heavy for something so small.

Several things happened at once. A spiral of golden light shone from the centre of the stone, flowing around her. And a howling alarm clanged, ringing in the air.

The door to the room scraped open and horror rooted her to the spot. She'd been caught.

Chapter Two

The Magic-Keeper

Jude clutched the magic as three short, robed figures entered the room. They had golden outlines for faces, as if drawn by a child who had never got around to colouring in the details. Their hands, the only other part of them visible under their sparkling purple robes, had the same golden outline. Each figure clutched a longsword which, unlike the rest of them, looked all too solid, glittering with a green hue.

They were helplings, servants made of magic. Helplings were difficult to make, needing lots of ingredients to be mixed with the raw magic, and only activated after being struck by lightning. Almost every family in Farrowfell had at least one. Judging by how naturally these helplings held their swords, they must have been guards.

The helplings lined up in a row, blocking the exit.

'You have broken in,' said the one in the middle, its voice low and gravelly. Jude yelped. She'd never come across helplings that could speak before. Normally guard helplings attacked straight away and the only escape was to run. Could she possibly bargain with them? She banished the thought as quickly as it arrived. Helplings were made for a single purpose, until the day their magic faded into nothing.

'How's it going?' she said cheerfully, feeling in her pocket for her yo-yo. She needed to keep her movements slow so the helplings wouldn't notice. Her hand brushed the prickly surface of a stink bomb. There would be no point using that: she didn't even know if helplings could smell. 'Lovely home you guard here.'

As if responding to her voice, the golden glow of the room got brighter, shining on her like the rays of the sun. Her eyes watered at the sudden light.

The helplings still made no move to attack and Jude wondered what they were waiting for.

'You stole,' said the middle helpling.

'Technically, it's only stolen once I leave this house.' On the last word, Jude's yo-yo let off a high-pitched squeal as it shot through the air towards the helplings.

They clutched their ears, their movements jerky. Jude had trained herself to ignore the squealing, though the noise still set her teeth on edge.

The yo-yo flew back to her, the ringing continuing, though it wouldn't last long once the magic bouncing around inside was still. She crashed past the helpings, still grasping her stolen magic as she sprinted through the doorway and into the corridor. Excitement raced through her like fire, burning away any fears. A good thief was always ready for a chase.

Pulsing arrows of light shone on the walls. Once the distraction was over, the helplings would scramble to find her, the arrows leading them straight to her – but they would have to catch her first. She picked turns in the maze of corridors at random, wishing she'd paid more attention to where she was going on the way in.

The golden glow turned red and steam uncurled from the floor. There was a whistling, like a kettle boiling, only much, much louder. The magic in the walls of the Weston mansion would do its best to make sure she did not escape. When Jude tried to wrench open a door it remained firmly shut.

'Come on, you stupid house, let me out.' She threw her weight against the door but the house ignored her, the red shining a more vibrant shade of scarlet as though it was saying, *Ha, I'm not letting you go that easily.*

She gave up, picked another corridor, rounded a corner and came to a clattering halt. The helpings were in front of her, silently holding up their swords.

'Funny running into you again,' she said, backing away.

'You stole,' said the middle one.

'I thought we'd agreed I've done no such thing!' This time the helplings were ready for her yo-yo, sticking their fingers in their ears. Jude grinned, swinging the yo-yo low instead. It rolled across the ground, twisting around the ankles of one of the helplings. She yanked and the creature crashed to the ground, toppling into the other two.

She skirted around them, laughing, and burst into the grand entrance hall. Her footsteps echoed as she sprinted across the wide-open space to the front door.

Locked. Of course.

The house was determined to keep her.

Jude gasped for breath. She had eaten the last of her ghost magic when she'd entered the mansion, but she wouldn't be defeated by a locked door. Her own home had magic built into the walls and she knew there were ways around it. Magic houses were proud, vain creatures.

Gritting her teeth, she slashed a giant Y into the door's intricate carvings. She would whittle into the wood with her pocketknife, ruining the house until it let her out. The door creaked and groaned, but she kept going on to the next letter, an O. 'I'm writing, *you suck*, just so you know,' she called out. The door shuddered as she dug the carving knife deeper into the wood.

Finally, the front door swung open, the house giving in to her threats, and Jude fell out on to the front lawn, which was only half visible in the dusk. Her cheeks hurt from grinning. *This* was what she loved. The thrill of the steal, of the chase, the risk. This was what she was good at.

***

The Weston mansion was located at the bottom of a valley through which a river of black liquid flowed. At the far side of the valley the Westons had their own private port, which Jude headed towards. The port was a towering purple archway. Entering it would magically and instantly transport her to another linked port in Farrowfell. Ports were a brilliant invention – each was linked to multiple other ports, and all you had to do was make sure you knew which one you wanted to end up at. But they had a few drawbacks – because Farrowfell's port system had been built over many years, with port connections added for convenience rather than what made logical sense, it was sometimes impossible to travel between ports only a few miles from each other if they weren't a connected route.

As Jude strode up to enter the port, a woman sprang out of nowhere. She wore black robes, her silky blonde hair tied into a neat bun on the top of her head, and had a mask of feathers on her face.

'Hello, Judiper,' said the woman, blocking Jude's exit. 'You shouldn't have stolen that magic.'

Jude stared at the woman – she'd thought that, apart from helplings, the Weston mansion was empty. If she'd known otherwise, she never would have attempted her steal. 'What magic?' she said, jutting out her chin. 'And how d'you know my name?' She hoped the questions would buy her a bit of time to figure out how to get away. If she reached for her yo-yo too quickly the woman would probably attack.

'I know lots of things about you, my dear Judiper Ripon.' The woman smiled. From the steely tone of her voice, it was clear this was someone used to getting what she wanted.

Jude scowled at the repeated use of her full name: she hated being called Judiper.

'Aren't you going to ask me who *I* am? I am a magic-keeper.' The woman held out her arms, as if expecting a round of applause.

Jude grimaced – this wasn't good news. Magic-keepers worked for the Consortium, Farrowfell's government. They were in charge of dishing out licences to people who made magic, and carrying out inspections to ensure the dangerous raw magic that fell from the stars was properly turned into tamed magic. Had the Consortium somehow got wind of her steal and sent someone to stop her just as she was getting away?

'Have we met?' asked Jude. 'Did you once chase me out of Mergio Market with a broom?'

'What? No. I am a *magic-keeper*.'

'And I'm the giant ball of fire that's going to hit Farrowfell tomorrow morning. Look, lady, if you're not going to try and fight me or arrest me, you might as well just let me go.' Jude twirled her fingers around the yo-yo, ready to launch it.

'I don't think—'

Jude hurled her yo-yo at the woman – a nice conk to the head would distract her for a moment. Instead, the woman's hand moved so quickly that it was a blur, and she batted the yo-yo away with ease. Jude tried again, swinging the yo-yo around in a fast motion and releasing it. The woman ducked backwards.

'Nothing you can do will surprise me, because—'

As quickly as she could, Jude chucked her stink bomb at the woman. It bounced off the woman's side and fell to the ground. Both of them stared at the small ball which, instead of releasing deadly fumes, lay innocently in the grass. Jude could have cursed. She'd swiped the stink bomb from Aunt Morgol's collection but her aunt had probably gone so cheap when purchasing it she'd bought a dud.

'Now that we're done with that foolishness, let's get down to business. I don't work for the Consortium – I am an independent keeper.'

'I didn't realise independent keepers were a thing,' Jude said. 'What's the point? You can't give out licences, and you saying tamed magic is safe to use probably doesn't mean much.' As she spoke, she scanned the area for an exit path. The woman was standing in the way of her route to the port, so her only option was to run in a random direction and hope for a chance to double back on herself.

'Magic-keepers are involved in more than just quality control,' said the woman, her voice smug. 'In this case, *you* stole magic I am personally protecting.' She nodded at the pocket where Jude had put the decision-making magic.

The stink bomb had started letting off little puffs of smoke, which drifted away slowly in the windless air. Jude held back a grin – finally, things were going her way. She needed to keep the woman talking until the stink bomb was working properly. 'So, you guard rare tamed magic rich people are hoarding?' she said, as the stink bomb started to whistle. She raised her voice, to cover the noise. 'Sort of like a human helpling? Nice – I can appreciate a sell-out.'

A plume of scarlet smoke erupted from the stink bomb and at once the magic-keeper bent over, retching. Jude used the distraction to dodge around the woman, catching a small whiff of the sewer-like stench exploding from the ball.

With a grin, she leapt into the port.

***

The journey to Ripon Headquarters involved jumping across several ports scattered around Farrowfell. Travelling through ports always made Jude feel nauseous because she liked to keep her eyes open and see the blurry world she was passing through, enjoying the brief glimpses of fields and lakes, houses and barns.

Finally, she was vomited out of the Ripons' private port, set fifteen minutes from Ripon Headquarters in the middle of rugged moorland. She regained her balance and patted her pocket. The decision-making magic was still safely there.

She peered at her yo-yo, looking for any scratches. Inside the hard shell of the yo-yo was a tiny ball of tamed magic whose uses were limited – it could either produce the high-pitched squeal, or else help her direct the yo-yo towards an enemy.

All tamed magic needed to be activated to work, and lots of tamed magic was activated upon being eaten. But this wasn't the only way to use magic. Simple magic used in toys like Jude's could be activated just by movement. (Even though Jude hated calling her yo-yo a toy, she had seen several others just like it being sold in a toy shop for about ten kira.)

The yo-yo was one of her most prized possessions. It was the last present her mother had given her – on her eighth birthday. She'd said it was an important tool that would help with thieving. She hadn't given Jude a gift since, or remembered her birthday, her focus shifting to growing the Ripons' empire instead.

Of course, Jude's mother had never been the most involved parent anyway. But she did *used* to try making mother-daughter bonding time, like the occasion she took five-year-old Jude along to an abandoned warehouse to pick up some smuggled goods. The plan had gone wrong and they'd ended up being chased by guard helplings across Farrowfell. It was one of Jude's favourite memories.

As Jude started the walk home, the magic-keeper sprang up before her, arms folded.

'You can't escape me that easily,' the magic-keeper said, tapping her foot and shaking her head.

Jude tried not to howl in irritation. She'd wanted to bring home stolen magic, not a magic-keeper. Her family wouldn't take kindly to her leading a stranger who had a connection with the Consortium back to Ripon Headquarters. 'How did you follow me?' she asked.

'That stolen magic has a tracker on it,' said the woman smugly.

Jude's shock was replaced with annoyance. She hated smug people. 'Look, lady, if you're not a Weston you shouldn't care about what I stole. Buzz off and mind your own business.'

'The magic under my protection is cursed with a powerful spell,' said the magic-keeper, and she leaned in. Her voice got softer, mixed with something like pity. 'The decision-making magic will never work for you.'

Jude shrugged. 'That doesn't matter. I'm just going to sell it.'

The magic-keeper snorted. 'That's not all the curse does. You stole it for your family, did you not? In which case, you *and* they will all be cursed. Your lives will slowly fall apart until you have nothing – unless you return the magic and seek forgiveness for stealing from its owners.'

Jude had never heard such nonsense in her life, and that included the time her cousin Spry had tried to convince her if she ate enough rubber magic and jumped off the roof she could bounce all the way to the moon.

Still, she couldn't ignore the woman, with her Consortium links.

The Consortium. An idea blossomed in Jude's mind.

Jude grinned as she turned on her heel and sprinted back into the port, yelling, 'The Consortium!'

The magic-keeper followed her into the port. Jude kept her eyes closed. When she got out on the other side, she wanted to be ready.

It wasn't a direct route to the Consortium from Ripon Headquarters, and Jude lost the magic-keeper on the journey through different ports – but at least she had heard Jude's destination and would hopefully meet her at the end.

Finally, Jude was hurled out on to a road lined with trees that bent forward, their branches snaking together like locked fingers to hide the night sky. An enormous palace of glowing gold rose like a mountain at the end of the road: the Consortium, the government of Farrowfell.

The street was busy with government officials heading home for the day. There were several Farrowfell Guards lined up on the road, wearing their dark blue uniforms and staring straight ahead. When Jude was younger, she'd gone out of her way to avoid them, as guards and Ripons generally didn't mix. But over the past few years it had become impossible to go to a public place without seeing at least one guard stationed to protect people from the increasing number of Lilthrum attacks.

Lilthrum were raw-magic monsters that occasionally popped up in Farrowfell. Jude had grown up hearing stories of attacks in far-flung places she had never heard of. Sightings used to be rare but not any more, although Jude had yet to come across a Lilthrum in the flesh.

None of the guards gave her a second look.

'Come to turn yourself in?' said the magic-keeper,

straightening her mask. Good – she had taken the bait and followed Jude; not once had she said she was going to call the guards. All she had delivered were empty threats – which meant she might be wary of getting the Consortium's attention. 'You've used some sort of magic to find out my name and stuff about my family, haven't you?'

'Why do you think that?'

Jude raised her voice so the people passing by would stare. 'How else would you know my full name? Using magic to find out personal details about someone who hasn't been officially arrested is illegal under section forty-three of the Right to Privacy from Magical Meddling Act.' She could quote this law backwards – her family knew it well.

'How do you know that?' asked the magic-keeper.

Jude snorted as she tossed the decision-making magic from hand to hand. You had to know all the laws if you were going to break them properly. 'So, lady, you'd better leave me alone before I get both of us arrested.' She had no intention of getting caught but she was willing to bet the magic-keeper wouldn't call her bluff.

The magic-keeper held up her hands, her voice slightly muffled behind the mask. 'Fine. But, remember, now the curse has been released I cannot stop it – only you can.' As if responding to her words, the decision-making magic glowed a deep scarlet. Jude yelped, almost dropping it. The woman reached into her pocket and slipped something under her mask into her mouth. A second later she vanished in a puff of white smoke.

Chapter Three

The Ripons

Ripon Headquarters was a sprawling mansion, gloomy and cold, many of the rooms rarely used. It had special tamed magic built into the walls, which made it impossible to find unless a Ripon sent an invitation with its location. The protections meant they never had unexpected guests – which was good, because Headquarters wasn't a welcoming place. In the winter only a few fires were lit, which meant Jude had to bundle up just to get from her bedroom to the dining room. Wind from the moors whistled through the windows and the freezing air nipped at exposed skin. In summer, barely any light could force its way through the thick grime coating the windows.

Grandleader had ordered Ripon Headquarters to be built when he'd made his first million kira. He said the fact that the house wasn't comfortable would make the Ripons tougher. Jude didn't understand his reasoning – surely it couldn't hurt to have a couple of comfy sofas here and there – but at least Headquarters was plenty big enough for her entire family: Grandleader, an uncle, two aunts, two cousins, her parents, Moorley and her. Once a week, the entire family would sit down for dinner together. Jude was the first to arrive in the dining room for that week's gathering. Her excitement at sharing how she'd successfully carried out a solo heist, something even Moorley hadn't done, was slightly dampened by the magic-keeper's story of the decision-making magic being cursed. She was sure it was a load of rubbish – her family had been stealing rare magic for years, and in that time had only come across cursed magic twice. Both times the curse had been weak, fading away quickly. One curse made the stealer turn purple, and the other made everyone who ate the magic speak in rhymes for twenty-four hours. A curse on her entire family, ruining their lives until she asked forgiveness, seemed like an impossibly complicated spell.

All the same, the warning hovered around the edges of Jude's mind, popping up just as she was about to forget.

The long oak table of the dining room had already been set by the Ripon helplings. A few hovered by the door like flies. Jude wondered if they were congratulating themselves for managing to place the plates *on* the table and not underneath it as they had done last time.

'You know, some helplings can actually talk,' she said. Even with their fading magic the helplings would never be replaced because Grandleader had grown up with them. To a Ripon, there was nothing more important than family, however annoying they were.

Grandleader would sit at the head of the table, so Jude perched herself as close to his throne-like chair as she dared. Too near and one of her aunts would push her down, reminding her of her place. She was the Ripon who contributed the least to the family business, making her the *least important*.

First to arrive was Aunt Victi, a bullish woman who seemed to always be ever so slightly sweating. At the end of her nose was a large wart that twitched whenever she was annoyed, which was often. In her mind, everyone needed to be as independent as they possibly could. When Jude was six, she'd told her she was useless because she couldn't cook a three-course meal.

Aunt Victi marched up to a helpling that was putting some bread and butter on to the table and elbowed it out of the way. 'The day we get rid of our servants and serve our own food will be the day we can respect ourselves again.' Her wart twitched as she started sawing at one of the loaves of bread.

She was followed by Trudie, her oldest child. Jude generally avoided speaking to Trudie. There was a six-year age difference between them, which felt like a chasm. Plus, Trudie took *ages* to get out a sentence, which was never worth waiting for because she was a fountain of knowledge for the dullest facts in the world. Jude was relieved when she sat at the other end of the table.

After Trudie came Spry, her younger brother. He was seventeen, with curly black hair and a mischievous grin. If Jude had to pick a favourite of her two cousins, it would be him. He was brilliant at inventing things but also had a wicked sense of humour and loved pranks. He often played these on Aunt Morgol, a humourless woman who had probably never cracked a smile in her life.

Aunt Morgol was next to sweep into the room. She was the oldest of Grandleader's three daughters and had never married or had children, which was probably for the best, given she made no effort to hide her dislike of her nephew and nieces. She had sallow skin and thin lips, which were usually pursed in displeasure as people broke the rules she had made up. Her entire wardrobe consisted of stiff dresses in various shades of grey and her hair was always tied in a bun so tight it caused a vein in her forehead to pop out.

'Has no one called a plumber about the broken pipes

yet?' she sniffed as she sat down. 'I went to my book club today and the *stares* from the other women. You'd have thought I'd shown up with three heads.'

It had only been a few days since the water had stopped working and Jude quite liked the novelty of bathing in Ripon Lake, even if it did have an odd pong.

'I'm working on it,' said Spry through gritted teeth, as if they'd already had this discussion. 'I'm just trying to find the pipes.'

'What do you mean *find* the pipes? They're in the walls,' snapped Aunt Morgol.

Uncle Runie arrived next. He was Aunt Victi's husband: short, with a shining bald head, and liked to wear colours so bright and loud it sometimes gave Jude a headache to look at him. Today he was wearing a lurid green waistcoat over a yellow silk shirt that looked like the sun had vomited on it.

'Hi, Jude, how are you?' he said. He didn't wait for Jude to reply, and just sat down next to Spry. He often tagged along with Spry as he came up with wild new ideas, not acting like a parent at all. Jude didn't understand why he'd married Aunt Victi because they were so different – unless he'd thought all her speeches about overthrowing the government were jokes and only found out they weren't when it was too late.

'How's the flying carriage coming along, kid?' said Uncle Runie to Spry as he grabbed a slice of bread from the stack Aunt Victi was adding to feverishly.

'Only crashed twice today,' said Spry, giving Uncle Runie a thumbs up. 'Second time right into Lake Windomore. Scared some old ladies wrestling with a grippyjock.'

Grippyjocks were water animals that lived in the clear lakes and rivers of Farrowfell. They liked to grab on to unsuspecting swimmers and hug them. Jude thought of them as fishes with arms. She'd been scared of them when she was younger, until she realised the way their eyes popped out of their heads when they finally got a cuddle was one of the funniest things she'd ever seen.

Jude's mother entered the room, sweeping into a chair next to the head of the table, her shining black hair tied in a knot above her head.

Rosalittia Ripon was the youngest of the sisters, as beautiful as the rare flower for which she had been named. She had plump lips and enormous brown eyes that could show scorn with the quickest glance. While Aunt Morgol and Aunt Victi took after Grandleader, Jude's mother looked like Grandma. Jude had never actually seen Grandma in person as she had died before Jude was born. But the single painting displayed in Ripon Headquarters was a large oil portrait of Grandma, and Aunt Victi said it was a good likeness.

Jude's mother barely glanced at Jude as she sat down. As ever, being ignored sent a pang through Jude. Her mother used to at least say hello, or sometimes ask about her day. These days it was like she didn't care any more.

Things would change now, though, because Jude had the decision-making magic. Her mother would see what she could do.

Jude's father sat near the bottom of the table. His hair was a nest of black, sticking out in random directions. Jude mostly looked like him, although she did her best to avoid speaking to him if she could. He'd always had a horrible temper, but over time it had got so bad that Jude never knew what would set him off.

Then came Jude's sister Moorley, dressed all in black as usual. Though she had their mother's beautiful features, she spent so much of her life scowling her face had probably forgotten it was supposed to be attractive. Aunt Morgol had told Jude many times that it was a shame she didn't have her mother's looks. Jude didn't care; a good thief wasn't supposed to be seen at all.

Moorley slinked over to one of the chairs at the end of the table. Jude studiously looked away from her; since Moorley had said she would never be a true Ripon, they'd barely spoken. Not that they'd ever been close. It was hard to be pleasant to Moorley when Jude was forever unfavourably compared to her.

Worse still, Moorley never acknowledged how much better everyone treated her. Instead, she kept trying to tell Jude what to do – *Jude, eat your vegetables, Jude, do your homework, Jude, stop trying to turn the helplings into mice.* But even though she was annoying, Jude had always assumed that, deep down, Moorley was on her side. That was why Moorley's comment to Grandleader had stung so much.

Grandleader arrived last, five minutes late, but also right on time. Dinner never started without him. His hair was silver like moonlight and despite being in his early seventies he had a youthful glow to his wrinkle-free skin. He was scarily intelligent, a sharp businessman – he'd told them years ago they shouldn't call him Grand*father*, but Grand*leader* instead, because he had done so much for the family.

Words of praise from him had to be earned, which made them all the more valuable. The most important thing to him was the business and Jude knew she would never win his affection if she wasn't involved in any heists.

The rest of the Ripons fell silent as a helpling held out the chair at the head of the table for Grandleader. No matter how old or confused they were, all the helplings treated him with respect.

'Evening, family,' Grandleader said. He picked up his knife and fork but did not cut into the steaming chicken pie before him. 'We have a problem,' he said. He was softly spoken but his voice carried. 'A shipment of magic was attacked by bandits earlier this evening. Our buyer was expecting it in three *days* and now we've lost it.' He paused, leaning forward slightly, his voice now almost a whisper. 'So, whose fault is this?'

Jude studied the cracks in the wooden table – she didn't want to meet his eyes.

'Is someone going to answer me?' Grandleader's voice was quiet. Jude tried to keep as still as possible. She knew it wasn't *her* fault the shipment of magic had got lost, but that wouldn't necessarily stop her getting the blame. None of the adults, not even her own parents, would stick up for her if she was accused of having something to do with the missing magic.

The silence stretched on.

Uncle Runie shifted, his waistcoat crinkling. 'Perhaps it was a case of being in the wrong place at the wrong time—'

'We should have been prepared,' snapped Grandleader. 'The buyer won't be happy.'

'We've made record profits this year,' said Uncle Runie timidly. 'We can afford to take the loss on this one—'

'It's not about *money*,' said Grandleader. 'In return for the shipment, the buyer was going to give me the location of a very *special* person, someone I've been searching for for *years* – that all the magic in my possession couldn't track down. Who was in charge of that shipment?'

Jude's father cleared his throat and ice swept over Jude's back. She hoped he just had something caught in his throat. Then he spoke up. 'That would be me, sir.'

Two bright spots of red flushed her mother's cheeks. Jude's face burned as Trudie snorted into her untouched dinner. Aunt Morgol shot a look of glee at Aunt Victi, who smirked. Now the rest of them knew they weren't in trouble, they were ready to be entertained by Jude's father being told off.

'How did this happen, Seam?' said Grandleader, setting down his knife and fork and drumming his fingers on the table. *Tap, tap-tap, tip-tap.*

'Runie was supposed to be guarding the shipment.' Her father half-spat the last words and glared at Uncle Runie.

'That's a lie,' said Uncle Runie, though he shifted in his seat and scratched his head, his eyebrows furrowing together. 'Well, actually I can't remember if I was – either way it doesn't matter, you were the one in charge.'

'That's ridiculous.' Jude's father's chair flew backwards as he shot to his feet, slamming his hand so hard on the table that water splashed from the jug in front of him. 'You were playing with those stupid moonstones when you should have been focused on the magic—'

'Don't you try to pin the blame on my husband,' snapped Aunt Victi. She turned to Uncle Runie. 'And, *you* – defend yourself better, because I'm not doing it for you.'

Uncle Runie blinked a few times. Jude had never seen him get involved in an argument before. He was usually too busy daring Spry to do stupid things.

'It *is* your fault, Runie!' roared Jude's father, and he grabbed the table, squaring his feet like he wanted to throw the entire thing. He strained for a few awkward seconds but the table was heavy and didn't budge.

Jude wished that dinner would end even though her stomach was growling with hunger.

'Sit down, Seam,' said Grandleader quietly. Her father's face glowed red and Jude willed him to listen to Grandleader.

Her mother's head was in her hands. Jude's father glanced at her before sinking into his seat as if it caused him great pain.

'Good. Now, explain,' said Grandleader.

'There was no reason for those bandits to be on that road.' A vein on Jude's father's forehead throbbed. 'We had all of our usual protections in place. It was simply . . . bad luck.'

'Bad luck? There is no such thing as luck.' Grandleader's tongue clicked against his teeth as he spoke, drawing out the word *luck* like it was a rude word.

Jude's stomach turned. It was a coincidence, surely. The missing magic couldn't be a result of a curse on the decision-making magic because there was no curse. The magic-keeper had been trying to trick her.

'No one gets the better of Ripons. *No one.*' Grandleader banged his fist on the table and Spry jumped at the noise. He knocked over his glass of water, droplets splashing on Jude. She barely noticed, her heart leaping around in her chest like a frog. This *couldn't* be her fault. 'So does anyone have any suggestions of how we come back from this? Anyone?' Grandleader's eyes darted around the table, very briefly resting on Jude before he moved on.

'We could tell the buyer there's been a delay?' piped up Spry.

'The buyer was already annoyed we were going to take a few weeks to get him the magic – I suspect he won't want to wait longer. Now, if none of you can come up with a solution, I shall have to punish Seam.' Grandleader's last words were spoken matter-of-factly.

'No,' whispered her father, his eyes darting around the room like he hoped someone would speak up for him. 'Please ... I ...'

Jude's breath caught. Would Grandleader send her father to the basement? She had never been down there but Spry had told her all about it. There was twisted tamed magic in the walls, feeding off human fear to turn the basement into a nightmare world.

'I stole decision-making magic,' Jude blurted. It wasn't exactly the glorious moment she'd been hoping for, but if ever there was a time to speak up, it was now. 'It's rare – maybe the buyer will accept a substitute—'

'Oh, do be quiet,' said Aunt Morgol with a single flick of her hands.

Jude simmered, about to argue back, when Moorley spoke.

'We could give the buyer fake magic,' said Moorley. She mirrored Grandleader, leaning forward and speaking quietly. 'By the time they've figured out what we've done, you'll already have your location, Grandleader. They're buying illegal magic – they should expect to get ripped off.'

A slow smile spread across Grandleader's face. 'Excellent, Moorley. This is the kind of thinking I want.'

Jude bit her lip. She wanted to scream at the unfairness of it. Aunt Morgol hadn't told *Moorley* to shut up. Her idea wasn't even that great. Grandleader probably could have come up with it on his own. Now she would get praised because she was Moorley and everyone loved Moorley. Nothing Jude did ever mattered because her sister always got there first.

'Moorley, as you're the only one who has come up with a sensible suggestion, you'll have the honour of coming along to the meeting with the buyer. Only *true* Ripons are invited, of course.' Grandleader's gaze lingered on Jude's father.

Jude knew the words were directed at her father, but all the same they stung. She had never been invited to a business meeting because she was too young. It was just one more way she wasn't properly part of the family.

'Dinner is over.' Grandleader rose. He snapped his fingers at the helplings, who rushed to clear away the cold pies.

Jude dug her nails into her palms. No one would care about the magic she had stolen, not now, not when Moorley had managed to get through to Grandleader when he was angry.

Bitterness boiled inside her.

It wasn't *fair*. How was she ever supposed to become a true Ripon if she never got to be properly involved in the business?

It was time to take things into her own hands.

Chapter Four

Moorley and the Parents

Trudie went up to Moorley, droning on about her marvellous quick thinking.

'Might have a look at those pipes,' Spry said to Aunt Victi.

'That's my boy.' Aunt Victi patted him on the back with what, judging from the pained expression on his face, must have been a little too much energy.

Jude stood sulkily to the side while Spry said well done to Moorley on his way out of the room.

Jude's mother appeared next to them. 'Come to the evening room in half an hour – family meeting,' she muttered to Jude and Moorley. She kept her eyes fixed on Uncle Runie, who was trying to balance all the plates of dessert the helplings had left on the side table. 'We need to discuss things with your father.'

Before Jude could ask more, her mother had walked away and Aunt Morgol had taken her place.

'Jude, go and lock up for the night.' Aunt Morgol's hands were on her hips as she tapped her foot. Out of the corner of her eye Jude could see Moorley and Trudie slipping away. 'Make yourself useful.'

'I *was* making myself useful,' said Jude, trying not to sound whiny. Aunt Morgol did not respect whiners. 'I told Grandleader about my decision-making magic . . .'

But Aunt Morgol wasn't listening. Jude scrunched up her face. If she didn't do as she was told Aunt Morgol would complain to her mother – or worse, Grandleader.

Jude stomped down to the entrance hall, stinging with the unfairness of it all. The grand front door swung open when she got closer. Every night, the house objected to being locked up, flinging open windows and doors the same way a toddler chucks their toys to the floor. The door was so heavy Jude needed to put her weight on it, forcing it closed centimetre by centimetre. A helpling sidled up to her and attempted to assist by pulling at the door.

'Wrong way,' grumbled Jude as she finally managed to shove the door closed and slide all the locks into place. The Weston mansion had actually been *helpful* to its owners. Why couldn't her house be the same?

Many of the old houses of Farrowfell had tamed magic in the walls, which was activated either by sunlight or moonbeams. Unfortunately, Ripon Headquarters was made with tamed magic which responded to both. That meant it never went to sleep and had developed a horribly stubborn personality from being so cranky.

As Jude went around the ground floor forcing all the external doors shut, fires in the brackets on the walls flared up. They cast a glow that barely lit the dark-panelled corridors before her and went out with a soft *puff* the moment she was a few metres past. It meant she travelled in a small circle of light.

Aunt Morgol had come up with the system so they wouldn't waste magic lighting entire corridors when all they needed was a little patch. Grandleader approved of her cleverness in trying to save money – and if Grandleader was on board, no one would argue.

Jude's last part of locking up involved wrestling a stubborn garden door. She narrowly dodged a window which swung open at her head.

'Oi!' she said, slamming the window shut so hard the panes rattled.

Despite hating the job, she wished it could go on for longer because at least she could avoid going to the evening room and the meeting with her parents. It would likely be a painful ten minutes of her father ranting about how they should have stuck up for him.

No matter how many times her father lost his temper, Jude could never get used to it. She remembered a time when he'd only lost his temper for worthwhile things, like when the helplings accidentally served charcoal instead of chocolate for dessert.

Jude dragged her feet as she headed to the evening room, which was a living room they only used after dinner. Tall armchairs were grouped around an empty fireplace, one they never bothered lighting. Jude shivered as she entered to find her parents perched on the edges of the armchairs in silence, her mother's hands folded in her lap like a ruler sitting before her subjects.

'What are *you* doing here?' said her mother. Her father frowned at her.

'Er . . . you said it was a family meeting,' said Jude.

'No, I wanted Moorley,' her mother said, her eyebrows bunched together in confusion. Then her expression cleared. 'Oh, were you standing next to Moorley when I told her to come? Well, there's no harm in you being here, I suppose.'

Jude burned with embarrassment – she hadn't even *wanted* to come, but that didn't change the fact that her mother had called this a family meeting even though she wasn't inviting Jude.

Moorley skulked into the room as if Jude's resentful thoughts had summoned her. She leaned against the far wall and stared at their parents.

'Congratulations, Moorley,' Jude's father said, his voice stilted as if he was being forced to read a ransom note. 'You've made me proud.'

Jude twitched, preparing herself for the sudden screaming. She glanced at the door, which Moorley had left open behind her. Perhaps she could use that to her advantage and slip out without her parents commenting.

Moorley folded her arms, her face expressionless.

'Well, Moorley? Aren't you going to thank me for my praise?' Her father's voice had an edge. Jude couldn't understand why her sister wasn't bouncing off the walls, delighted with herself for pleasing Grandleader, why she narrowed her eyes.

Moorley unpeeled herself from the wall. She gave their father a small bow. 'You know I live to make you proud.' Her voice dripped with sarcasm but she kept her eyes on the ground, as if too humble to meet his gaze.

'You make me proud too,' said Jude's mother. 'You spoke up just as Grandleader was about to rightfully punish your father for—'

'Nothing *rightful* about it!'

'—his careless mistake—'

'It wasn't my fault.'

'—and it would do each of you well to remember that, as the youngest of my siblings, I've had to work much harder to prove my worth. As the oldest, *Morgol* should be ranked above me – only my brilliance has helped me jump ahead of her. But it is a constant competition and I *must* come out on top.' Jude's mother clicked her tongue against her teeth, her eyebrows arched as she looked at Jude's father. 'If Moorley hadn't thought of that solution, all our hard work would be for nothing. Grandleader is so close to the biggest ... success he's ever had. None of us can afford to slip up now.'

'It was just bad luck,' muttered Jude's father. 'It won't happen again.'

Bad luck. An icy feeling spread through Jude – but no, her father was right. It was a one-off piece of bad luck. A coincidence. Nothing to do with the decision-making magic.

'You should have been guarding that shipment with your life,' snapped Jude's mother. Her eyes slid to Moorley. 'Now, Moorley, when you go to that meeting with Grandleader, remember you are there to make us proud. This is an honour for all of us. And Jude ...' Jude's mother paused to look at her. Jude's stomach flipped. The embarrassment of being forgotten disappeared in an instant. 'Stay out of the way.'

Disappointment crashed through Jude. 'I could come to the meeting too—'

'You'll have a chance, I'm sure,' said her mother, cutting her off. 'In the meantime, just do what you do best. Keep quiet.'

She got to her feet, dusting invisible bits of dirt off her flowing white trousers before she left the room, only looking at Jude to side-step around her.

Jude's eyes stung. Her father paused on his way out, ruffling her hair like she was a dog. The moment the door closed, Moorley's shoulders slumped and she sighed.

'What's *your* problem?' said Jude, bitterness spiking through her.

Moorley looked up, as if surprised Jude was still there. 'Nothing,' she said, rubbing her forehead. 'They're right, you know – you should just keep quiet.'

'*You* don't keep quiet,' snapped Jude. 'And they all listen to you, for some reason.'

Moorley sucked in her cheeks. 'Look, Jude, maybe it's for the best that you're not too involved in the business.'

Jude's nostrils flared. Climbing the ladder and then pulling it up after herself was so typical of Moorley. Because *she'd* achieved something, apparently it meant Jude couldn't as well.

Before Jude could say any of that, Moorley continued. 'I know you stole some of my ghost magic. And at dinner you said you stole decision-making magic – where from?'

Jude eyed her, suspicious. Why was Moorley taking a sudden interest? This might be the longest conversation they'd had in two years. 'The Westons – they're superrich.' Despite it only being Moorley, Jude couldn't help puffing out her chest a little.

'Nice,' said Moorley, and Jude thought she actually sounded impressed. 'But really, you should keep your head down. Don't take any more stupid risks – shouldn't you be focusing on studying? Maybe you should ask for a new tutor?'

And there it was. Moorley just wanted to tell her what to do, act like she was higher up in the Ripon rankings than Jude. 'You're not Mum,' said Jude at once. 'I'll do what I like.'

'I didn't mean—'

A blood-curdling scream from somewhere in the house interrupted her. They both looked up at the ceiling. There was another scream, followed by yelling.

Moorley strode out of the room. Jude followed, wondering if she should grab a vase or something as a weapon.

The noises were coming from above. They hurried up the stairs and entered a corridor flooded with water seeping from a laundry room.

Uncle Runie was standing by the door. Jude pushed past a helpling holding a mop the wrong way around to see what was going on.

Spry was wrestling with a pipe which had broken away from the wall. Water gushed from several holes and he was completely soaked. 'The important thing is, I got the water working again!' he yelled above the noise.

'Who was screaming?' said Moorley.

'Aunt Morgol,' said Spry, trying in vain to block one of the holes in the pipe with what looked like wads of tissue paper. Uncle Runie was roaring with laughter. 'On the bright side, she definitely got the bath she wanted.'

***

When Jude woke the next morning the events of the previous night crashed down on her again. She rolled over and groaned into her pillow – and was promptly doused in icy water.

'Ah!' she yelled, getting tangled in her bedsheets as she twisted around to find herself staring at a helpling holding a bucket above its head. 'What are you *doing*?' she screeched.

Her bedroom door burst open and Aunt Morgol strolled inside. 'No, no, no,' she said, her hands on her hips. 'I wanted you to heat the water and pour it in a *bath* – how you got *bath* and *Jude* mixed up—'

'What is going *on*?' said Jude as she scrambled out of bed.

'I was trying to teach this helpling how to fetch water from a well,' said Aunt Morgol. 'So we could all have nice fresh baths while your useless cousin tries to fix the plumbing. But clearly I got unlucky by picking the *stupidest* of all our helplings.'

The helpling walked up to Aunt Morgol and poured the rest of the water over her head.

'You're *useless*!' shrieked Aunt Morgol. 'Useless!' She glanced around Jude's bedroom. 'What a state this room is in. Clean it *up*.'

She stormed out, Jude's door slamming shut behind her. Jude blinked a few times. Her bedroom wasn't dirty, just slightly messy. Like the rest of the house it was gloomy, but she'd tried her best to make it cosy, dragging in a large scarlet rug to give it a splash of colour. The rug was now half hidden under books strewn across the floor that Jude had started reading and never finished.

Clearly, I got unlucky by picking the stupidest helpling.

Aunt Morgol would have been lucky to find a *smart* Ripon helpling. But all the same Jude couldn't help thinking of the decision-making magic and the curse the magic-keeper had warned her about. If there *was* a bad-luck curse, then the loss of the shipment of magic that was so precious to Grandleader wasn't her father's fault. It was hers.

She crossed over to her desk, reaching into her top drawer and throwing aside the rubbish she'd collected when she went through her real-life-drawing phase (using magic to make the things she drew into three-dimensional objects – only she had no artistic talent so everything came out all lumpy).

Buried underneath it was the decision-making magic. It seemed innocent enough, a slightly transparent, small yellow stone. It did not appear cursed. But then she wasn't sure what cursed magic was supposed to look like. She guessed it was unlikely to have a big sign on it saying, 'This magic is cursed'.

'Load of rubbish,' Jude muttered to herself unconvincingly.

***

Grandleader's business meeting was scheduled for two days later and Jude was determined to sneak along – to this one, and many meetings after. She would learn from her other family members and figure out how to be better than them. Then, when she was finally *invited* to a meeting, Grandleader would be so impressed.

But he could never find out what she had done. Invites to meetings were a reward. He wouldn't think much of her disobeying that rule.

While Jude waited for the meeting to arrive, she figured she would pretend to have listened to her mother and keep her head down. It wasn't easy because the whole family seemed to be on edge. Aunt Morgol blamed her for setting fire to an unused study even though she was sure she'd seen Spry heading in that direction. Aunt Victi was in a foul mood because two helplings had gone missing and Grandleader had told her to find them. Uncle Runie twisted his ankle trying to get free cake from a bakery that was doing a promotion.

'I didn't even get a cake,' he muttered as he wrapped a bandage around his ankle.

Jude had taken to carrying the decision-making magic around with her. Occasionally she would pull it out, just to stare at it. Surely it couldn't be the cause of the family's recent string of bad luck? If it was ... well, the bad luck wasn't *that* bad, was it? It definitely wasn't the start of all their lives falling apart or whatever it was the magic-keeper had said.

She considered trying once more to tell someone about her steal, but there wasn't any point if she couldn't announce it at a family dinner. It was likely that whoever she told would try and take credit for her hard work, and she'd been hoping for a big scene where everyone would witness her brilliance.

When the time came for Grandleader's business meeting, Jude choked down the rest of her invisibility magic, washing the taste away with a glass of warm milk. She slipped down to the entrance hall where Spry, Trudie and Aunt Victi were waiting. Grandleader must have decided they were worthy enough to be invited along.

Spry was fiddling with a bit of folded metal, his tongue sticking out as he concentrated.

'Did you know ... the average helpling needs to be shocked ... by lightning ... six ... times ... in its lifespan ... in order to keep its ... magic running ... properly?' Trudie was speaking so slowly Jude felt like she had aged ten years just waiting for her to get to the end of the sentence.

Aunt Victi rolled her eyes. 'The person who invented helplings has caused the most damage to society out of anyone or anything in history.'

Spry looked up from his scrap of folded metal. 'More than the damage caused by Lilthrum?' he asked, raising his eyebrows. 'You know, a Lilthrum was spotted near Mergio Market the other day. It tried to drag away this little old man who sells toys. Apparently the guards fought it off and the old guy is still recovering.'

Jude's mouth fell open. She knew Lilthrum sightings were becoming more common but no Lilthrum had ever been as near as Mergio Market before.

'Oh, pish,' said Aunt Victi, her wart twitching. 'It's probably not even Lilthrum that people are seeing – just a trick of moonlight.'

'Yeah, moonlight that tries to eat people,' muttered Spry as Moorley arrived wearing one of her standard black outfits. 'You're cutting it fine,' he said to her.

Moorley shrugged, though she bit her nails, something she did when she was nervous. Maybe she would be so edgy she'd mess up at the meeting. Jude smiled at the thought.

Grandleader followed a few minutes later, striding across the flagstones. He had the entire left wing of the house to himself. Jude had never been inside because it was off limits to the rest of the family. Above the golden door leading to his quarters hung the portrait of Jude's grandmother. There was kindness in the smiling eyes that stared down.

Below Grandma was a giant version of the family crest – cupped hands holding overflowing coins, the motto in curling handwriting underneath: 'If you're born a Ripon, you're a Ripon for life'.

A memory floated back to Jude of a rare occasion, years ago, when her mother had had a bit of time to spend with her. They had made cookies, just the two of them. Jude had asked what the motto meant as the cookies baked over hot coals.

'Your grandmother came up with it.' Her mother brushed her hair back with gentle fingers. Grandma was almost never mentioned in Headquarters, and the reference was enough for the memory to lodge itself into her brain. 'It means that no matter what, you'll always be a part of this family.'

'So even if you decided you didn't want me any more?' Jude said.

Her mother smiled knowingly, as if she knew something Jude didn't. 'I think it means, even if you didn't want us any more.'

'Why wouldn't I want you any more?'

'Exactly,' her mother replied, stroking her hair again. 'Why wouldn't you?'

The memory sent a pang through Jude.

'Let's go,' said Grandleader, leading the little group into the driveway where a carriage was waiting. They had a few carriages, which were powered by different kinds of magic. As tonight was windy, Jude guessed the one propelled by magic that reacted to wind would have been selected. Two helplings sat at the front, one to steer and the other to hold flickering torches as the last dregs of evening light faded fast.

The cushioned seats of the carriage were the size of benches and there were four rows, plenty of room for Jude to slip in at the back.

The towering gates of Ripon Headquarters closed behind them and the carriage jolted along the winding, dusty road. It would have been quicker to walk to the port, but there was no question of that. Grandleader liked to arrive at business meetings in style.

They reached the port and the carriage clattered through, spitting out on the other side with a bump. Houses were more frequent in this part of Farrowfell, nestled in the hills, windows lit with a welcoming golden light. Ripon Headquarters was imposing and grand but it could never be called *welcoming*.

The carriage passed through several more ports until at last it turned down the road that led towards the Consortium's palace, which was home to the three sections of government: the lawmakers, the elected rulers and the judges. Having three branches was supposed to make sure no one ended up with too much power, though Aunt Victi still thought the Consortium was corrupt and had suggested a family outing to burn the place down several times.

Jude expected the carriage to turn down a side road, but it continued heading straight for the main entrance. She frowned – Grandleader's buyer worked for the government? The Ripons had never done business with the Consortium before. She'd assumed Grandleader wanted the name of a criminal contact in exchange for the illegal magic. What could someone who worked for the Consortium tell him?

The carriage bumped past the main entrance to a little side door hidden behind a hedge. A portly man stood in the doorway wiping his ink-covered hands on his greasy apron. Something about the way he was standing, leaning a little forward and shifting from foot to foot, made Jude think this was the man Grandleader had arranged to meet.

They had arrived.

Chapter Five

The Consortium

The man's face was shining red, and underneath his apron he wore a pinstripe suit that was at least one size too small. He looked like a sausage squeezed too tightly. Jude wondered if that was why he was so red. He dabbed the sweat on his brow with a lily-white handkerchief but it didn't seem to make much difference.

'Good evening.' The man's voice quivered. Jude had never seen someone look so obviously as though they were doing something they were not supposed to. 'Please, follow me.'

He opened the door and stood to the side, then

seemed to remember that he was supposed to be leading the way. 'Sorry, force of habit. It's the polite thing to do, you see, to let guests go first.'

'Indeed,' said Grandleader, raising his eyebrows.

The man led them through corridors with vaulted ceilings, down a spiral staircase, and through several more corridors. The floorboards creaked as they walked, and the sunshine yellow walls were lined with paintings of stern men and women. Jude squinted at the caption of one as she passed: 'Madam Gillywater, Lawmaker, 1403'.

'Quickly now,' said the man, speeding up. They entered a small sitting room crammed with furniture. Jude managed to slip inside before he closed the door.

There were chocolates on the tables and frilly lace covered the chairs. Thick orange blossom perfume scented the air. The fire crackled. Jude's clothes were already beginning to stick uncomfortably to her.

The man sat down but Grandleader remained standing. The rest of the Ripons crowded behind him, their hands tucked behind their backs.

'T-tea?' said the man.

'That would be delightful,' said Grandleader, the words not matching his tone. The man snapped his fingers and a helpling entered, pouring steaming cups of tea.

Grandleader passed his cup to Moorley, who wordlessly took a sip. The rest of the Ripons waited, and when Moorley didn't die she handed the tea back to Grandleader. He would never eat or drink outside food without someone else tasting first.

'Now, Everiste, we've gone to great troubles to get your magic for you.' Grandleader settled on one of the chairs. Moorley looked at Spry, then at a chair. Spry shook his head: Aunt Victi and Trudie had remained standing.

Jude kept still in a shadowy corner of the room. She couldn't believe she was finally going to get to see Grandleader in action, doing a proper deal. Maybe at a family dinner she could casually mention something he'd said while negotiating, pass it off as something she'd come up with on her own and Grandleader would think she had the same brilliant business mind as him.

Grandleader pulled a small brown package out of his pocket and tossed it from hand to hand. Everiste licked his lips, his eyes following the movement. 'I'd like the location of his home now. I suspect it is somewhere . . . not in Farrowfell? Highly protected against magical interference – possibly somewhere surrounded by Dark Rivers?'

'The magic first, please,' whispered Everiste, holding his hands out. 'You know, I've never done anything like this before. I'd never heard of the Ripons, to be honest. But someone mentioned you'd been helping them balance their books because you're cheaper than buying from the gatherers – they said you could get me *anything*.' He babbled on, wringing his hands together.

Grandleader tilted his head. Jude wondered if he was going to protest, tell Everiste that he wanted the location before he gave the magic. But instead, he smiled. 'Of course.' Grandleader tossed the package to Everiste, who scrambled to catch it. 'Now, the location.'

Everiste started to unknot the string, his hands trembling.

'The location, Everiste,' repeated Grandleader, his voice getting cooler.

Everiste shook his head, the loose skin on his neck flapping like a rooster's. 'I need to check the magic is here first – you're crooks, after all. It would be silly of me not to make sure . . .'

'Hmm,' said Grandleader. He set his tea down then raised a hand, clamping his fingers against his palm. Everiste gurgled, clutching at his throat like the breath had been sucked from his lungs. The air crackled with magic as Grandleader got to his feet and strode forward, shadows appearing to bunch around him.

Red veins popped in Everiste's eyes and black lines snaked across his skin. He squealed like a dying pig as he collapsed, his face turning purple. Grandleader stood over him.

'I don't like being called a crook,' he whispered, placing a muddy black boot on Everiste's face. 'I'd like the location, now.' Grandleader's boot left a mark on Everiste's greasy skin.

With a small smile he crossed back to his chair, picking up his tea again. The moment he sat down Everiste gasped for air, panting as his face slowly returned to its natural red. Trembling, he got to his feet.

Jude's breath came out in ragged gasps and she clamped her hand over her mouth. She knew Grandleader could be ruthless – one time, a buyer of illegal magic had tried to pay less than he owed, so Grandleader had framed him for a crime and got him arrested. But Jude had never seen Grandleader use magic like this – he hadn't even eaten anything. Fear flooded through her, switching off her invisibility magic. She took a deep breath, and it returned a moment later. Luckily everyone's focus was fixed on Everiste and not her corner.

Grandleader *must* have eaten magic. She'd missed him slipping something into his mouth that was all.

Everiste shook as he bowed so low Jude wondered if he was trying to scrape the floor with his forehead. 'Please ...' he said. 'Please ... I only know Harrimore Hardman's location because I was the one in charge of giving him a new identity in the first place ...' He looked up, his mouth opening and closing like he was scared to finish the sentence. 'I want to make sure that you won't harm him.'

Grandleader smirked. 'Of *course* not. I've waited a very long time to meet him.'

Everiste nodded, though Jude could tell he wasn't convinced. 'Harrimore is in Silithar,' he said, naming the hostile kingdom to the north of Farrowfell. 'In a house at the base of the Crying Mountains. He's a brilliant man – the Consortium turned to him when the snufflepox came and it only took him a few weeks to figure out a tamed magic recipe for the medicine.'

Grandleader took another sip of tea then placed his cup down. 'It has been a pleasure doing business with you.' He held out a hand, but before Everiste could shake it, the door to the study slammed open. A man dressed in the dark uniform of the Farrowfell Guards, flanked by two guard helpings, strode inside. At once Jude's instincts screamed at her to flee and she had to remind herself she was invisible. It would do no good to panic; strong emotion would stop her magic from working.

The man held up a scroll and read it so quickly the words rolled into a meaningless blur. Jude heard enough to get the gist – he was trying to arrest everyone for an illegal purchase of magic.

The Ripons blinked as the guard lowered the scroll. 'Did you hear me? You are under arrest.'

Aunt Victi, Spry and Moorley turned to Grandleader. A smile still played on his face, as if the whole thing amused him. 'May I ask, my good sir, who you are?'

Everiste had hidden behind a chair like he hoped no one would notice him there.

'I am a commanding guard of the Consortium,' the man smirked. 'And as I said, sir, you are under arrest.'

Jude's heart pounded.

Grandleader just smirked. 'You're all corrupt,' he said, his voice bored. 'Every last stinking one of you in this miserable, filth-filled palace.'

And then five more guards burst through the door, all holding glittering blue swords pointed towards the Ripons.

Chapter Six

The Curse

'Ripons, we've got what we came for,' said Grandleader calmly. 'It's time to leave.'

Spry dropped a stink bomb and Jude had just enough time to suck in a breath of air before the toxic gas spread. The guards gagged, leaning over and retching. Meanwhile the Ripons, holding their noses, ran past them to the exit. Grandleader strode out like he had all the time in the world.

Jude used the confusion to burst into the corridor after them. An alarm clanged and the hall flooded with more guards, both human and helpling. Most other government workers had probably gone home for the evening.

She wanted to be out of sight of the main corridor, so she opened a nearby door, and found herself looking at a closet. *Perfect.* She dived among the brooms and dustpans and took a few deep breaths, her heart racing as a broom clattered down. She winced at the noise, hoping any passers-by would think she was nothing more than a particularly clumsy helpling rooting through a closet for cleaning supplies.

A Ripon business meeting had been interrupted by the Farrowfell Guards once before, when Aunt Morgol didn't do the proper checks and decided she wanted to buy magic from a too-good-to-be-true cheap seller who ended up being an undercover guard. That had happened because Aunt Morgol had been greedy. But this . . .

Was bad luck.

Jude took the decision-making magic out of her pocket. All the bad things that had happened over the past few days – they were because of her. If she ignored the curse, would it get worse? Her stomach churned at the thought of what Grandleader would do if he found out. The memory of Everiste shaking on the floor flashed in her mind.

No, Grandleader would never *hurt* her. She was his own flesh and blood, and he loved the Ripons above all else. But if she really had cursed her family then it would mean Moorley was right: all she did was mess things up.

Had the magic-keeper told her how to get rid of the curse?

Yes – she'd said Jude needed to return the magic and say sorry to the owners.

So, basically, all Jude had to do was march up to the Weston mansion, knock on their door, lob the magic at them, tell them she was sorry for stealing, then leg it before they could call the guards.

It was simple enough. She could go now, tonight.

Cautiously, she pushed open the closet door and stepped into the corridor just as a guard sprinted past. She flinched back but he didn't spot her. The guards were looking for hardened criminals, not a twelve-year-old.

Jude had no idea how to get out of the Consortium but she remembered having to go down stairs to get to Everiste's office. She hurried along corridors until she found a circular staircase, the spirals so tight she felt dizzy as she went up. The stairs led to an enormous hall with a domed ceiling made of glass that revealed the night sky above. Tapestries of spun gold hung from the walls, with the crests of the three branches of the Consortium woven into them. This had to be the entrance hall.

Jude tried to walk casually to the front door, but she picked up her pace when she got outside. In the distance was the Consortium's port. By the time she reached it, she was half running. It was time to get rid of the bad luck once and for all.

***

In fifteen short minutes she was strolling out of the Westons' private port. The Weston mansion was like a ghost in the night, the lights shining from all the windows like beacons.

'Hello, Judiper,' said a voice. She jumped, spinning to find the magic-keeper standing behind her.

'How did you know I was here?' said Jude.

'The magic you stole has a tracker on it, remember?' said the magic-keeper. 'I saw you were here and I got curious.'

'I'm bringing it back,' said Jude as she marched to the front gates. They swung open for her.

'This must be a new experience for you,' said the magic-keeper, her tone conversational as they headed to the front door. 'Not breaking in.'

'Yeah,' said Jude shortly, letting the comment wash over her. The magic-keeper knocked on the front door.

A helpling opened it, bowing low before disappearing into the depths of the house.

Jude and the magic-keeper stood in silence, the light from the house spilling out over them. Stars twinkled in the night sky and a cold wind blew.

After a minute the helpling returned with a girl

and boy about Jude's age. The girl had silky blonde hair tied with a pink ribbon, and wore a pink dress that flowed to her ankles. She had rosy cheeks and skin that glowed with good health. The boy was taller, with dark brown hair, thick eyebrows and high cheekbones. Both had brown eyes, which were narrowed suspiciously at Jude.

'All right?' said Jude, waving sheepishly. They stared at her in silence. 'I'm Jude Ripon. I stole some magic from you the other day and I wanted to say I'm sorry for that. Here is it as good as new. I haven't even taken a bite.' She got the decision-making magic out to show them.

The girl gaped, her eyes wide and her mouth hanging open a little bit, as if viewing a rare creature in a cage. The boy's scowl would have made Moorley proud.

The silence stretched on. Perhaps the Westons had been made speechless by her apology. Or maybe they were so rich they paid their helplings to speak for them. That might explain their talking guards. 'More importantly, is my curse lifted?'

'It's not enough,' said the magic-keeper. Jude wondered why the boy and the girl didn't seem surprised to see the magic-keeper, or question why she was there. Though, if the magic-keeper worked for the Westons and hung around their house waiting for people to break in, they were probably on good terms. Probably met for tea once a week, plaited each other's hair and gossiped about all the other poor thieves they'd cursed.

'What are you talking about?' said Jude.

The magic-keeper snorted. 'The magic did not belong to Eri and Fin.' She nodded at the girl and boy in turn. 'It belonged to their parents – you need to say sorry to *them*.'

'OK, fine, where are their parents?' said Jude, impatient again. 'I'll apologise to all the Westons if it means I can get rid of the curse.'

'It is not as simple as you think,' said the magic-keeper. The girl and boy, Eri and Fin, looked away, as if the conversation had moved on to a topic that was painful for them. 'They've been missing for over a year.'

'But—'

'There's no other way to lift this curse,' continued the magic-keeper, as if Jude hadn't spoken. 'So I suggest you help Eri and Fin find their parents – and fast.'

With that cheerful comment, she ate some magic and vanished into smoke.

Chapter Seven

Eri, Fin and Grandleader

Jude briefly considered just going home. The magic-keeper had made it sound like lifting the curse would be straightforward, and this definitely didn't *sound* straightforward. But she couldn't continue to put up with the bad luck, not when it was affecting the Ripons' business. She needed to stop it before everything got a thousand times worse.

Plus, for all she knew, no one had looked for Mr and Mrs Weston properly. They might be easy to find.

'Shall we get cracking, then?' Jude said to Eri and

Fin when it became clear neither of them were going to start talking. She rolled up her sleeves.

The Weston siblings looked at each other like they were unsure what to do. Fin gripped the door as if ready to slam it shut.

'You're a Ripon,' he said at last, his voice cracking.

Jude could have cheered. 'Oh, you *do* speak.'

'You're really here.' Eri's face was white with shock. Jude might as well have announced she was a ghost come to haunt their home. 'A Ripon.' She shook her head. 'Sorry – we just ... weren't expecting visitors ... It's the middle of the night ...'

Grandleader had done everything he could to make sure the wider public did not know the Ripon name. He wanted them to remain a mystery, unlike other crime families in Farrowfell, like the Sillians and Fordimores. Still, the Ripons had reached such a level of success they were beginning to have meetings with the Consortium, and since the Westons probably had lots of Consortium connections, it made sense that Eri and Fin had heard of them.

'I know this is all a bit ... odd,' said Jude, struggling to find the right word to sum up the situation. 'But *you're* the ones who keep cursed magic in your home.'

Fin's hands were still on the door. Despite not wanting to admit it, Jude knew she needed the Weston siblings more than they needed her. She had to get the conversation back on track before Fin decided to leave her outside in the dark.

'Look, I want to lift my curse and you want your parents back,' she said quickly. 'We can work together. If your parents have been missing for over a year, it's because they're in trouble – and I know all the people who cause trouble. You need someone like me.' She preferred to look on the bright side of things – hopefully, Mr and Mrs Weston had simply got lost in their enormous home or taken a nice trip and lost track of time.

Eri looked at her brother. A silent understanding seemed to pass between them. Fin nodded grimly, pulling back the door to reveal the marble entrance hall. 'Desperate times call for desperate measures,' he muttered. 'Just . . . don't steal anything, OK?'

Jude rolled her eyes. If she *wanted* to steal their gold she would have already done it.

'Maybe we should have some tea?' said Eri, her voice earnest. She stalked away, her hair swishing side to side as she walked. Her back was too straight, like she had a stick keeping her perfectly upright. She was so *polite*. Too polite. Jude didn't trust people like that – she could never tell if they were being genuine or hiding something. A criminal might cut your purse and steal your money but at least you always knew where you stood with one.

Fin kept pace with Jude. She struggled to think of

something to talk about. She had never actually come face-to-face with the people she stole from. She didn't like it. It wasn't natural.

They headed into a room with a few couches grouped around a crackling fire. Judging by the number of windows, the room would be full of light during the day. A grandfather clock ticked in the corner, and hanging above the mantelpiece was a portrait. Two adults who were obviously Mr and Mrs Weston had their arms wrapped around Fin and Eri, as if protecting them from all the evils in the world. Mrs Weston had a halo of golden hair and a face full of joy. Mr Weston had eyes that sparkled, even in the painting.

Jude felt a tinge of envy. The room was cosy and comforting. And the Fin and Erin in the painting looked completely sure of their parents' love – *they'd* probably never had to prove themselves.

Eri rang a bell and a helpling entered the room. 'Tea, please,' she said with a small nod. The helpling gave a deep bow and left.

Jude raised her eyebrows at the helpling's politeness as she settled on one of the soft couches. 'Wow, yours are super-obedient. Ours normally throw at least three things before they do anything – except when Grandleader asks them to do something.'

'Who is . . . Grandleader?' asked Fin, wrinkling his nose as if Jude had a bad smell hanging around her. Jude might have taken offence, but the water coming out of the pipes Spry had finally fixed now came with a scent of sulphur, so she probably did.

'Never mind,' she said. 'Look, the magic-keeper said I need to apologise to your parents and then I can be on my merry way, bad-luck free. So all we need to do is find them and that'll be the end of it.'

The helpling returned with two delicate china cups filled with steaming tea, presenting one to Eri and one to Fin.

Eri frowned. 'One for Jude too, please.' She sipped from her cup, her little finger sticking neatly in the air. 'They probably haven't forgiven you for your ... er ... last visit.'

'That's fine, I don't want any tea,' said Jude. 'I'm sorry, but how old are you?' She was distracted by the way Eri daintily dabbed a napkin on her lips. She didn't act like a kid at all – and even the adult Ripons didn't care that much about table manners.

'Eleven,' said Eri. 'Fin is twelve.'

'Excellent,' said Jude, staring as Eri folded the napkin over so the edges lined up. She shook her head – she needed to focus. 'So, er, where did you last see your parents? And when?'

'Are you going to tell your family about this curse?' said Fin suddenly. He stood with his back to the fire so his face was in shadow. Eri set her teacup down with a clang and the steaming liquid sloshed across her hands. It must have burnt her but she didn't flinch.

'Why?' Jude frowned as Eri blotted at the mess she'd made with more napkins, neck bent to hide her face.

'How do we know we can trust you?' said Fin, sitting next to his sister as she continued to dab at the last and tiniest of tea droplets. 'How do we know your family won't try to take revenge on us for cursing them?'

The Ripons *would* take revenge on the Westons if they found out – right after they'd punished Jude. Her father would scream until his voice was hoarse, her mother would lose the last bit of respect she had for Jude – and Grandleader would send her straight to the basement.

'Believe me, I won't be saying a word about this to my family,' said Jude in the most reassuring tone she could manage.

Fin's face darkened and Eri dropped her sodden napkin on the table, placing her hand on his arm. 'Please,' she said quietly to him – though not quietly enough because Jude had very good ears. 'We need her.'

'Too right you do,' said Jude with a grin, leaning back. It was nice to be needed. 'You should really learn how to whisper,' she continued as Eri looked startled. 'Now, tell me about your parents. Do they have any enemies?'

Eri picked her teacup up again, though her hands shook slightly. 'You know how there have been more Lilthrum attacking people?'

Jude had a sudden fear Eri was going to tell her

that Mr and Mrs Weston had been dragged away by Lilthrum – in which case they would almost certainly be dead and Jude would never get to apologise. But then, she realised, if that *was* the case, Fin and Eri would now be the rightful owners of the decision-making magic and her apology earlier would have worked.

Eri was still looking at Jude, waiting for an answer.

'Yes, I've heard about the Lilthrum attacks,' Jude said. *I don't live under a rock*, she wanted to add, but didn't. Eri probably wouldn't appreciate snark.

Eri nodded. 'Well, our parents were helping the Consortium look for the reason *why*. One night they thought they had found an answer. They said goodnight and told us they'd see us in the morning. When we woke up, they were gone.' Her voice was thick, like she was holding back tears. She gulped from her cup then set it down with a clink. 'Are you sure you don't want tea?' she said, clutching her bell.

Jude didn't do well with emotional people, especially those she didn't know. She decided to barrel on. 'So, we know your parents were up to something dodgy.' There went her hopeful theory that they were sunning themselves somewhere on a beach and had forgotten to write home.

'How d'you work that one out?' said Fin as he gently forced the bell away from Eri and put it on the table next to the sodden napkins.

'If they were up to something nice and normal, they

wouldn't have been sneaking out at night. Nothing lawful happens at night.' It was basic common sense.

'That's completely untrue.' Fin narrowed his eyes. Eri seemed to have recovered herself because she elbowed him again. 'Ow!'

'You're not being very polite, Fin!' she said.

The clock struck twelve and panic shot through Jude. If someone at Ripon Headquarters locked up the house not knowing she wasn't home, she'd be left outside for the night. She didn't fancy facing whatever wild animals roamed the moorlands surrounding Ripon Headquarters.

'I'm going to head home now but we'll figure something out,' she said.

'The more time that goes by, the worse your curse is going to get,' warned Eri.

'I know,' said Jude irritably. 'I'll be back as soon as I can. I want to break this curse, and you want your parents back. It's a win-win for both of us.'

***

Eri gave Jude a torch of fire that wouldn't go out, even if the wind blew, to light her path. Jude started her journey home, which required jumps through several ports. She mulled over the meeting as she went. She hadn't been lying to Eri and Fin: she *did* want out of the curse – whichever way she could. But the more she thought about it, the stronger her feeling was that the Weston parents had got themselves into a dangerous situation. Her instinct was to run the other way.

Halfway through the journey home, Eri's wonderful torch of fire went out and Jude was left to make the rest of the trip home in darkness. To make matters worse, it started to rain just as Jude trudged through the fields near Ripon Headquarters.

'*Stupid* curse,' she muttered, wondering how exactly it worked. Was there a patch of rain just above her? How had the magic-keeper created such complicated magic?

The front door had not yet been locked and she heaved a sigh of relief as she slipped inside and headed for the staircase.

'Where have you been?' said a soft voice behind her.

Jude spun around. Grandleader was standing by the entrance to his part of the house, like he'd been waiting for her. The last time she had spoken to Grandleader one-on-one had been her twelfth birthday three months ago. Any other time she would have been thrilled to see him, but not when she was sneaking back from trying to lift the curse she had put on the whole family.

'Just for a walk. You know, to be at one with nature.' Jude shrugged, trying to keep her voice level as she edged towards the stairs.

'You came to the Consortium even though I did not invite you.' Grandleader cracked through Jude's excuse as easily as breaking an egg. He stood with his hands behind his back, the meaning clear: he expected all her secrets to spill out – or else.

Her heart hammered.

You're a Ripon for life.

'How did you …' Jude trailed off, not wanting to be rude.

'My dear Jude, *good* invisibility magic is made with water from the clearest stream in Farrowfell, which flows from the top of the Crying Mountains.' Grandleader raised his hand and the entrance hall was flooded with light, revealing the amusement on his face. 'That rubbish your father bought on the black market is a cheap knock-off.'

Jude's shoulders slumped, relief flooding through her. Grandleader was, if not impressed by her antics, at least entertained. 'I just wanted to watch the deal. You know – see what being a Ripon really is.' Her voice shook on the last word, the image of Everiste twitching on the ground flashing across her mind.

There was a long pause as Grandleader's eyes flicked over her. 'Let's have some tea,' he said eventually.

Jude bit her lip, unsure if she should be excited. If she let it slip where she had really gone after the deal … well, she didn't even want to think about how angry he would be.

She followed Grandleader to the draughty dining room and they sat on opposite sides of the table while a helpling poured tea. It gave Grandleader a flower-patterned cup with its own saucer and Jude a chipped mug.

The difference between the Westons' cosy tea room and their dining room was stark. There were no happy family photos here, nothing to suggest the room was lived in. Just the Ripon family motto engraved into the walls.

Jude held the mug with both hands. She hadn't wanted the tea offered by Eri but she would have gulped gallons for Grandleader.

'How are your studies coming along?' said Grandleader, taking a sip from his cup.

The question was so unexpected Jude almost choked on her drink. 'Good – I, erm ... learned more about the Wild Lands the other day.' She'd been bored and had flicked through a textbook, skim-reading facts about the Wild Lands that surrounded Farrowfell, before deciding she would take a nap. Her last private tutor had quit after just one day and Aunt Victi had taken over Jude's education. They'd only managed three lessons on how useless the government was before Aunt Victi said Jude should be independent enough to teach herself.

'Mmm.' Grandleader set his cup on its saucer with a clink. 'It is clear to me how much you care about the family, Jude. Your priorities are in order.'

Jude blinked, putting down her mug. She had

never heard such high praise from Grandleader – on her twelfth birthday he had congratulated her on making it to twelve, which she didn't think was much of an achievement. Moorley had already done it three years earlier.

'But you're still very young, my child,' Grandleader continued, waving away the helpling trying to refill his tea. 'There will be time aplenty for you to be more involved in the family business. And when your day comes, I know you will do wonderfully – you're a Ripon through and through.'

Jude repeated the words in her head.

A Ripon through and through.

Had anyone ever heard words so beautiful? She wished Moorley had been here to hear them. Or her mother.

'I think you can learn something from tonight, though,' said Grandleader. 'For example, what do you think the family business *is*?'

'Er . . .' Jude wondered if this was a trick question. 'Smuggling illegal magic from other kingdoms and selling it on the black market? And stealing rare tamed magic from rich people?'

Grandleader tilted his head. 'I've never liked the idea of any tamed magic being made illegal. Some has terrible side effects, of course – but if you know the risk, what's the harm? And some is banned because it helps with criminal activity – well, you can see why I wouldn't care about that.' He tilted his head. 'As the business has grown, I've begun to wonder ... should *any* kind of magic be illegal?'

Jude didn't understand the question but she knew the right answer. 'No?' she said, trying to figure what he was asking. The only other kind of magic was *raw magic* – the dangerous magic that became tamed magic by being mixed with exactly the right ingredients in exactly the right amounts.

'Bad *magic*,' continued Grandleader. 'There is no such thing. Only bad *people*.' A cold light burned in his eyes. 'And the Consortium agrees, you know. In secret. They put their brightest minds together to conduct ... research. Research I would very much like to see. Knowledge should be for *all*.'

Jude nodded along. She would have agreed with anything Grandleader said, still repeating those glorious words in her mind.

A Ripon through and through.

Grandleader got to his feet, leaving his cup for the helplings to clear up. 'I'm glad we had this chat.'

He'd talked to her like she was an equal. So she thought she would risk asking a question about the meeting she had snuck into. 'Grandleader ... who is Harrimore Hardman?'

Grandleader paused by the door, his shoulders tense. She immediately wished she could take the question back.

Then he turned and gave her a brief smile. 'He's someone I think will have some very good ideas ... for the business.'

***

Jude waited for Grandleader to go to his quarters before she slipped to her bedroom. She and Moorley had their rooms in a separate wing of the house. Habit meant Jude opened and closed the door leading to their corridor as quietly as possible. Moorley's door was ajar and she was hissing at someone in a low voice.

'We're supposed to sell rare tamed magic,' Moorley was saying. 'But Grandleader just wanted a location from tonight's meeting ... There's something weird going on, you must have noticed.'

'No, there's not.' It was Spry's voice that spoke back. 'We're making record profits, remember?'

'Do you *really* believe we're making all that money from selling tamed magic?' Moorley's voice was sceptical.

There was a pause, and when Spry spoke again he was hesitant. 'Well ... no. But whatever's happening, the best thing for us to do is stay out of the way.'

Jude felt a moment of triumph. She knew something Moorley didn't. Grandleader had told her *why* he was looking for Harrimore Hardman – Harrimore would have good ideas to help them take the family business to the next level.

'But has Grandleader said anything to you about a *special* family meeting?' Moorley's voice was now so low Jude had to strain her ears to hear. 'With everyone except you, me and Uncle Runie?'

'No. Like I said, we should just stay out of the way.'

Jude didn't have time to leap back as the door opened, and Spry stared at her. There was a brief moment of shock on his face, replaced a second later with an easy smile.

'You're wandering around late,' he said, quirking an eyebrow at her. 'Moorley, you should probably use anti-eavesdropping magic next time,' he said in a louder voice, as Moorley stood in her bedroom doorway and scowled at Jude. Spry whistled as he walked away.

'What did you hear?' asked Moorley. Then she shook her head. 'Never mind – it's really late, you should be asleep. You look exhausted.'

She was using her superior big sister tone, the one that made Jude immediately want to do the opposite of whatever she was saying. She'd spent years nagging at Jude and trying to stomp on all her fun.

'Goodnight, Moorley,' said Jude.

Chapter Eight

The Disappearance

Jude wanted to visit Fin and Eri the next day, to see if they could figure out the last place Mr and Mrs Weston had been seen. But in another round of bad luck, Ripon Headquarters decided to let in an invasion of grefers from the moorlands. Grefers were rat-like animals with the ability to walk on their hind legs and jump impossibly high. They seemed to think they were ghosts and had an annoying habit of sneaking around and popping up to shriek at you when you were at your most vulnerable. Jude had been disturbed in the bathroom many times.

Clearing the house was an unpleasant process that

involved sneaking up on the grefers with nets and trying to avoid the slime they spat. Jude had known Aunt Morgol would try to draft her in to get rid of them, so she'd gone up to the attic to hide – and run right into her aunt.

'Bad luck there, Jude,' said her aunt, a gleam in her eyes as she handed Jude a net. Moorley, Spry and Trudie were also told to help. Only Trudie was too busy spouting useless facts about the creatures to notice any running past, and Spry kept releasing the ones he'd caught in places he knew Aunt Morgol would be to scare her.

'Ripon Headquarters hasn't done anything this stupid in months,' moaned Spry as he slumped into a chair beside Jude. It took two days to get rid of the grefers, and Aunt Morgol had kept a beady eye on them all to make sure none of them tried to sneak off. 'This is such bad luck – I wanted to go to a festival in North Farrowfell and now I've missed it.'

What was worse was that Jude *knew* she could stop the bad luck if only she could sneak out to Fin and Eri and figure out how to find their parents. But when she tried later that day to slip out of a back door, Ripon Headquarters wouldn't let her go.

'I'm training the house how to lock down in case of an attack,' said Aunt Victi, appearing behind Jude. 'Only now it thinks it needs to *stay* locked down. All the time.'

At that point Jude considered climbing out of a window but couldn't get any to open wide enough to let her out. She tried to steal more ghost magic from Moorley but for some reason her sister had locked her door – Moorley *never* locked her door.

Jude started to get more frustrated. For a brief moment she considered telling Uncle Runie about the curse – he was less likely than the other adults in her family to immediately start punishing her – but then she decided to sleep on the problem, and when she woke the next morning, it was to find Ripon Headquarters had finally finished its lockdown. Relief flooded through her as she hurried out of the house before it could change its mind.

It had been three days since she'd first spoken to Fin and Eri. The curse hadn't seemed to get noticeably worse in that time, but she couldn't risk finding out what it would evolve into. For the entire journey to the Weston mansion she was on edge, expecting something terrible to happen. Finally, she was knocking on the front door.

Fin raised his eyebrows when he saw her. 'Didn't think you were coming back,' he said gruffly as he led Jude to the sitting room. His clothes were rumpled with stains of black and grey paint splotched across them.

The fire hadn't been lit but there was no need for it as the room was already warm, filled with sunlight, which streamed in through the windows. Doors on the far side of the room had been opened, leading out to neat gardens filled with blooming flowers. A fresh breeze flowed through and a helpling hummed as it sashayed in and placed a vase filled with sunshine-yellow buttercups on the mantelpiece.

Eri was sitting on the couch reading a textbook and making notes. She put down the book and smiled. Today she was wearing a turquoise dress, her silky hair tied up with a glittering ribbon. Jude ran a hand through her own frizzy hair, which had swelled even further in the humidity. She felt sweaty and unprepared next to Eri.

'You're home-schooled?' said Jude, pointing at the textbook. 'I am too – well, technically.'

'No – I'm just making sure I don't forget everything we learned,' said Eri, stacking her notes in a neat pile. 'It's the Gathering holidays.'

The Gathering holidays were so-called because it used to be when children would take time off school to help their parents recover from collecting raw magic. Magic-gathering was now a proper job, with the gatherers having to pass a series of difficult tests to make sure they were prepared to enter the dangerous Wild Lands, but the holiday remained.

'Oh. Well, if I had no parents around, I definitely wouldn't worry about stuff like school. Who looks after you anyway – the helplings?' When Jude was younger and no one had time to babysit, the helplings had given her food and made sure she didn't burn the house down.

Eri flushed, staring at the ground. Fin cleared his throat. 'Mum's best friend has been staying here,' he said. 'She's our guardian. We're very lucky.'

Jude looked around, expecting a stern old woman to pop up and scold her. 'Where is she? You haven't told her about me, have you?' She didn't want an adult involved – they would probably want to turn her over to the Consortium for stealing, or else try to tell her what to do. She had enough of that at home.

'No,' said Fin abruptly. 'Obviously not.'

'She's at work,' said Eri, locking her fingers together. 'She works a *lot* – at the, erm . . . bank.'

'I guess you've been off speaking to all your thief friends?' said Fin suddenly.

'Thieves don't have friends,' said Jude with a sniff. Of course they had no idea about basic things like that, poor things, all sheltered and cosy in their mansion. She sat on the couch (it *was* a very comfy couch) and crossed her arms. 'So tell me – why were your parents so interested in the Lilthrum? Why'd your parents think it was their problem? Surely there's loads of people at the Consortium who could investigate?'

A helpling bent by Eri's side and offered her tea and gingerbread. Jude held out a hand for the sugary golden biscuits, her mouth watering. The helpling held the tray above its head, way out of her reach. It probably would have stuck its tongue out at her if it had one. The moment its back was turned she snaffled several biscuits and crunched them triumphantly.

'Well, it was the right thing to do,' Eri said, like it was obvious.

'People don't do good things just because.' Jude sprayed crumbs as she spoke because she was determined to finish her treats before the helpling noticed. 'They get something out of it as well. So, what was your parents' plan? They want power or something?'

'No, they did not want power,' said Eri, setting down her tea and leaning forward as if trying to see how much of a mess Jude had made. 'You do good things because they're good things to do.'

Jude snorted, then tried to cover it up with a cough.

Fin had been sitting quietly, his dark eyes fixed on Jude. He shifted. 'Our parents were – *are* – experts in magic. They've spent their lives studying it and they occasionally advise the Consortium on issues related to it. If anyone was going to find an answer to why there's more Lilthrum, it'd be them.' He ran his fingers through his hair. 'Can we trust you? Really?'

'I'm here, aren't I?' grumbled Jude. 'Got this stinking curse on my family. I have no choice but to help you.'

Fin stared at her with his head slightly tilted, as if still expecting her to attempt to run off with the grandfather clock ticking in the corner. 'Well, then . . .' He took a deep breath. 'We think our parents discovered something bad. Something dangerous.'

Jude furrowed her eyebrows. 'Huh?'

Eri pursed her lips, staring at the floor. Fin got to his feet and headed to one of the windows, his back to Jude as he looked out at the manicured lawn beyond.

'Why are you both acting so weird?' asked Jude. For the first time since she'd arrived she felt nervous. How much did she even know about the Weston siblings? They kept cursed magic in their home; they were friends with a magic-keeper who took her job much too seriously.

She palmed her yo-yo, feeling its comforting weight.

Fin turned around, sucking in his cheeks. 'The night our parents disappeared, they were worried – scared. They kept repeating, "This can't be true", and, "We need to do something."'

'Do something about what?' asked Jude.

'They didn't say,' said Fin. 'We guess they were going to go and fix whatever was wrong . . . and disappeared trying.'

'Why didn't you question them?' said Jude, annoyed. This was vague nonsense that would get them nowhere.

Eri was drinking her tea again, her face hidden by the mug. Judging by her bobbing throat she was gulping it like water. When she set the mug down her face was flaming. 'We weren't supposed to be listening. They didn't know we were at the door.'

Fin stared at the ground.

Jude scratched her head. 'I don't get it,' she said as she looked from Eri to Fin. 'What's wrong?'

Eri's eyes were wide. 'They didn't want us to know! They told us we should *never* eavesdrop, that people who do only hear bad things. We betrayed their trust and then they disappeared.'

Jude couldn't believe what she was hearing. *This* was why Eri looked so guilty? The last time her mother and father went away for a business trip, she'd only found out because she had listened at the door. Eavesdropping was the most natural thing in the world! 'You're serious? You can get magic made which makes sure no one can listen in on you – if they didn't bother with it, they clearly didn't care if someone was eavesdropping.'

'It's not just that,' said Fin, though clearly it was enough for Eri, who looked like she was wishing the ground would swallow her whole. 'When Mum and Dad were leaving I . . . I yelled at them not to go. I said some . . . some stuff I wish I hadn't.' He rubbed the end of his nose. 'I wish I could take it back.'

Jude leaned in, intrigued. 'Oooh, what'd you say?'

Fin's look of shame turned into a glare. 'None of your business.'

'Sorry,' Jude said, not sorry at all. 'Right, so your parents were looking for a reason why there's more Lilthrum, found out something bad, tried to fix whatever it was – and went missing. This isn't a lot to go on.'

'We've tried everything we can think of,' said Eri. 'We even hired private detectives.'

Jude had a sudden mental image of Eri ordering a bunch of expensive detectives to sit down on newspaper while she explained how she had once eavesdropped on her parents *even though they had asked her not to*.

'We've tried looking ourselves,' continued Eri. 'We've asked everyone they have any sort of connection to if they knew anything. We've searched all the places we could think of; we went to the library . . .'

Jude frowned. 'The library? What – you thought the answer would be in a book?'

Eri's face could have cooked eggs. The helpling bustled over, picking up the empty biscuit plate and Eri's mug. 'I think I should help clear up,' said Eri, trying to yank the plate from the helpling. 'Look, his hands are full—'

'We thought we could figure out what our parents were doing,' Fin cut in, picking at the dried paint on his skin. 'We thought we could be smarter than the best detectives in Farrowfell. And after a year we have absolutely nothing to show for it.'

Eri stopped struggling with the helpling, her shoulders slumping. 'We're desperate,' she said, her voice cracking.

It was a shame Jude couldn't use the decision-making magic to figure out what to do. But even if the curse hadn't stopped it from working, she wouldn't be able to return it to Mr and Mrs Weston later if she ate it.

She frowned as she looked at Fin and Eri, a thought occurring to her. 'Hang on – why didn't you use your decision-making magic to help you figure out how to get your parents back? You know – before I stole it?'

Eri looked at Fin, her eyes wide.

'Well ... it's cursed,' Fin said with a shrug. 'And since it belongs to our parents, only our parents can lift that curse – until then we can't use it either.'

Jude bit her bottom lip. From the sound of it, Fin and Eri had tried everything they *legally* could do to find their parents.

'What we need,' she said, 'is some magic to help us find them. Like a tracker – but for people.'

'Using magic to track people is illegal under the Right to Privacy from Magical Meddling Act,' said Eri at once.

'Yeah, I know,' said Jude automatically. 'Wait – why do *you* know that?'

'You don't think we researched using a magical solution for this?' said Fin. 'We weren't born yesterday.'

Jude rolled her eyes. 'So, where's the magic?'

'Didn't you hear Eri?' said Fin, pausing from picking at the paint. 'Using tracking magic to find people is illegal—'

'So clearly you *were* born yesterday, because otherwise you'd have ignored that stupid rule.'

'It's the *law*,' said Eri. If possible, her back had got straighter. Jude probably could have used it as a ruler.

'Well, *I'm* going to find out how we get our hands on some of that sweet, sweet illegal magic,' said Jude, getting to her feet. 'And I have just the person in mind.' Farlow Higgins, the criminal who had told her about the decision-making magic in the first place. He'd got her into this mess. He owed her.

'A thief,' said Fin. 'Thought you said thieves don't have friends.'

'He's definitely *not* a friend,' said Jude as she headed to the door. 'Are you two coming or not?'

Eri grimaced as she looked at Fin.

'Whatever,' said Jude, rolling her eyes. Cowards – fancy being scared of buying a little illegal magic! She strolled out of the room and into the entrance hall, the front opening of its own accord.

In daylight, the Westons' grounds looked like something out of a storybook. Several thrushes pecked at the water in a bird bath, occasionally raising their heads to let out bursts of song. Rabbits played across the grass and a few helplings were planting flowers with multicoloured petals.

'Wait!' called Eri as she and Fin hurried up to walk beside her.

'Where do we find your friend?' said Fin. 'Down a dark alley? Stealing from babies?'

'Thieves are people just like you, Finobert – is that your full name?' Jude frowned. 'Finjamin? Finstar?'

'Fin *is* my full name,' he scowled.

'Eri's short for Erisabeth,' chipped in Eri, almost tripping over herself as she tried to keep up.

'Great – well, as I was saying, thieves are people, Finolay. They have jobs just like everyone else. And our thief in question has a little shop in Mergio Market.'

Chapter Nine

Mergio Market

Mergio Market was set in the shadow of one of the mountains that bordered Farrowfell. Rivers of black gushed in waterfalls over the mountains and snaked all the way through the land, breaking and branching, black veins webbing across the hills and valleys. These Dark Rivers stopped raw magic from falling in Farrowfell, acting as a natural barrier to the dangerous magic.

The Dark Rivers did not flow in the Wild Lands surrounding Farrowfell, and this was where raw magic fell. Only gatherers working for the Consortium made the journey to these highly magical lands, to track down and bring back small amounts of raw magic. The Consortium carefully controlled these trips because the Wild Lands were dangerous, home to the Lilthrum who would injure or kill any visitors. The Consortium then gave raw magic to people with special licences, people who could shape the dangerous liquid into tamed magic.

A number of these people worked at Mergio Market, a bright place crammed full of all kinds of shops which had sprung up to replace the original stalls many years ago. Farrowfell's winters were often freezing and having outdoor stalls simply wasn't practical.

Jude looked the other way when they passed a few ordinary-looking clothes shops which belonged to the Ripons. These were used as fronts for their illegal sales and she didn't want the shopkeepers asking who her new friends were and passing the information back to Grandleader. The shopkeepers had signed up to work for Grandleader for life – they were intensely loyal, or else risked his wrath. If anyone tried to leave the service of the Ripons, they might find their house burned down or themselves framed for a crime they hadn't committed … Grandleader could be inventive with his punishments.

As ever, there were Farrowfell Guards hanging around, clutching their swords and peering at people walking past. Their uniforms were spotless, not a strand of hair out of place.

Jude ignored them as she led Fin and Eri into an alleyway off the main street, where Farlow Higgins had his shop.

'I was right about the dark alley,' muttered Fin as they walked down the cobbled lane.

Jude headed for the dingiest shop at the end, which had a layer of grime so thick on the windows it was impossible to tell what was inside. The door of a bakery was flung open, snapping against the wall with a bang. A man clutching two halves of a loaf of bread in each hand was shoved out.

'I ain't paying five kira for this broken bread! I'll give you two and be done with it,' said Farlow Higgins, waving the halves of bread above his head. He was tall and skinny, and wore a thick, shabby coat even in the middle of summer. The coat had many pockets, making it easy for him to pinch things and slip away without anyone seeing. He'd done odd jobs for Jude's family in the past.

'You're the one who tore it up in the first place!' roared the baker, a small, round man with rosy cheeks who had followed Farlow out.

'Er – maybe we should wait here,' said Eri, grasping Fin's arm and dragging him backwards.

Jude rolled her eyes as she marched up to Farlow. 'Here, I'll buy the bread,' she said, holding out a few coins to the baker. She didn't want to waste time listening to the nonsense Farlow would come up with trying to talk himself out of trouble. 'You'll want to get rid of him as fast as you can. If he stays too long, he'll definitely steal from you.'

The baker took her money and flapped them both away.

'Why'd you tell him that for?' said Farlow, stuffing one of the loaves into his biggest coat pocket and tearing into the other one. 'I was going to nick a few of them cakes in the window too.'

'Proving my point,' said Jude, shaking her head when Farlow tried to offer her some of the crust. 'So, remember that tip-off you gave me about the Weston magic?'

Farlow, who had probably never looked innocent, even as a newborn baby, looked even shifter. 'What about it?'

'Where'd you hear about it in the first place?'

Farlow shrugged, not meeting her eyes as he tore another chunk of bread and stuffed it into his mouth. 'Some bloke down the pub. You get it or not?'

'Yeah, I did,' said Jude stiffly. She wouldn't tell him it was cursed – Farlow had a big mouth and this was the sort of gossip he loved.

Farlow broke out into a genuine smile. 'Good for you, kid,' he said, spraying bread crumbs at her.

'Can we go somewhere more private?' asked Jude, aware of the baker's curious gaze.

'Let's go inside.' Farlow nodded at his shop. 'Though

I gots to warn you, there's two kids over there staring at us and they don't look happy. Like they just got told the date of their own deaths.'

'That's Fin and Eri.' Jude raised her voice to call to them. 'He won't hurt you.' Eri jumped and Fin edged forward cautiously.

'Where'd you find them?' said Farlow as he led them into his shop, a dingy space crammed with ugly paintings of rugged moorlands. A layer of dust coated the floor, the windows so dirty daylight barely managed to enter the room. He'd probably never made a single kira from the paintings, but that didn't matter – in the back of the shop he made very good money from selling stolen goods.

'Doesn't matter,' said Jude as Eri got out a snowy white handkerchief, wrapped it around the door handle and closed it gently behind her. Fin's eyes flicked over the paintings and he grimaced. Jude decided to launch straight into the reason for her visit. 'Your sources tell you where to get all kinds of magic, right? Even the super-illegal stuff?'

'You looking for your next heist?' said Farlow as he slipped behind the counter. 'Blimey, kid, I never thought I'd say this, but don't push your luck. Supposed to wait a couple of weeks between jobs.'

'I didn't know you cared,' said Jude, oddly touched.

'You call that *caring*?' said Eri, her mouth twisting.

'Anyway,' said Jude, ignoring the comment. 'Do you

have any idea where I can find magic to track someone down? Someone who's missing?'

A sipling waddled across the counter, right over Farlow's resting hand. Siplings were tiny animals that looked like teddy bears, though they weren't creatures anyone would want to cuddle as they made their homes in piles of dirt or rubbish. Farlow didn't seem to notice a second sipling following the first, his bushy eyebrows drawing together as he frowned. 'What d'you want tracking magic for? It's dangerous.'

A pulse of worry shot through Jude. Was Farlow getting *responsible* on her? Did this mean he wouldn't help? 'Never mind. You know how to get it?' She lowered her voice to try and sound grown up and reassuring.

'What's wrong with your voice?' whispered Eri out of the corner of her mouth. Jude elbowed her.

Farlow bit his lip. 'Well – normally when you eat magic, there's a few side effects. The more complex the magic, the bigger the side effects, see? Tracking magic got banned because it ... well, you'd find the person you were looking for, but ...er ... lose yourself.'

'Like ... like you'd forget where you were?' said Jude, exchanging a confused look with Eri. Fin was staring intensely at Farlow, as though he thought that if he focused hard enough he could read his mind.

'No – more like you explode,' Farlow shrugged. 'But not always, if that makes it any better. It was completely random, who exploded and who didn't. They ended up figuring out that taking anti-nausea magic solved that side effect, no problem, but by then it had already been banned, and then that law about magic primacy—'

'Privacy,' said Jude and Eri at the same time.

'Yeah, that one, came out and made tracking magic illegal. But this is super-rare magic, kid – you know what sorts of ingredients you need to mix in to make it? Stuff like the nose of a pugglypuff, which has the best sense of smell in the world, and pugglypuffs have only got one extra nose to spare and they won't give it up without a fight. In fact, I think I only know one place where you can find tracking magic.' Farlow was frowning at her again, his face full of curiosity. 'Which is why I'm interested in why you're asking.'

'Where can I get it?' pressed Jude eagerly, deciding she would ignore all Farlow's dire warnings and focus on the positive part: he knew where she should look.

'Well, it's hidden inside what's probably the most highly guarded place in all of Farrowfell. Way harder than your last steal—'

'Where?' repeated Jude.

'Ripon Headquarters,' said Farlow, his head tilted.

Jude's stomach swooped, her ears filling with a roaring sound. She'd stolen magic from her family before but that was stuff they left somewhere easy for anyone to swipe. This would be way harder – and if she got caught, she didn't know what would happen.

Or maybe she did. This wasn't something she'd be accidentally doing, like cursing the family. This would be a proper betrayal.

Farlow was smiling at her expectantly, a glint in his eye.

'You OK, Jude? Shall we buy the anti-nausea magic first?' asked Eri. She placed her hand on Jude's shoulder.

'Yeah, of course,' Jude said, her voice coming out too bright and cheery. For all she knew, Grandleader might appreciate her initiative, or be amused by her, like he had when she'd snuck along to the Consortium meeting.

She shrugged off Eri's hand, clearing her throat and trying to sound as business-like as possible. 'What's this tracking magic look like?'

Farlow shrugged. 'Supposed to be quite big – like a good-sized rock. Bright green, I think. Can't miss it.'

'Great,' said Jude, her thoughts still hurtling in circles. She'd stolen the decision-making magic to impress her family and where had that led her? To cursing her own family and attempting to steal from them to cover it up. No wonder they all loved stupid, perfect Moorley more than her.

'Er . . . Jude?' said Fin, breaking into her spiral.

She forced the thoughts away. She'd never been one to overthink and she wasn't about to start now. 'Let's go and get some anti-nausea magic,' she said.

Chapter Ten

Madam Cada's Magic Made

Jude led Fin and Eri through the bustling streets of Mergio Market. 'The best medicine shops are right in the centre, so that's where we'll go,' she said. Farlow's shop was near the outskirts of the market, so they had quite a long way to walk. Mergio Market wasn't the biggest market in Farrowfell but all the streets were arranged in such a higgledy-piggledy way, looping back on themselves, twisting into dead-ends randomly, that it was impossible to take a direct route through it.

As they went, a scream pierced the air.

Jude jumped, looking around for the source of the noise.

'What was that?' Eri came to a halt.

'I think it came from that way,' pointed Fin past a line of bakeries. There was another scream of absolute, pure terror, which sent shockwaves through Jude. The people in the street turned in the direction Fin had pointed. Several dropped their shopping bags and sprinted away.

'Good to know,' said Jude quickly. 'So, we're going the other way.' She made to follow everyone else, but Eri grabbed her arm.

'What are you doing?' she said. 'We need to go and help.'

'What?' said Jude. 'You run *from* the screaming.' The few shoppers who had frozen at the noise joined the others in running away from the centre of the market.

'It's a Lilthrum!' someone screamed as an inhuman shriek cut through the air.

Jude froze, locked into place as she tried to register what was happening. She'd grown up listening to nightmare stories about Lilthrum but she never thought she'd be close enough to hear one roar.

A Farrowfell Guard rounded the corner. His sword was hanging loosely from his fingers and there was a dark stain on his uniform. 'What are you doing?' he screamed at them, sweat dripping from his forehead. 'It's coming – run! *Run!*'

There was another shriek, closer this time, and the sound was enough for Jude's brain to start working again. She turned on her heel and fled, and didn't need to check to see that Fin and Eri were following her.

People were stampeding away from the centre of the market where the inhuman roaring and shrieking seemed to be loudest.

'There's another one!' someone screamed, pointing upwards. Jude paused to see something enormous and silver leaping across the shop roofs. It was shaped like a human, but longer and narrower, as if someone had taken a person and stretched their body too far.

'We need to get inside!' said Jude. She chose a random side street, bursting into a shop. Fin and Eri followed and they slammed the door behind them.

'Lock it!' ordered Jude. Eri's hands trembled as she slid the bolts across.

Jude rested her head on the glass. Had her curse somehow drawn the Lilthrum to Mergio Market? Could other people be hurt by her bad luck? Would it continue to get worse? A few grefers on the loose, a house lockdown, she could cope with. This was something different entirely.

'Excuse me,' said a quiet voice from behind. 'Why are you locking my door?'

A woman, who Jude assumed was the shop owner, had drifted in from the back room. She had wrinkled sand-brown skin, a shade darker than Jude's, and wore shawls of various colours. Beaded necklaces swung as she moved, and her raven-black hair had strands of grey. She was wearing what appeared to be bird feathers draped across all her clothes.

'There are Lilthrum outside,' panted Jude. Fin's eyes were fixed on the door and Eri had her hand clapped over her mouth as she took deep breaths.

'Ah, I wondered what all the screaming was about,' said the woman with a smile. Jude stared at her. She didn't seem at all bothered by the fact that there were raw-magic monsters lurking in Mergio Market. Unlike Jude, whose legs were shaking.

Jude tried to focus on her new surroundings. The shop was dimly lit, the air thick with the smell of incense. Candles burned in little pots on the floor. On groaning shelves, behind dusty glass, were pre-prepared medicines for basic things like sniffly noses or headaches. On the counter were a few plants waving stubby green leaves.

'Is this . . . is this a medicine shop?' she asked cautiously.

'It is indeed,' said the woman, her voice soft and dreamy, the beaded necklaces clinking as she held out her arms in welcome. 'I am Madam Cada. And *this* is Madam Cada's Magic Made – the *finest* pharmacy in all of Farrowfell.'

It was lucky the shop they'd taken shelter in was a pharmacy, which was just what they needed . . . Except, the curse wouldn't allow good luck, would it? Jude had a prickling feeling down the back of her neck. There was something off about Madam Cada. Though her voice was dreamy, her eyes were sharp, sizing the three of them up.

'Are these harwaki plants?' said Eri as she sidled up to the plants on the counter. She didn't seem to notice anything wrong. 'I've got one at home – I've been trying to grow it for ages, but it keeps dying.'

That distracted Jude. 'What do you mean, *keeps* dying?' she said, unsure she'd heard Eri right.

'Harwaki plants rely completely on the selflessness of their owners to stay alive,' said Madam Cada as she stroked the spiky leaf of one. 'I work with raw magic on a daily basis to make tamed magic. Raw magic brings out your worst traits and my greatest failing is selfishness. If my plants were to die, I would know the raw magic I work with had corrupted me.'

Jude frowned at Eri. 'What're you doing that's so selfish?'

Eri jutted out her jaw. 'Nothing. I feed mine all the time and I water it and I give it lots of sunlight.'

Despite the dim lighting, Madam Cada's eyes glittered as she straightened. 'Did you know you can be *too* selfless? Too much of a good thing can be bad.'

Jude rolled her eyes at the idea that Eri's big flaw was that she might be too selfless. It sounded like the sort of non-existent flaw Moorley might be told she had. No Ripon could ever be called selfless – they all had too much of a survival instinct for that – but

Jude imagined Eri would probably warm to her silent, serious sister.

'We want to buy some magic,' cut in Fin. 'It shouldn't take too long to make – it's pretty basic.'

Jude nudged him; she didn't want to buy anything from Madam Cada.

'What?' he muttered. She opened her mouth, then closed it. They didn't have many options – it wasn't like they could waltz past any Lilthrum in the centre of the market to find a shop more suited to her tastes, and they didn't have time to be picky, not with the curse hanging over her head. It looked like Madam Cada was the best they were going to get.

Madam Cada turned her gaze on Jude. Her eyes were two different colours: one brown and the other purple and glassy. 'What is the magic you want, my dears?' she asked. The rings on each of her fingers glinted in the flickering light from the candles.

'Magic to combat nausea,' said Eri. 'But really bad nausea – like you'd get if you were to spin in circles a thousand times.'

One of the harwaki plants folded its leaves in on itself, as if giving itself a hug. 'I can make that for you,' said Madam Cada, arching an eyebrow. 'But it will take a bit longer if you want me to make enough for three.'

'It's just for me,' said Jude. She, of course, would be the one eating the tracking magic so only she needed the anti-nausea spell. 'But they'll be paying,' she added, nodding at the Westons. She'd already bought Farlow Higgins the bread – she didn't need to keep throwing her money away.

Fin snorted but said nothing.

'Fine.' Madam Cada pointed at Jude with a crooked little finger. 'You, come and help make the magic.'

Jude scrunched her face up. 'Why?'

Madam Cada's voice lost its dreaminess. 'My assistant didn't show up today and I don't like chopping the ingredients.'

'Er ... aren't only people with licences allowed to actually make magic?' asked Eri.

She trailed off at the look Madam Cada gave her. 'If you don't like the way I do things, you can go somewhere else.' She nodded at the door, which had somehow unlocked, swinging open long enough for them to hear the faint sounds of yelling before Fin closed it again.

'Fine, I'll do it,' said Jude quickly, shooting Eri a look to tell her to stay quiet.

Madam Cada's smile widened. 'Good. Plant girl, boy, you two wait here. I have some harwaki feed in one of the drawers if you'd like to give it a snack. Not too much, mind you.'

Jude dragged her heels as she followed Madam Cada into the back room. She found herself in a vast kitchen with stone floors and a large fire roaring in the corner.

Steam whistled from the cauldron hanging above the fire.

'Now ... chop these.' Madam Cada set a bundle of leaves and a knife on the counter in the centre of the room. 'Have you ever seen magic being made before?'

'No.' Jude did as she was told, lining the leaves in a row and slicing. A foul smell floated from them, a mixture of rotten eggs and three-week-old milk. She gagged, eyes streaming from the stench.

'Not even in school?' Madam Cada frowned. 'The education system has gone downhill since my day – and don't be foolish, hold your breath.'

Jude knew Theory of Magic-Making was a class in most schools, but her education so far had been patchy to say the least.

'I like using strong smells in my anti-nausea magic,' continued Madam Cada. 'Smells that unsettle the stomach. It's the same reason people who make cleaning magic often use dirt as a key ingredient. The ingredients you use need to be linked to what your magic does in some way, you see.'

Madam Cada pulled back the bolt on a cupboard and took out a little box, which she held away from her body as she crossed the room. She leaned over the cauldron, tipping the contents of the box into it. Jude's breath caught as something glimmering silver disappeared into the cauldron and a smell of freshly baked cake with a chocolate frost filled the air ... Jude didn't even know *how* she could tell the cake had a chocolate frost but she could imagine the moist sponge, chocolate dripping down the side ... Exactly like the cake her mother bought on her seventh birthday. A warm feeling spread through her at the memory.

Jude's mouth watered. Without thinking, she took a few steps forward. But then Madam Cada added a few herbs into the pot and almost at once the smell disappeared.

'That's raw magic,' Jude said, staring at the pot. She'd always imagined raw magic would smell horrible, like old milk and sewage – something that reflected how evil it was. But it was ... lovely.

'Yes.' Madam Cada put the box back into the cupboard, shutting the door and drawing the bolt. 'Keep chopping.'

Jude sliced with the knife but she couldn't keep herself from shooting glances at the cauldron hanging innocently over the fire. There were folktales about raw magic, how it was conscious, swearing revenge on the humans who twisted its nature by taming it. Jude had never given much thought to the tales before, but her mind was replaying the story about the man who had angered the stars by making too many clouds. They'd been furious at him for hiding them from sight as they were very vain and took revenge by releasing so much raw magic that the man drowned in a sea of shining silver liquid. Ever since, so the tale went, raw magic fell from the stars like a tap that could never be turned off.

Madam Cada interrupted Jude's thoughts as she scooped up a handful of the chopped leaves. 'Smells disgusting – excellent, excellent indeed.' She dropped the mix into the pot, stirring, then adding what looked like rotten eggs.

The room got hotter and sweat stuck Jude's clothes to her body. She slipped her favourite black trench coat off.

'Come and stir,' said Madam Cada.

Jude hesitated, not wanting to get closer to the raw magic than she needed to. Now that the delicious smell had gone, the way it had been able to tap into her memories felt creepy.

'It's OK to be scared,' said Madam Cada with an understanding smile.

That annoyed Jude. She wasn't *scared*. With a huff, she marched up to the cauldron and peered over the edge at the silver mass churning in circles. The raw magic was cloudy, and sparkled slightly, like its surface was catching the last ray of sunlight.

Jude clutched the long spoon and stirred. Madam Cada threw in spices and began to sing, the words soft and soothing. As the mixture swirled, Jude's arms grew heavier. Tiredness crept through her and she stifled a yawn. It was like energy was being sucked from her.

'Can I stop?' she said. Madam Cada was muttering to herself, occasionally throwing in extra spices. She ignored Jude, continuing to mutter, her eyebrows knitted together in concentration.

Five minutes passed, or longer – Jude didn't know. Her knees buckled but it was like her hands were locked on to the spoon, her arms continuing to stir.

Madam Cada batted her away. 'Taming raw magic is not easy. It drains you, yes?'

Jude sat on a high stool, relieved she no longer needed to stir. 'Why's it so hard?'

'Because you have not been taught.' Madam Cada sniffed. 'Taming raw magic drains more than just your energy – but it is better than the alternative.'

'What's that?' Jude yawned again, eyes drooping. Her thoughts were sluggish.

The cloudiness in Madam Cada's eyes was replaced by deep clarity. 'Drinking it raw, of course.'

Drinking raw magic was taboo: the magic that fell from the stars was not fit for humans. Jude had heard the stories of what happened to those who drank. They died, or else ended up in a state of living death, shells of the people they had once been, unaware of the passage of time, until eventually their bodies gave up.

'How do you make it tamed and . . . not raw?' said Jude to take her mind off the thought. 'Like this? Just stirring and adding some key ingredients?'

'No, that is not all.' Madam Cada stopped stirring, resting the spoon on the edge of the cauldron. Her eyes lost their focus and she shivered, her mouth going slack.

'Er ... Madam Cada?' said Jude, waving a hand in front of her face.

Madam Cada shook her head, sucking in a piece of spit dangling from her bottom lip. She continued speaking as if nothing had happened. 'To tame magic we put some ... humanity into it. We put in things magic does not understand, like compassion and kindness. We strip away the parts of raw magic that chip at your soul.'

'How do you do that?' asked Jude.

Madam Cada shrugged. 'I believe that's not something the Consortium wants young children knowing. Not that I agree with them, but it's part of my licence terms not to reveal that secret. Now, come and see the magic.'

Jude looked into the pot. Most of the liquid had boiled away so only a small glob remained, right at the bottom. The silvery sheen had gone, replaced by a dark blue hue. It was thicker now, more like a jelly. Madam Cada scooped it out with a hand and folded it over.

She took it over to the counter and stroked a finger across the jelly-like surface as she set it down, her shoulders slumping. 'The rawness is still there. My work isn't good enough.' With a quick movement she grabbed a hammer hooked on to a nail on the wall. Before Jude could stop her, she smashed it down on the blue jelly.

Annoyance swept through Jude – why was Madam Cada destroying the magic they'd spent so long making? But when Madam Cada lifted the hammer the magic was still intact. She smashed again, and the magic twisted over itself, forming a little ball. The hammer came down a third time and Madam Cada stood back, wiping her brow.

'Go back to your friends,' Madam Cada said, panting. 'This will take a while to finish.' She started to sing again as she smashed down the hammer. Jude was glad to leave the strange woman to her job.

She found Eri feeding little bits of yellow goo to the harwaki plant. The leaves curled around the food, and when they unfurled the yellow goo had disappeared. Fin was sitting cross-legged on the floor, sketching in a notebook.

Jude leaned against the counter. She'd never really thought about how tamed magic was made. It was always just there, made for her, ready to be eaten.

Eri looked up. 'That didn't take long. How was it?'

It had felt like *days* to Jude, but when she looked at the clock she saw only a few hours had passed. She shrugged, not knowing how to explain, and focused instead on Fin's picture. It was good. He had outlined Madam Cada, the broad strokes of his pencil capturing the thoughtful look in her eyes, her slack jaw, the flowing hair.

He looked up, meeting Jude's eyes, and shifted his arm to cover his picture.

'You know there's magic that can make you draw really well,' said Jude, irritated at him trying to hide it from her. 'Captures the image perfectly.'

Fin ignored her, his head carefully bent over the sketchpad.

***

While they were waiting for Madam Cada to finish, a Farrowfell Guard came into the store to tell them that Mergio Market was clear of Lilthrum.

'Was anyone hurt?' asked Jude.

The guard shook his head. 'But someone was … taken. We'll find them, of course,' he added hurriedly. 'There's no need to panic.'

'Who?' said Fin.

'A toymaker,' said the guard. 'Felix Snuggleton.'

A shiver went down Jude's back. She remembered Spry mentioning a Lilthrum had tried to drag away a man who sold toys but it hadn't succeeded. Had it come back to try again?

No, that couldn't be right. The Lilthrum didn't *target* people. They were mindless monsters, killing anything that crossed their paths and sucking their remaining lifeforce.

Jude pushed the unsettling thought away. The Lilthrum weren't her problem.

'Have a safe journey home,' said the guard as he left.

Finally, Madam Cada bustled in from the back room and placed the magic proudly on the counter. It didn't look like much, a turquoise sweet about the size of Jude's thumbnail. She slipped it into her pocket and hoped it would be enough to protect her from exploding.

'Thank you,' said Eri as Fin paid. Madam Cada smiled as the coins clinked in her till.

'Do come again,' she said.

They exited the shop. Their shadows stretched before them and a slight chill hung in the air as the sun set. The streets were largely empty, and even though they'd been told the centre of the market was safe, they came to a silent agreement to take a path around the outskirts. Farrowfell Guards were posted every few metres, their hands on their swords, as if ready for another attack.

Jude still had no clue how she would steal the magic from her family, but at least she'd made some progress. She was one step closer to finding the Weston parents and getting rid of the curse.

They reached Mergio Market's port, and Eri and Fin stopped and looked at her.

'Shall we go back to our house and work out a plan?' asked Eri.

Jude couldn't think of anything worse. Owning up to eavesdropping had made Eri burn scarlet; the thought of stealing might make her explode, even without eating tracking magic. She didn't want to waste time trying to pretend Fin and Eri's ideas were any good, not when she could go straight home and come up with an idea that might actually work. 'Stealing is more of a solo thing,' she said delicately.

Fin shook his head. 'You're trying to find our parents. We'll do whatever we can to help. Just tell us what.'

'That's sweet, it really is, but I don't think stealing is something either of you can help with.' Jude stepped towards the port. 'And I work best alone.'

Chapter Eleven

A Different Type of Curse

On her journey home through the ports, Jude got straight to work. The Lilthrum attack at Mergio Market had unsettled her, but the more she thought about her next heist, the more she found herself getting excited at the possibility of outsmarting the rest of her family. If it went well, maybe she would be able to tell Grandleader about it one day. He would be impressed by her cleverness, see what a good thief she was and how much she could help the business. By the time she stumbled out of the Ripons' port she was buzzing with ideas – the best one she had was tricking a helpling into showing her where the Ripons kept their most priceless magic.

When Jude finally got back, it was to find Spry and Uncle Runie surfing mattresses down the main staircase. They were doing handstands or jumping as they went.

'Want to join?' Uncle Runie called.

'No, I'm OK,' said Jude. Normally, it would have been the sort of thing she loved. But she wanted to get cracking on kidnapping a helpling.

Uncle Runie frowned for a moment, and she wondered if he was suspicious. But then Spry managed to do a front roll as the mattress slid down the stairs and his attention was back on his son.

'What in the name of Farrowfell are you doing?' Aunt Morgol appeared at the top of the stairs, her hands on her hips as she looked at Uncle Runie and Spry. Her eyes narrowed as they locked on Jude. 'Judiper – I've been looking for you! Where *have* you been? The house threw a tantrum and knocked over all the cabinets in the tea room. I need you to go and clean up.'

Here was the curse, yet again trying to ruin her life.

'That's what the helplings are for!' whined Jude. She didn't have *time* for this.

She bet the Weston mansion never threw a tantrum. It was probably super-nice and cheerful all the time.

'Why don't Uncle Runie and Spry have to clean as well?'

'Because Uncle Runie is an *adult*,' said Aunt Morgol as Uncle Runie did a backflip and collided into the banister.

'What a hit!' Uncle Runie cheered. 'Ooh, that's going to bruise!'

'And Spry has been so helpful in sorting out the pipes,' she continued.

Jude scowled as she headed across the entrance hall to the passageway behind the stairs. So much for getting on with her plan.

'Wipe that scowl off your face!' Aunt Morgol's voice floated after her.

Jude huffed, the fires in the brackets flickering to life as she went. Stupid house. Stupid Aunt Morgol.

The passageway led to the tea room at the back of the house. It was a large space that overlooked the grounds. Aunt Victi had put down some sort of poison so the lawn stayed alive but never grew. In daylight Jude would have been able to see acres of yellow, sickly grass stretching off into the distance. Now, however, on the other side of the windows was darkness.

The tea room itself had a few armchairs grouped around a table too low to actually be of any use. The mahogany cabinets were standing upright against the far wall but their contents were all over the floor; loose leaf teas all mixed together.

A helpling was clutching a dustpan and brush as it kicked the tea leaves into a pile. Jude sized the helpling up; if she wanted to kidnap it, she'd need a giant net or something. It definitely wouldn't come easily.

Moorley popped up from behind one of the armchairs, also holding a dustpan.

'What're you doing here?' said Jude with a start as she took the helpling's dustpan and brush. Moorley was the last person she wanted to see. 'Aunt Morgol isn't making you clean too, is she?'

'No, I volunteered,' said Moorley. Jude rolled her eyes. Of course *perfect* Moorley would have volunteered. 'Aunt Morgol wants us to rescue as much tea as possible so nothing goes to waste.' She scooped up some of the tea and put it in a jar.

'Gross,' said Jude with a shudder. There were several bits of fluff mixed in with the leaves. She pitied the person who tried drinking it.

'Where were you all day?' said Moorley as Jude bent down and half-heartedly brushed a few bits of tea around.

Jude said nothing. What on earth did it have to do with Moorley? And why was she making small talk when she couldn't possibly care? She wished Moorley would hurry up and leave so that she could get on with planning how she was going to steal that tracking magic. If her helpling idea didn't work out, her next best bet was searching Ripon Headquarters from top to bottom – there were many rooms she never went into and any might contain the rare magic she was after. It would take forever, so she needed to get going as quickly as she could.

'Aunt Victi's been talking about a new steal,' said Moorley after the silence stretched on. 'There's some rich guy in North Farrowfell who has got his hands on memory magic – it lets you relive your favourite memory like it's the first time.'

Jude eyed her. Moorley didn't normally volunteer information like this – she hardly spoke to Jude. 'Sounds cool,' said Jude as she stopped brushing and sat back. Moorley seemed to have a good system going with the cleaning. She didn't need more help. 'Why are you telling me about it?'

'Just wondering if she'd mentioned it to you,' said Moorley, her voice casual.

Jude narrowed her eyes. Moorley was trying to rub her face in the fact that *she* was told about the family's plans. 'No, she hasn't,' Jude said, not bothering to keep the bitterness out of her voice.

Moorley glanced at her, then scooped another handful of tea leaves into a jar. 'You're right, this is gross.'

Jude was about to say something cutting, then she paused. The other Ripons *did* trust Moorley. That meant she knew a lot more family secrets than Jude. Maybe she could use it to her advantage. Perhaps she didn't need to kidnap a helpling after all, or waste time searching the entire house.

'The magic we steal,' Jude said as casually as she could. 'Where do we keep it?'

'We don't – we sell it,' said Moorley.

'I know,' said Jude through gritted teeth. She had to stop herself from saying, *Obviously*. 'But before we've found a buyer. Where do we keep it? Somewhere in the house?'

'Yeah, the basement,' said Moorley, like it was the most obvious thing in the world.

'The *basement*?' said Jude in horror, thinking back to the stories Spry had told her about it. 'But that's what causes all the nightmares.'

'What?' Moorley looked at her as if she'd just announced she was off to try growing another head.

'You know – the basement,' said Jude impatiently. 'Where there's nothing but empty corridors stretching in all directions like a maze and the magic in the walls is dark and twisted, and the only way to leave is if someone comes to let you out – otherwise you're trapped down there for ever. Spry *told* me this . . .' She stopped because Moorley was chuckling and Moorley hardly ever laughed. 'What?'

'He was *joking*,' Moorley said. 'I don't think he's ever been down there.'

Jude made a mental note to get Spry back. Maybe she would put a grefer in his bed.

'I mean, there *are* loads of protections over the basement,' continued Moorley. 'Like, you can't go down there on your own – you need someone to stand at the door and keep it open. All the protections are designed to stop non-Ripons taking stuff – I guess they used to be triggered *any time* someone took magic out or put some in, including Ripons, but that probably got really annoying really fast. And obviously the biggest protection is being in Ripon Headquarters in the first place. If an intruder started wandering around, we'd all know.'

'And how does the house know the person's an intruder and not a guest?' asked Jude.

Moorley shrugged. 'If they're not with a Ripon, they're probably not supposed to be here. ''Course, the system isn't foolproof – remember that time Spry brought that friend over and they went to the bathroom, and the house thought they were trying to steal and locked us all down for a week?'

Jude had a vague memory of listening to Aunt Morgol complain about how they were all going to starve as she opened yet another one of their tinned foods.

'Aunt Victi's trained the house since then to spot people who shouldn't be here – if it looks like they're with a Ripon then it's all good.' Moorley brushed up the last of the tea leaves. 'I think we're done.'

'And what a great job we did,' said Jude, getting

to her feet. Her mind was sparking with new ideas – maybe she did need Fin and Eri after all.

Jude grinned. Things were falling into place.

***

When Jude arrived at the Weston mansion the following day, a helpling led her to a long room at the back of the house. It had glass walls with a view of the neat gardens and, beyond, rolling green fields. Eri was watering her harwaki plant whose leaves were the colour of yellow vomit, nowhere close to the lush green of Madame Cada's plants.

'You're here!' said Eri, standing up so quickly water spilled from her metal can and splashed on to the ground. 'Have you got the tracking magic?'

'No,' said Jude. 'I changed my mind. You and Fin are going to help.'

'What?' said Eri, biting her bottom lip. 'You said you wouldn't need our help.'

Irritation flashed through Jude. She'd been expecting Eri to be grateful. Being involved in a heist would probably be the most exciting thing either of the Westons had ever done. 'Yesterday, you were super-eager. What changed?'

'I like planning,' said Eri, setting down the watering can. 'Actually *doing* things – not so much.' She took four deep breaths. Jude raised her eyebrows, wishing she didn't have to deal with someone who was obviously a liability. 'Right, well, let's get a pen and paper and start plotting our exact schedule so we'll know what our roles are and—'

'Calm down,' said Jude with a wave of her hand. 'There's nothing to plan. You and Fin – or just one of you, I'm not fussy – need to come to Ripon Headquarters and hold the door to the basement open for me. The alarms won't go off because the house will know you're with me, and none of the protections are designed to stop a family member from stealing.' That design flaw wasn't because Grandleader trusted them all. It was because he knew no Ripon would ever dare to steal from him – but Jude was trying to *save* them all.

She just hoped Grandleader would see it that way.

'No plan?' Eri's eyes were wide. She cleared her throat. 'Right … well …' She stroked the leaf of her harwaki plant. 'OK, let's do this. No time like the present, right? I'll get Fin—'

'Hold your grefers,' said Jude. A good thief knew timing was everything. Her entire family would be home tonight, which would make the steal much riskier. Plus, if she accidentally triggered a hidden protection in the basement, they'd catch her in seconds. 'We need to wait for the right moment, when most people are out of headquarters. I've brought you both some invisibility magic, and when the time's right I'll send a message.' She tossed a ball of invisibility magic to

126

Eri, who fumbled the catch. It clattered to the ground, rolling a few feet before coming to a gentle stop. 'Careful. I went to a lot of effort to get that.' Eri didn't need to know she'd simply waltzed into her father's study and swiped it. To anyone *not* in a criminal family with highly shady connections, it was magic almost impossible to get.

Eri's hands trembled as she picked up the magic. 'It's true what they say. Breaking one rule means you break another – and then before you know it you're on the run from the law and—'

'It's just a bit of invisibility magic,' cut in Jude, trying not to smile at how dramatic Eri was. On the one hand, she felt slightly sorry for her – Eri obviously didn't know how to cope with anything vaguely criminal. On the other hand, it was very entertaining to watch.

Eri's entire body trembled, reminding Jude of a scared rabbit. 'I'll go and get Fin,' she said. 'You should let him know what's happening.' She almost tripped as she hurried from the room.

Jude wandered around absent-mindedly, peering at Eri's collection of plants. Alongside the harwaki plant there were others Jude had not come across, some with stems so thin they looked like they could snap with a single bend, or others with wilting flowers which looked as though they were hanging their heads in shame. Eri clearly did not have green fingers.

At the end of the room was a door. Jude pushed it

open, curious, and entered a room with walls covered in paintings, of sun-swept fields filled with daffodils, of people laughing and smiling, their faces so lifelike it was hard to believe real people had not been placed inside the canvas.

The floor space was filled with easels, upon which half-finished paintings rested.

Jude looked at the paintings with interest. They had a neat signature in the corner: Fin Weston. They were all a thousand times better than the stuff Farlow Higgins sold. She couldn't help being impressed. Fin was grumpy and judgemental, but he was talented, that was for sure.

Fin had painted himself and Eri, along with their parents, several times. The style of the pictures reminded Jude of the family portrait hanging in the Weston family room. She guessed Fin had painted that picture – perhaps with a little magic to guide his hand. In a few of the pictures was a blonde woman who looked vaguely familiar. Jude squinted at the picture, trying to figure out where she knew the woman from. With her blonde hair and straight nose she had a strong resemblance to Eri.

'What are you doing?'

Jude spun around. Fin was standing in the doorway, clutching a paintbrush with bristles sticking out, like he'd been pressing too hard.

'I was just looking . . .' said Jude, surprised by the anger in Fin's voice.

'Leave,' said Fin, his voice strangled. 'This is my space – you had no right . . .'

Jude wondered if Fin was one of those tortured artist types who didn't want anyone to see or buy their work until they died. But the stricken expression on his face made her feel like she'd done something terrible. She decided it would be best not to argue. 'I was just looking,' she said again as she left the room.

Fin glowered, closing the door and dropping his paintbrush on a side table.

Jude went to stand by the harwaki plant. At least Eri didn't have a weird need for privacy over her hobby.

Fin folded his arms, hovering by his painting room as if worried Jude would attempt to slip back inside. 'Why are you here anyway?'

Jude repeated what she'd told Eri. The awkward silence that fell afterwards was broken by Eri's return. 'Oh – there you are, Fin. Listen, Jude has this idea—'

'She told me,' broke in Fin. 'Happy to be involved. Let us know when you're ready for us.' With that, he charged from the room.

'Who's the blonde woman Fin drew?' said Jude to Eri, who looked very confused. 'She looks just like you.'

'My mother?' said Eri, her eyebrows drawn together.

'No, another lady,' said Jude. 'An aunt or something?' she guessed.

'Oh . . . that's Aunt Annelia.' Eri's cheeks burned red.

Jude raised her eyebrows – was Eri's aunt involved in some sort of scandal? She'd love it if that was the case – the Westons seemed like too much of a happy family. Surely, there had to be *something* wrong with them.

'Your aunt? You never mentioned her.'

Eri's cheeks flamed brighter, and Jude wondered if it got tiring having a face that always gave away exactly what you were feeling. It was certainly a novelty – the Ripons considered openness a weakness.

'How come your aunt isn't looking after you instead of that random family friend?' Jude pressed on as something else occurred to her. 'The family friend . . . who's still not here.' It was odd, because Jude imagined the Westons' family friend was probably someone really hardworking, who took their responsibilities for looking after Eri and Fin seriously. Yet she never seemed to be home.

'Miss Fletcher is at work,' said Eri, her cheeks flushing red. 'And Aunt Annelia is, um, dead.' She cleared her throat. Her voice shook and Jude immediately felt bad. They'd lost not only their parents but their aunt as well.

'I'm sorry,' said Jude lamely. She kept putting her foot in it – first with Fin and his paintings, and now this. She tried casting her mind around for something suitable to say. 'How did it happen?'

Eri looked at her, shocked.

'Er – I mean . . .' Maybe Eri needed to hear something

wise about how everything would be OK. 'Time heals all wounds?' Jude winced even as she was speaking. She'd never been very good with emotional things.

'We ... weren't that close. Mum and Dad didn't really like having Aunt Annelia around – they never agreed with her plans.' Eri had a far-off look on her face.

Jude shifted from foot to foot. She'd done what she had come to do, and there was no need for her to hang around and continue to deal with the awkward conversation. 'I'd better get going.'

'Oh, no! Stay a little bit,' said Eri. 'Have some tea with us – and maybe ... maybe play some moonstones with me?' She looked a little uncertain. 'I mean, unless you have something more important to do?'

'Of course I do,' said Jude, wrinkling her nose and feeling slightly offended. Everything she had to do was important. 'We've got a curse to lift, your parents to save ...'

'Well, you can't do anything about the other two things right now.' Eri shrugged. 'So why don't you just hang out here? It'll be fun!'

'Erm ...' For the first time in her life, Jude didn't know what to say. She had fun all the time – stealing things, messing with the helplings. But she never just *played* with other kids. 'Yeah, OK.'

***

Fin got over his grumpiness to join them in several games of moonstones. The idea was to scatter the moonstone rocks about and try to chuck the master moonstone on to them, to make them light up. They could fly around on their own, which made the game more difficult. The Westons had a more expensive version than the one Jude owned, and their moonstones could chase the players as well. Jude briefly lived in a world where no one came along to tell them off for disturbing a brainstorm session on how to make more money, because at home fun always came second to the family business. She couldn't remember the last time she had enjoyed herself so much. She wondered if they might meet up to play again, once this was all over, before she reminded herself that if everything went to plan she'd be too busy planning heists and being a true Ripon to play games.

When Jude got home, the corridors of Ripon Headquarters seemed even gloomier than normal. The layers of dust were more obvious, the lack of family portraits highlighting how different the Ripons were from the Westons. For the first time coming home didn't feel comforting. Would it have been so bad to put a few family photos up? To make things just a *bit* nicer here?

Jude headed up the staircase, turning a corner only to find herself being pushed aside by Aunt Morgol, who barely broke her stride as she continued marching.

Aunt Morgol never missed an opportunity to tell her off. Jude stared after her, wondering what was going on. Then she shrugged; she wasn't going to question her first bit of good luck in ages.

Further along the corridor, Spry and Trudie were having a conversation in hushed tones. They stopped when Jude got near.

'What's happening?' said Jude. It was odd to find Spry and Trudie together. They were about as close as she and Moorley.

'Nothing,' muttered Spry, his eyes not meeting hers as Trudie turned and walked quickly away. 'Go to your room, Jude.'

Jude considered telling Spry she could do whatever she wanted, but since she *did* want to go to her bedroom, she said nothing. Instead she headed in the direction Trudie had gone. There were echoes coming from a different corridor and Jude paused. It sounded like yelling.

She grinned. She loved watching arguments.

It was a detour, but Jude headed down the corridor to find Uncle Runie and Aunt Victi in the middle of a row.

'The Lilthrum suddenly turned and saw me and I *had* to run—' Uncle Runie was saying.

'I don't *care*,' said Aunt Victi. 'You shouldn't have let Rosalittia get hurt trying to help you—'

'What could I do that Rosalittia couldn't – she's the one who *drinks*—'

'And now *she's* the one who's injured!' roared Aunt Victi. 'More bad luck we don't need.'

There was a ringing in Jude's ears. Her mother had been attacked by a Lilthrum.

This was all her fault.

The Lilthrum were becoming more common, but not common enough that the coincidence of them attacking her mother made any sense. This was the curse's work – there was no other explanation.

Jude hurried forward, forgetting she wasn't supposed to be listening. 'Mum's been hurt by a Lilthrum?' she said, looking from Aunt Victi to Uncle Runie. 'Is she at a hospital—'

Aunt Victi spun around to face her. 'Jude!' she said. 'Go to your room – how dare you listen in on us?'

'Where's my mum?' said Jude, trying to sound firm.

But Aunt Victi rolled her eyes and walked off.

'Uncle Runie, what's going on?' asked Jude.

He shook his head. 'You should listen to your aunt . . .' he said, biting his bottom lip. He looked like he wanted to say something else but remained silent.

Jude could tell she wouldn't get anything useful out of him. Instead, she turned to follow Aunt Victi, who was striding in the direction of the evening room.

Jude held back as Aunt Victi got to the door and knocked gently. It swung open and she slipped inside, closing it behind her.

What was she doing?

There was a grate in the unused study next door, high on a wall. It looked directly into the evening room and Jude had used it in the past to listen in on her parents.

Jude hurried into the study and carefully pushed a table underneath the grate, wincing at the scraping of the table's legs against the floorboards. Hesitation slowed her from stepping up. What if she didn't like what she saw?

She bit the inside of her cheek. She needed to know what was happening.

Jude climbed on to the table, standing on her tiptoes to peer through the metal slats of the grate. At first she couldn't see much – just Aunt Morgol reading a book. She adjusted her angle and there was her mother, a chalice held up to her face.

A few drops of the silver liquid splashed on to her mother's front. When she put the chalice down, her beautiful face briefly changed into a shining creature of silver with sunken holes for eyes and a gaping mouth. Horror rooted Jude to the spot. She wasn't looking at her mother at all – she was looking at a monster in the place where her mother had stood.

Aunt Morgol looked up. 'You've got a bit on your dress, Rosalittia,' she tutted.

'Bore off, Morgol,' replied her mother. She took another gulp from the chalice and her supple skin returned, glowing with good health.

Jude didn't understand. Uncle Runie had said

she'd been attacked by a Lilthrum – had she *become* a Lilthrum?

'Jude – what are you doing?' said a sharp voice behind her.

Jude jumped. Moorley was looking at her with wide eyes.

'Nothing – I . . .' Jude trailed off. She didn't know what to say.

'Have you seen?' whispered Moorley, nodding at the grate.

'Mum's turned into a monster,' said Jude, too shocked to be guarded in front of Moorley. 'I didn't realise Lilthrum attacks changed you into a Lilthrum—'

'They don't,' said Moorley. She was trembling. 'That's Mum in there. She's not a Lilthrum – she's human. But, Jude, think about what a Lilthrum is . . . what it's made from . . .'

Jude's heart tripped over itself as she took in what Moorley was saying. She couldn't believe . . . she *wouldn't* believe it. No way – it wasn't possible, it wasn't right.

But Moorley's clenched fists confirmed her fears.

Their mother was drinking raw magic.

Chapter Twelve

The Library of Farrowfell

Jude jumped down from the table, shoving past Moorley and half walking, half sprinting to her bedroom. There was a roaring in her ears, like she was standing on a beach as waves crashed against the shore. She closed her bedroom door, wishing she had a lock – but that wouldn't be enough to protect her, nothing would be enough to protect her . . .

From what? Her own mother? She wasn't a monster, she wasn't evil. She drank raw magic, so what? Clearly the stories Jude had heard about the effects of drinking it weren't true – her mother hadn't dropped dead, she hadn't turned into a half-living shell . . .

Except Jude knew there was something terribly, horribly wrong with what her mother was doing. That maybe all her family was doing – Aunt Morgol had been so casual about her mother drinking, like it was an everyday occurrence.

But drinking raw magic was taboo for a reason.

There was a soft knock on her door. Jude spun around as Moorley slipped inside.

'Are you OK?' she asked gently. Jude stared at her. Their mother was drinking *raw magic* and Moorley didn't look anywhere as shocked as she should have been.

'You *knew*,' said Jude. Moorley didn't say anything but her grim face told Jude she was right. 'You knew Mum drinks raw magic – do they *all* do it? *Why?* And why didn't someone tell me – why didn't *you* tell me—' Jude stopped. Of course Moorley hadn't told her. Why would she? Did she drink it as well? Was she also part of their special, horrifying club?

'They all do it . . . Well, not Uncle Runie or Spry. They haven't given in just yet – but I bet they will one day. For the honour.' Moorley lowered her voice even more, so quiet Jude could barely hear her. 'It's what makes you a *true* Ripon. It's how you rise up in the family.'

'How do you know this? How *long* have you known this? Have you . . .' Jude trailed off. 'Did you?' She felt sick. She'd always been jealous of Moorley but she didn't want to drink raw magic. She remembered the brief moment she had seen it in Madam Cada's shop, how a few seconds of smelling it had conjured up the enticing memory of her seventh birthday.

But if raw magic was supposed to be so terrible, how come nothing bad had happened to her family? Apart from her mother very briefly becoming a shining, silver monster—

'No,' said Moorley, her throat bobbing. 'I'm too young ... For now. But Spry told me they told him to drink some, just after he turned sixteen. It was ahead of a heist they'd invited him on – apparently they said stealing would become the easiest thing in the world, he'd never have to worry about being caught again. He said no – Uncle Runie didn't want him to – and now look how they treat both of them. They leave them out of anything really important. I'm turning sixteen soon but if they tell me to drink it, I won't – and neither will you.' Her voice became fierce, but Jude wasn't really listening.

'Why do they do it?' Jude asked, rubbing her forehead. 'To make them better thieves? I mean ... I know you can do anything with raw magic but we can get whatever illegal tamed magic we need.'

'But with raw magic ... you can do *anything*,' said Moorley. 'No restrictions. No tracking down tamed magic that's only made for one specific purpose. All you have to do is take a sip ...'

'I need . . .' Jude swallowed. 'I don't know . . . I need to speak to Mum. I need to hear this from her.' Maybe her mum would tell her it was all a big misunderstanding, that Moorley was wrong, and now Jude knew the truth she would no longer be left out of the family—

'*No,*' said Moorley, blocking her way. 'You need to keep *quiet*, Jude—'

'I wish everyone would stop telling me to keep quiet!' Jude burst out, years of frustration finally boiling over. 'When did *you* find out about this?'

Moorley's dark eyes were unreadable. 'I didn't want you to know,' she said at last. 'They don't care about anything but raw magic. They don't care about each other, they don't care about me, they don't care about you – I just wanted to protect you from that—'

'Just go,' said Jude. She suddenly felt tired, desperate to curl up in a ball and sleep. She didn't want to hear Moorley's excuses. Moorley squared her shoulders. 'You won't speak to anyone about this? Promise?'

Jude didn't want to promise but she also knew Moorley wouldn't leave until she agreed. 'Yes. Fine,' she said reluctantly.

Moorley's eyes scanned her for a second, then she opened Jude's door. She whispered something before leaving, so low Jude barely caught it, but she was fairly sure Moorley had said, '*I* still care about you.'

***

Jude hardly slept. If her family was corrupted by raw magic, what was she risking by stealing from them? If she was caught, her punishment might be a thousand times worse than anything she'd previously imagined.

She considered breaking her promise to Moorley and marching up to her mother and demanding answers. But she knew what would happen if she tried: her mother would dismiss her.

At some point in the night, Jude decided what to do: she would go to the Library of Farrowfell and do some research, find out whether the stories she had heard about raw magic were true. Maybe there wasn't anything *really* evil about what her family was doing. The Ripons had always been ahead of the game – they were the best criminals in Farrowfell after all. Maybe they had discovered how to use raw magic safely, figured out how to harness its power to their advantage. For all she knew, they could be pioneers and one day share their discovery with the world and change everyone's lives for the better.

At the very least, she needed to get more information – she knew less than anyone in her family. She needed to *understand*.

***

The Library of Farrowfell was an enormous, elegant building set on the edge of a sparkling blue lake so massive it resembled a sea. The library glowed gently in the morning sunshine; it had more magic in it than any other building in Farrowfell. Jude only knew about that particular feature because she'd once had a tutor obsessed with buildings. The lessons had stopped when Jude decided to take matters into her own hands and teach herself basic magic-use. Her tutor had been left with no eyebrows and a firm resolve never to return to Ripon Headquarters.

Jude passed under one of the freestanding stone archways of the library. Little clouds of dust kicked up from the cobbled stone path leading to the columns of the open-air entrance.

In the middle of the empty space was a long desk, behind which a boy with dark brown skin sat, his eyes closed, his chest rising and falling in a steady motion. He looked to be about Moorley's age and was dressed all in black with a paper pinned to his chest that read: 'Hi, my name is NONE OF YOUR BUSINESS'.

'I want to go to the Hall of Knowledge,' said Jude. The private tutor had once taken her to the Hall of Knowledge on a field trip. All she had to do was ask her question out loud and the Hall could tell her the answer if the knowledge was contained within one of the books in the library. 'Can you give me directions?'

'Library's closed,' said the boy without opening his eyes.

'What d'you mean it's closed?' said Jude. The

library was *never* closed during daylight hours. Even on holidays, through storms and droughts, the library stayed open. Couldn't the curse take a few days off?

''S closed,' repeated the boy. 'Come back next week.'

Jude balled her hands into fists. She couldn't wait an entire *week*. 'Please,' she said. 'This is important. This is . . . life and death.' The boy had to understand that the understanding of the world she had been living in was crumbling, and all she had left was a tiny hope that she would find answers in the library that would make everything make sense.

The boy finally opened his eyes to look at her. 'You don't look smart,' he said.

'What's that supposed to mean?' Jude glared at him. She hadn't come to the library to be insulted.

'I mean we've had to turn away a few kids who came because they want to get ahead on their schoolwork. But you don't look like the type of kid who thinks studying is life or death.' The boy shrugged, closing his eyes once more. 'Now buzz off, I'm sleeping.'

Jude stuck her tongue out but the boy started snoring – he'd already fallen asleep. She looked at the main entrance behind him. She could easily slip down to the Hall of Knowledge, ask her questions and leave.

The boy gave a little grunt, a small bit of drool hanging at the corner of his mouth. Jude smirked as she crept past him.

It was immediately obvious why the library was closed. The room Jude was standing in looked like it had been hit by some sort of earthquake. Rubble and books were strewn about on the ground. Bookstacks lay on their sides. There was a dark stain on the floor that looked horribly like blood.

She picked a corridor at random and it soon became clear that the destruction fanned out in every room. Her progress through the massive halls was slow because she had to pick her way carefully over upturned desks and chairs.

It didn't help that the librarians hadn't thought to put up something as helpful as signage. She had a vague idea that the Hall of Knowledge was on the other side of the library, but it was hard to aim that way when the corridors kept branching off in random directions. She hadn't made it far before footsteps echoed behind her.

'I told you,' said the boy, panting as he caught up with her. 'This is all off limits.' His finger glowed golden; he'd obviously used some sort of magic to find her.

'What happened?' said Jude, signalling to all the destruction around.

The boy pointed at his name tag. *NONE OF YOUR BUSINESS.*

'Yeah, well, the library is a public space and I'm public. I want answers,' she said. She decided to head down the corridor that looked the least damaged but marched towards it, the boy hurrying by her side.

'I'm going to have to ask you to leave,' he said. She ignored him, entering a huge hall filled with yet more books.

A group of library staff passed her and she slowed down, expecting to be told off. The librarians said nothing. They all had worried expressions on their faces and wore the same black uniform as the boy. From what Jude remembered, the uniform of the librarians was brightly coloured.

'Why do they all look like they've seen a ghost?' said Jude, coming to a stop by a large roped-off section where rows of stacks had been pushed over. Books lay in heaps on their backs with their spines cracked. A few helplings were clearing up the mess.

'Not a ghost – a monster,' said the boy shortly. 'There was a Lilthrum attack yesterday.' He nodded at marks raked across the floor by something with claws so sharp it could cut stone. 'That's why we're closed. Trying to rebuild without the public in the way.'

Jude took a deep breath. This was her curse – *she'd* brought the Lilthrum to Mergio Market, and near her mother, and to the library. It was like they were stalking her. 'Why would they want to attack this place?' she asked quietly as she ran her fingers over a deep gash on the wall. Only something with razor-sharp claws could have cut into the stone so easily.

'Lots of people here.' The boy's throat bobbed. 'Lilthrum are made of raw magic, aren't they? So they're attracted to humans, just like raw magic is. Have you ever seen a Lilthrum attack someone up close?'

Jude shook her head, her mind flashing back to the calm way her mother had sipped liquid raw magic after her attack.

'Well, before the Lilthrum try to kill you, they stick their horrible claws in you and try to drain you of everything that makes you human,' said the boy. 'And when there's nothing left, and you're a hollow shell just like them, *then* they kill you.'

'So the clothes you're all wearing . . .' Jude trailed off. She didn't really need to ask the question. The Lilthrum had done more than just damage the library. They had killed.

There was nothing good about raw magic. And if her family had anything to do with it, that meant . . .

No. She wouldn't finish the thought. Surely there had to be something she was missing.

'We're in mourning,' said the boy. 'Three people died.' He pulled back the excess material of his clothes to reveal a knife tucked into his waistband. 'We're prepared now, though. Never again.' His voice shook slightly as he pulled out the knife, grasping the hilt as though he expected it to catch fire. He would probably do more damage to himself than any Lilthrum if he tried to fight with it, Jude thought.

Three people – dead. Jude remembered the attack in Mergio Market, the moment she'd caught sight of the silver monster jumping across the roofs. How horrible for that to be the last thing you saw. 'I thought the Consortium were putting guards everywhere ...' She trailed off as the boy snorted.

'Most of the guards aren't even properly trained – a lot of them have never seen combat in their lives,' he said. 'And there's no point sticking guards everywhere if the Consortium still doesn't know *why* there are so many Lilthrum around – for every Lilthrum they kill, two more show up.'

From what Jude had heard, Mr and Mrs Weston had got the closest to figuring it out – and then disappeared before they could tell anyone.

Finding them was about more than just lifting the curse. Finding them could help the Consortium work out how to stop the attacks in the first place.

Jude looked in the direction of the Hall of Knowledge, but the answer to her question about raw magic seemed to be all around her. She was grasping at straws, trying to come up with a theory about how her family drinking raw magic could *somehow* be a good thing.

'I'll go now,' she mumbled.

The boy's shoulders slumped. 'Good,' he said. He'd obviously been expecting more of a fight and that made Jude feel bad. All she wanted was to know that her family would be OK. She didn't want to walk over anyone.

They headed towards the entrance.

'What're you so desperate to research anyway?' said the boy as they walked.

'Raw magic,' said Jude shortly, annoyed with herself for wasting time at the library when she should have been focused on lifting the curse.

The boy frowned. 'What's there to know? It falls from the stars and gatherers collect it. Before we tame it, it's bad. Evil.' They reached a fork of five corridors and the boy picked the middle one without hesitation.

'Evil . . . how?' asked Jude, paying him more attention.

The boy shrugged. 'It has plans of its own – plans I'm willing to bet aren't good for humans.'

They headed back into the entrance room so fast Jude assumed her method of randomly selecting corridors had led her in a giant circle. The boy slipped into his chair.

'So what happens if people drink raw magic?' said Jude, hovering by him. The boy seemed to know quite a lot about the subject.

'Well, some people believe drinking raw magic will kill you outright,' said the boy. 'But there's loads of other theories. I think the best one is Professor Rutherford's. That drinking raw magic makes you much stronger than any tamed magic – but the magic twists your soul, brings out all your worst traits until you're not human any more.'

Jude frowned at him. What were her parents' worst traits? Her father seemed angrier these days, yes. Her mother never paid her any attention. Had drinking raw magic made them monsters? And if so, more importantly, if they stopped drinking, could they go back to being the parents she remembered? They'd never been perfect but they had certainly been better than they were now.

Fierce longing swept through her. It wasn't that her mother and father didn't care about her or that they loved Moorley more. It was the raw magic twisting them, corrupting their minds. If they stopped – if they stopped . . .

'How d'you know all this?' said Jude, trying to keep her voice steady.

'I work in a library. Read lots of books.' The boy tilted back in his chair, his eyes narrowed at her. 'Why are you so interested? You said it was a matter of life and death before.'

'I was being dramatic,' said Jude, bluffing. 'It's for a school project. Extra credit.'

The boy didn't look convinced.

'But maybe the books are wrong,' said Jude, talking quickly. 'Maybe raw magic isn't that bad. Maybe there's a way to stop it from twisting your soul.' No matter what the evidence around her showed, she wanted to cling on to the idea that what her family was doing was not as terrible as it felt.

The silver, glistening, dripping from her mother's mouth . . .

The sudden switch to her flesh peeled away, leaving only a monster . . .

It's what makes you a true *Ripon.*

The boy was looking at her oddly. 'Raw magic hates humans,' he said slowly. 'The more you drink, the greater hold it has over you.'

She'd made herself look suspicious with her interest. 'Right. Well. I'll be back when the library's open. Thanks for your help.' She turned on her heel and walked away, feeling the boy's eyes boring into her back. Her head swirled with more questions. Even if she saved her family from the curse she had put on them, they had cursed themselves a different way, hadn't they?

She headed home, her mind still locked on raw magic and what it might have done to her family. What might it do to her if they asked her to drink it? What were her worst traits? She knew that technically the whole stealing thing didn't make her a good person, but she hadn't ever robbed anyone who didn't deserve it.

No one deserves it. For some reason Fin's voice spoke in her mind. She stumbled through the front door.

'Shut up,' Jude mumbled as she turned a corner and almost collided with her mother.

'Excuse me?' Her mother raised her eyebrows.

Jude stared at her mother in astonishment. Apart from looking a little haughtier than normal, her mother seemed absolutely fine. There was nothing to suggest that she had been on the brink of death or that she had been drinking raw magic. Her hair shone and a smell of orange blossom and sweet spices wafted around her. She was more beautiful than ever.

'Where are you going?' Her mother folded her arms.

'Nowhere,' said Jude. The boy at the library was wrong, he had to be. Her mother wasn't a monster. 'Are you OK? How are you feeling?'

Her mother tilted her head, confusion flickering across her face. 'What in Farrowfell are you asking me that for?' She placed a hand on Jude's shoulder and steered her in the direction of the sitting room. 'Aren't you supposed to be studying or something? Go back to your tutor.'

Jude took a shaky breath. She hadn't had a tutor for six months.

'Yes, I just had a quick break.'

'Right,' said her mother, but Jude could tell she wasn't listening – and the observation made her heart ache.

Chapter Thirteen

The Second Steal

A family heist – that Jude wasn't invited to – was scheduled for that night. It meant Jude could focus once more on stealing the tracking magic. She swiped a message ball from the post room and tucked a letter to Fin and Eri in the hollow centre, giving them Ripon Headquarters' location and telling them to arrive at 9 p.m. She found she was looking forward to seeing them again, to focusing on their family instead of her own.

She hurled the message ball from the attic window. It bounced on the ground, the force making its magic come to life. It started to roll and would continue to travel through ports until it reached the Weston mansion.

Then she got together everything she would need for her steal: her yo-yo, the anti-nausea magic and a wooden rabbit to give to Fin and Eri. It worked a little bit like the message ball; the magic inside could be set off by the rabbit being dropped. The rabbit would scurry along and find her, giving her warning if Fin and Eri spotted anyone coming.

The wooden rabbit was part of a set, its pair a little wooden rat, which she would keep hold of. That way, if anything went wrong while she was inside the basement, she could let them know. The rabbit and rat were actually toys Uncle Runie had bought for her from Mr Snuggleton's Toy Store in Mergio Market a few years ago, but as she'd never had anyone to play with, they had gathered dust in a corner of her bedroom.

When evening arrived, she went to the entrance hall to wave her family off. Spry was out with Moorley to source supplies for his flying carriage project, and Grandleader had gone off on business without mentioning further details. Everyone else was going on the heist.

It took ages for the Ripons to actually leave because Jude's father was arguing with Aunt Morgol about the best route and Spry had apparently not fixed a broken wheel on the carriage. Jude kept looking at the clock, worried her family would still be home when Fin and Eri arrived.

At last, however, the family were ready, an hour later than planned. Jude sighed with relief as they headed out of the front door.

'Why do you look so happy?' Aunt Morgol squinted at her. 'What have you broken?'

'Nothing! Have a great time!' she said cheerily. 'Bring me back a souvenir.' She closed the door and hurried up the staircase. She had told Fin and Eri to arrive at one of the side doors of Ripon Headquarters. They knocked right on schedule.

'Hello,' said Eri, her face scrunched with worry. She was wearing pink, but in a muted tone, as if she'd wanted to wear something appropriate for stealing but hadn't quite managed it.

Fin was dressed head to toe in black. Jude was half surprised he didn't have a mask over his face. He peered around him as she stepped back to let them inside the gloomy room, a large space lined with bookshelves filled with dusty volumes on all the laws in Farrowfell. The thick, velvet curtains hanging at the windows were moth-eaten, but the small fires in the brackets on the walls did their job in not showing the dingy space.

Jude sucked in her cheeks as the door shut behind Fin and Eri, expecting a wailing alarm to go off. Instead the curtains fluttered a little as if the house was saying hello.

'Got your invisibility magic?' Jude said, her voice low. She knew no one was around but it felt safer to speak softly.

Fin and Eri nodded, each holding up a small ball.

'Good – eat it, then follow me. Your job is simple. Just stand outside and keep the door open.' Jude gave Eri the wooden bunny. 'If anyone comes along, set this off.'

Both ate the invisibility magic and immediately started gagging.

'Oh – I forgot to tell you – it tastes disgusting,' said Jude as Eri heaved. 'Drinking it with orange juice helps.' She smirked, remembering how she'd learned that the hard way the first time she'd tasted invisibility magic.

'Then why didn't you bring us orange juice?' gasped Fin, but Jude was saved from one of his disapproving glares by the magic taking effect. A second later he disappeared, along with Eri.

'Oh, this is so weird,' came Eri's disembodied voice. 'Fin – where are you?'

'Ow! You poked me!'

'Oops.'

'Right – follow me,' said Jude. As they headed down the corridor, she wished the invisibility magic worked on sound too. Fin and Eri seemed determined to make as much noise as possible.

'Stop bumping into me!' hissed Fin.

'You're walking too slowly!' came Eri's snappish reply.

Jude had picked a side door near the entrance to the basement, so they didn't have to go far. Still, she heaved a sigh of relief once they reached the large empty room which housed the entrance to the basement. Jude had never been inside this room before; knowing where it led meant she was careful to avoid it.

The door to the basement had no handle. Instead, there was a large granite square in the centre of the room, standing out against the dark wood floorboards.

'I guess you . . . stand on the stone?' said Jude, folding her arms as she thought.

There was a shuffling noise and a yelp.

'We don't *both* need to stand on it,' came Eri's bossy voice. 'I'll do it.' A second later the square sank a few centimetres and the door in the far corner of the room slid open. 'Oooh, let's test this.' The square rose up again, and the door closed. 'Wow – I wonder how this works—'

'Eri,' said Jude through gritted teeth. 'Just stand there and stay still.'

'Looks like we've found the one thing you take seriously,' said Fin dryly.

Jude took a deep breath and walked towards the doorway, her palms clammy. Even though she knew Spry's stories about the horrors in the basement were lies, she couldn't shake her fear of what lay below.

Stone steps led into darkness. She tried not to hesitate as she crossed the threshold.

Flames flickered to life in iron brackets on the walls, revealing nothing but more steps leading down, down, down, deep underground.

At one point, she missed a step in the darkness. Her stomach swooped and she steadied herself by resting her hand against the wall, finding it damp with moisture.

She reached into her pocket, clutching the wooden rat in one hand and her yo-yo in the other, the feel of both giving her courage.

Drip. Drop. Drip. Drop. It sounded like a leaky tap. The air smelled almost salty, as though she was heading towards the sea.

Eventually, the flames revealed she had reached the end of the steps. She entered the basement of Ripon Headquarters.

Chapter Fourteen

The Basement

The moment Jude stepped foot on the stone ground, there was a low rumbling. Flames flickered to life on the walls, one by one, to reveal she was standing in an enormous hall with pillars holding up the ceiling high above.

Before her was an underground lake of glowing turquoise water. In its centre was a small island where a display cabinet stood. The cabinet was made up of hundreds of square slots of varying sizes. In some of the cubbyholes were small objects Jude knew at once were magic.

'That was easy,' Jude muttered to herself as she

walked towards the lake. Moorley had mentioned the protections weren't designed to keep Ripons out, but all the same she'd been expecting *something* to be lying in wait for her. Her footsteps echoed, and her yo-yo and wooden rat dug into her palms as she clutched them. As she got nearer to the lake, she saw most of the slots in the cabinet were empty.

She frowned. Her family's whole business was supposed to be based on selling magic they stole, so why did they hardly have anything in stock? In past years, she'd seen enormous hauls of stolen magic arriving at Headquarters, and she knew it sometimes took a while to shift the goods. Was this why Grandleader had needed the help of the man called Harrimore Hardman? To help him figure out where to source more magic? Because from the look of it, the family business was not doing well . . .

Except, Uncle Runie had said they were making record profits. How?

Her eyes were drawn to one of the larger slots where a glowing green rock had been placed. That had to be the tracking magic – it was exactly as Farlow Higgins had described. Excitement flooded through her, chasing away all other doubts. She could break off a small piece and no one would be able to tell the difference. Then she could use it to find the Weston parents, apologise and lift the curse.

She reached the edge of the lake. The water was still

and glassy but there was no boat, no way across. What was she supposed to do?

Something grabbed her wrist. She spun around and found herself facing a hooded creature in black robes. It towered above her – much too tall to be human.

Her first panicked thought was that a Lilthrum had managed to get past all the defences of Ripon Headquarters, aided by the curse. She yelped, snapping her hand away from the creature's grasp as she stumbled backwards. But she'd never heard of a Lilthrum wearing robes before.

Was this a new kind of silent monster, guarding the Ripons' treasure?

Why had she ever thought stealing from her family would be easy?

Her heart beat fast as she slid her finger into the slip knot of her yo-yo and swung. Though the discs flew wide, the yo-yo's magic curved it back to the cloaked figure. The string uncurled from the axle, twisting around the creature's body in a tight coil. Jude yanked at the handle, hoping the figure would fall to the ground. Instead the string slackened. She cried out in panic – her greatest weapon wasn't working – and dropped the wooden rat. The moment its little feet touched the ground it scampered away into the darkness.

The figure reached up slowly and pulled back its hood to reveal—

A golden outline for a face.

A helpling.

Jude's shoulders slumped as she exhaled with relief. 'What are you doing down here?' she said. 'You scared me!'

The helpling stared at her. There was a prickling at the back of her neck. This helpling was much taller than the helplings in the house and its golden outline was thicker, its face more defined. Its mouth was downturned, the lines of its eyebrows drawn together – she had never seen a helpling look ... *angry* before. *Why* hadn't her yo-yo worked? Had the helpling's magic somehow overpowered it?

Her relief began to ebb away.

She took a step back as the string of her yo-yo uncurled from around the helpling. It reached into the folds of its cloak to reveal a long, glittering green sword.

'I'm a Ripon,' she said quickly, holding her hands up. 'Jude Ripon. I'm not an intruder.'

The helpling raised its sword, slowly bringing it down in front of her, the tip centimetres from her forehead. She hardly dared breathe – she knew the helplings in Ripon Headquarters were old ... but *dangerous*?

The helpling pressed the tip against her forehead and she squeezed her eyes shut, the metal cold on her skin. She expected searing pain. Instead, a soft breeze blew over her, a welcoming sigh, like the sword had recognised her as a Ripon and wanted to say hello.

She opened her eyes, as the sword dissolved. The helpling bowed and gestured with its hand towards the lake. She took it as a sign she was allowed to cross.

'Jude! What's wrong?' Fin was running towards her, his invisibility magic gone. 'You sent your rat.'

The helpling spun around and raised its sword.

'He's with me,' she said quickly. 'He's a friend.'

The helpling bowed at her, and then at Fin.

'What's going on?' Fin panted as he reached her side.

'I, er … accidentally dropped my rat,' said Jude, keeping her eyes on the helpling. She didn't want to admit she'd panicked. 'But I think we're OK. How do I get across?' She directed the last words at the helpling. Once more it pointed at the lake.

'Swim?' Jude croaked. She had been taught to swim in Ripon Lake by Aunt Morgol, tossed over the side of a boat numerous times. But this was different. Though the lake was smooth there could be anything lurking beneath its surface.

Jude sidled up to the edge of the lake and frowned. The water was so still it looked almost solid …

Carefully she reached out and tapped the surface.

There was a dull thud. 'It's like ice,' she said, as she got to her feet. 'I can really just walk across?' She turned to the helpling, which did not indicate it had heard or understood.

She inched forward, expecting to tumble into icy water. Instead, it was like walking on normal ground.

She shuffled a few more steps, each one giving her courage. Then she broke into a run across the lake to the island in the middle, only relaxing when she arrived on its rocky surface.

A label attached to the green lump she had spotted from the other side of the lake revealed that it was, in fact, the tracking magic. Her hand shook as she tore a small piece of the spongy surface off. She tensed, expecting alarms to clang. Surely this was too easy. Even if she was a Ripon, Grandleader hadn't authorised her to take this magic. He would have ways of making sure no one disobeyed him.

But no sirens went off. She clutched the magic, her shoulders tensed.

'Do you have it?' called Fin from the shore. She nodded, holding it up. 'Wait – Jude – the lake.'

The surface of the lake was beginning to ripple, transforming into real water. She didn't have time to waste – clutching the magic and her yo-yo, she sprinted across part of the water which looked more solid than the rest. Blood pounded in her ears, the surface sinking beneath her weight – so close to shore—

Without warning, she plunged beneath the icy water. A searing heat wrapped around the hand holding the stolen magic, dragging her down.

The ripples of light on the surface got further away, and she kicked with all her might, trying to fight the invisible grip. It was no use – the force was too strong.

It wouldn't let her go, not while she was still holding the magic.

A tight band began to form around her lungs, squeezing. Her chest puffed as though it would burst any second – she needed air. She gave one more desperate kick. Her vision blackened for a moment.

Then something hooked on to her wrist, dragging her upwards so fast pain shot through her arm. Fin was swimming beside her.

She broke the surface of the water and took huge gulps of air. The lake was a swirling mass around them, the powerful water battering from all sides. The force around her wrist was still there, trying to drag her down, but Fin's presence lessened its pull. The force of the magic must be spreading out to try and drown both of them – making it weaker.

'Swim!' yelled Fin, as he started to splash. Jude followed his lead as waves of water slapped her face. She clutched the magic but a pounding wave snatched her yo-yo out of her grasp.

Panic shot through her. She couldn't be without her yo-yo. She tried to swim after it.

'What are you doing?' screamed Fin from somewhere to her right.

'I – need – to – get – my – yo-yo!' Jude called, accidentally gulping a mouthful of water and immediately wanting to retch.

'You are going to DROWN!'

Jude grabbed the yo-yo, gulping yet more water as she struggled to shore, the waves beating against her. Finally she crawled on to dry ground, heaving as she coughed up splutters of water.

Her clothes clung to her, the cold seeping under her skin. Numbness crept through her body and she stumbled to her feet, trying to jump up and down to bring back some warmth. Her legs wouldn't respond, so she settled for rotating her arms in circles.

Fin was gaping at her. 'What were you thinking? Going for that stupid yo-yo and risking your life like that.'

'I wasn't thinking,' snapped Jude, though shame forced her eyes to the ground. The yo-yo might look like a toy but it was a reminder that her mother had cared about her once.

Jude couldn't let it go that easily.

'Er . . . Jude . . .' Fin's voice shook.

She looked up to see the helpling pointing its sword at her – more specifically, at the stolen magic in her hand. Heat crackled in the air as she took a nervous step backwards.

'What do we do?' whispered Fin.

'Er . . .' Jude's mind was blank. 'Run!' She dodged around the helpling, sprinting across the basement and up the stairs. The backs of her legs burned but she forced herself to keep going.

She stumbled through the door, Fin following

through a second later. 'Eri, get off the stone!' Jude yelled as she turned around to see the helpling climbing the stairs, clutching its sword.

The door closed. There was a thud on the other side, followed by another. The helpling was knocking to get out. Jude winced with each knock but the door didn't open. After a few more thuds there was silence. Apparently the helpling had given up, or else couldn't open the door and leave the basement.

Jude exhaled with relief.

'Are you OK?' said Eri as she popped into view. 'Are you hurt?'

Jude shook her head, still feeling shaky. She wondered if the helpling would report back to Grandleader. Pushing the unsettling thought away, she slipped the anti-nausea magic out, turning it in her hand. If she could lift the curse quickly, she'd be able to explain to Grandleader why she had taken the magic and that the problem was solved and the whole thing was quite funny, actually, if you really thought about it. 'Ready?'

'Jude – wait. Maybe I should eat the tracking magic,' said Eri. 'Just in case the anti-nausea magic doesn't work and you explode—'

'It's OK,' said Jude, but she was touched at Eri's concern. She crammed the anti-nausea magic into her mouth, chewing it quickly. Nothing happened. 'How do I know if it's worked?'

'Spin in circles,' offered Eri. 'And see if you feel sick.'

Jude took the suggestion, feeling incredibly stupid as she spun in tight circles. None of the expected dizziness came. 'OK, it worked.' She held up the shining green stone of tracking magic, Farlow Higgins' warning about how dangerous it was floating to the front of her mind. 'Listen – if I explode, make sure ... well, I don't actually have any last requests. Steal something for me, OK? Keep my legacy alive.'

'You're going to be fine,' said Fin, but his nervousness was betrayed by the way he kept his eyes locked on the magic.

Jude popped the stone into her mouth, squeezing her eyes shut as she chewed as fast as she could. It had no taste and in a few bites was gone. She waited.

Nothing happened.

She cracked one eye open, then the other. Fin and Eri were staring at her.

'Well?' said Eri. 'Do you know where our parents are?' She pulled a sheet of crumpled paper out of her pocket, smoothing the creases out. 'Here's a painting Fin did, in case seeing them helps.'

Jude took the paper. Mr and Mrs Weston gazed up at her, a strong mix of Eri and Fin, the happiness on their faces somehow making the fact they'd been missing for over a year worse.

She felt nothing. 'It's not working,' she said, frustration boiling in her stomach. 'Why's it not working?' It *had* to work – she had snuck Fin and

Eri into the house, risked Grandleader's wrath. This couldn't all be for nothing.

Eri took the paper back. 'Maybe because it's such powerful magic it needs more time?'

Jude shook her head. She'd never eaten magic that didn't work. Was it fake? Moorley had suggested they give the man at the Consortium fake magic, but Jude had thought that was a one-off. Had her family realised how useful keeping fake magic was? But then why would they store it in such a high security location?

'This was supposed to be *it*,' said Jude. She wanted to scream. Instead, she dug her nails into her palms, trying to focus on any odd sensations inside her that might tell her the magic was working. Her head itched a little bit but she didn't think that had anything to do with the magic.

Somewhere in the depths of the house a door slammed. At once the torches on the walls shone brighter, the flames climbing a little higher.

'Someone's home,' said Jude, her heart lurching. 'The house is saying hello – you two need to leave. Got any invisibility magic left?'

They both nodded.

'Great. Eat it and follow me. You need to get out of here.' She ignored the gagging noises from behind her as she hurried down the corridor and back to the side door. She pushed it open and stepped aside. 'Go.'

'Jude – thank you,' came Fin's voice somewhere to her right.

'For what?' she said bitterly. She'd failed. The magic hadn't worked. She was going to have to tell her family about the curse. After a screw-up like this she would have no chance of ever being properly involved in the business. Her family would take over trying to lift the curse and she would be forced to the sidelines for ever.

Or the punishment might be worse. Like ... banishment. Saying goodbye to Ripon Headquarters and everything she had ever known. Grandleader didn't tolerate mistakes – and this was a colossal one.

'For *trying*,' said Fin. 'It means ... it means a lot.' An invisible hand took hers and squeezed, dropping it a second later.

'Bye, Jude,' said Eri.

Jude wanted to reply, but there was a lump in her throat. She'd failed her family – and also Fin and Eri. Their parents were going to stay missing but here they were, still thanking her. To her surprise, she was sad to say goodbye. She ... *liked* them. She liked how much Eri cared about things, how she overthought everything, how Fin listened to her, even how he rolled his eyes at her. It had been nice to feel like part of a team for once.

Before she could come up with the right words to express all that, the door had opened and shut, and she was alone.

She hurried to her bedroom. As she power-walked

along the gallery, she heard her family in the hall below. She paused long enough to work out that the steal had not been successful, that there had been more guard helplings than expected. Of *course* the heist hadn't gone right – the curse would never allow otherwise.

Jude closed her bedroom door, resting against the wall for a moment before she stomped across her room. *Why* hadn't the magic worked? What had she done wrong? Maybe she should have taken more – or maybe Mr and Mrs Weston simply weren't anywhere to be found—

She burped. Gas bubbled in her chest as she patted herself. Her hands glowed gold and a feeling of calm swept over her as her entire body tingled, like people were tapping at her skin with their nails.

At once she imagined Mr and Mrs Weston's faces from Fin's painting, their smiling eyes, the sharp angles of their jaws. The magic told her what to do – not in words but in feelings.

The magic was working!

She went to her desk where she pulled out paper and a pen and started to draw. She'd never been artistic but the magic guided her hand, helping her draw a map of Farrowfell.

Together she and the magic drew landmarks in thin black lines, her hand moving so fast it was almost a blur. She could hardly breathe as the tingling sensation began to build, starting to hurt. Like there was something beneath her skin trying to get out.

Her hand, now almost independent of her, drew a cluster of buildings and labelled them neatly with 'Mergio Market', in looping handwriting so different to her own.

Her hand drew the Library of Farrowfell.

And her hand drew one final, familiar building, and circled it. Jude didn't need the magic to label the building. She already knew what she was staring at.

Ripon Headquarters.

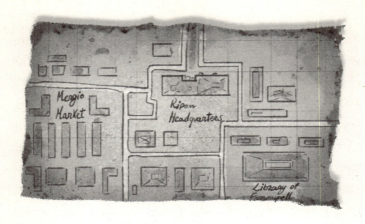

Chapter Fifteen

Ripon Headquarters

Jude stared at the map. It had to be wrong. There was absolutely no way Mr and Mrs Weston were inside Ripon Headquarters. She would know. The magic was lying – it was faulty.

And yet ... and yet ...

She crumpled the paper, wanting to throw it away and pretend she hadn't seen. But she couldn't. She couldn't hide the truth.

Ripon Headquarters was dark and gloomy, always too hot or too cold, and the gardens were choked with weeds, and now she knew there was a deadly lake in the basement. But it was her *home*. It was where she was supposed to be safest. It was not a prison for the Westons.

Her pulse skipped and she uncurled the map, smoothing it out on her desk. Her family were a lot of things – they were, after all, criminals. But they weren't *kidnappers*.

At the same time her heart sank into the knowledge that it was true. This was something her family was capable of. She knew it – she'd known it ever since she'd seen her mother drink the raw magic and seen a glimpse of the terrible monster within.

But what was Grandleader keeping the Westons for? Why had he trapped them here for over a year? The Westons had been looking for Lilthrum – how had that led them to Ripon Headquarters?

She hoped they were OK. Her mind flashed back to the coldness in her grandfather's eyes when he'd used magic against that man at the Consortium.

She paced her bedroom as a horrible thought occurred to her. One day, would she be just like Grandleader and the rest of them? She wouldn't have a choice – they would tell her to drink the raw magic and she would drink it to prove herself.

And then she would keep on drinking it, and she would become twisted and she would forget she had ever known any different. Just like her mother forgot she had daughters half the time and her father's temper was like a bubble, with only a small touch enough to make him explode.

She had no choice. She was only brave and strong because she was a Ripon. Without them, she was nothing.

She came to a halt in front of her window. It was pitch-black outside and all she could see was her own scared face reflected back at her.

You do have a choice, whispered a little voice in her head. A firm voice, which sounded a lot like Eri.

Her mind worked quickly. It would be the ultimate betrayal to free Mr and Mrs Weston. But even if she didn't need to find them to lift the curse, she knew she would try to save them anyway. Fin and Eri had become something like . . . friends. She cared about them.

Should she tell Fin and Eri she knew where their parents were? Once she did, they wouldn't trust her any more. Fin had always been suspicious of her and he had every right to be. She would have been suspicious too. She needed a little more time to come up with a plan.

But all the same, she wished she had someone to discuss it with. She wished Fin was here being gloomy and Eri was writing things down looking worried. She wanted to talk things through—

Her pulse quickened – Moorley! It wasn't the ideal option. She strongly disliked the thought of having to ask Moorley for help. But then . . . Moorley had seemed just as scared as Jude when she'd talked about their mother drinking raw magic – maybe she could help her figure out what to do next.

***

Jude slipped down the corridor to Moorley's room and knocked gently on the door. The torches barely cast any light, the shadows bigger than usual.

There was a scuffling inside, followed by a thump.

'Just a minute,' came Moorley's breathless voice.

'Moorley?' said Jude, confused. The door opened slightly and Moorley's dark eyes peered at Jude.

'Are you on your own?' she whispered, so low Jude barely heard.

'Yes – why?'

Moorley gestured at Jude to come inside, closing the door behind her.

Jude couldn't remember the last time she had been in Moorley's bedroom. It was the same size as hers but much neater, all the books lined up on the bookshelves, the bed made and the corners tucked in. Golden banners draped from the ceiling, as if Moorley was trying to make her room look like it was lit by rays of sun. White curtains hung around her four-poster bed and her windows were flung open, a cool breeze wafting in. A textbook lay on Moorley's bedside table, a flower carefully pressed between the pages as a bookmark. On one of the shelves was a row of pens on stands, displayed like precious trophies.

Moorley's eyes flicked to her bed. There was a small lump underneath the sheets. Jude moved before Moorley could stop her, pulling back the sheet to reveal a notebook lying open, its pages covered in figures.

'What are you doing with that?' asked Jude as Moorley snatched the book away.

'Er . . . nothing,' muttered Moorley.

Jude bit the inside of her cheek. As unpleasant as it was to admit, they were on the same side. She had to focus on the current problem. Besides, maybe Moorley had been right. Maybe Jude wasn't a true Ripon – and maybe she didn't want to be.

'Listen, Moorley, there's something I need to tell you. I . . . I did something stupid. You know that magic I stole from the Westons?'

Moorley snapped her head up from the book, giving Jude her full attention.

Jude started to tell her tale, her cheeks burning when she revealed the reason she'd been looking to steal magic in the first place.

Moorley folded her arms, her face expressionless, as Jude spilled the truth. It was a relief to finally share everything.

She got to the part about the basement and her discovery that the Weston parents were somewhere inside Ripon Headquarters. Here, Moorley stood so quickly Jude thought something had stung her. She paced back and forth, her hands twisting together.

'Mr and Mrs Weston were looking for Lilthrum? It doesn't make any sense. I've never seen a Lilthrum inside Headquarters – have you?' Moorley turned on her heel, facing Jude. Her mouth went slack and a flash of fear crossed her eyes. 'Except – there's one place inside Headquarters neither of us have been . . .'

Grandleader's quarters.

Jude's stomach swooped. It would be simple enough to take a look inside. Scout it out, see what they were up against. She had already survived the basement. Grandleader's quarters couldn't house anything worse . . . besides Lilthrum, potentially. But she would worry about that later.

Except that even the thought of sneaking inside sent a pulse of dread through her. What would Grandleader do if he caught her? What if he already knew about the tracking magic she had stolen and hadn't got round to punishing her?

'Look, we can do this – together. Grandleader's not so bad,' said Jude, trying to sound braver than she felt. Moorley snorted. For a moment they stared at each other, and the hopelessness of the situation crashed down on Jude's shoulders.

'Grandleader's got a business meeting tomorrow evening.' Moorley's voice was brisk. 'It'll be a good time for me to have a look inside and see what I can find. You can keep watch.'

Jude frowned. 'Wait – what do you mean? I'm coming too.' She didn't *want* to, but Moorley telling her she couldn't meant she had to.

Moorley shook her head. 'No, Jude. You're just a kid.'

And there it was, the reason Moorley had always irritated her. 'So are *you*,' said Jude. 'Stop leaving me out – you're as bad as the rest of them!'

Moorley froze, hurt flashing across her eyes. 'No, I'm not,' she said. 'I've been looking out for you. I've *always* looked out for you—'

'You haven't spoken to me properly in two years!' snapped Jude. 'You won't even talk to me properly now – what's so important about that red notebook?'

Moorley's mouth was a hard line. Jude thought she was going to do what she did best: ice Jude out. Instead, she sighed. 'I've been doing some research into the family finances,' she said. 'I made a copy of an accounts book in Dad's study a while ago. It says we're making double what we were last year – and last year we doubled what we were making the year before. But he hasn't said where the money's actually *come* from – it looks like he's scribbled insults to Aunt Morgol in the margins instead, so I guess she looks over all the numbers. And as for the outgoings, all the money is going to 'pile', whatever that means. Why isn't it going to towards proper stuff, like sorting out Ripon

Headquarters so it's not a dump any more?'

Her words came out so quickly Jude struggled to keep up. 'Grandleader always says we'll get soft if our house is too nice . . .'

Moorley snorted, making it clear she didn't believe that. 'Grandleader was looking for a man called Harrimore Hardman. From what I can tell, Harrimore is a recluse – I've not been able to find anything about him in the records at the library apart from the fact that he once worked for the Consortium. But I don't know when he worked there, or what he did or . . .' She shook her head. 'So, this curse of yours . . . I want to talk more about it. From what I know about magic-keepers, if they curse magic they leave things to run their course. Why do you think she cared so much?'

Because she was annoying, Jude wanted to say. But she knew that wasn't the right answer. 'She really wanted me to find Mr and Mrs Weston, because . . . they were investigating the reason for the increase in Lilthrum and might actually have an answer? But what's the link to our family? *Why* would they have kidnapped Mr and Mrs Weston?'

'Well, Lilthrum form when *too much* raw magic falls in one place,' said Moorley. 'That's why they're supposed to be so rare, because raw magic doesn't really collect in one place – it hates everything, including itself.'

'And our family drinks raw magic,' said Jude slowly. She felt like they were on the cusp of something, but it was just out of their grasp.

'But they've drunk raw magic for years,' muttered Moorley. 'Why would anything change now?'

'Maybe there's like a tipping point,' said Jude. 'Like once you've drunk a certain amount … something happens. So, which Ripon would have drunk the most?'

They stared at each other, not needing to say the word aloud.

Grandleader.

Chapter Sixteen

Grandleader's Quarters

Jude was on edge waiting for the next evening to arrive. She kept trying to convince Moorley to let her go along but didn't make any progress.

'If there's anything dangerous in there, it doesn't make sense for us both to put ourselves at risk,' said Moorley. Jude pressed her lips together but didn't push the issue. She kept her yo-yo and invisibility magic in her pockets, though, just in case.

Jude briefly considered that Moorley might have another motive for wanting her to stay out of Grandleader's quarters – how did she know, really, that she could trust her sister? She couldn't trust any of the other Ripons – even before she'd seen them drinking raw magic, she'd known they were all in competition for Grandleader's approval.

She hovered in the entrance hall, watching Grandleader's door. Moorley knew he had a business meeting because she'd overheard him telling their mother, but she didn't know what time. And Jude didn't want to risk missing him leave.

It was Moorley who had pointed out that no one would question Jude hanging around. The rest of the family hardly paid her attention; it was time to use that to their advantage. Before, Jude might have been offended. Now she swallowed her pride and tried to recognise that Moorley had some smart ideas. The portrait of her grandmother beamed down on her, the eyes kind as ever. But Jude wondered if Grandma would disapprove of what she wanted to do.

Minutes passed by so slowly Jude wondered if the big clock in the entrance hall was broken. Finally, in the late afternoon, Grandleader left the house. He seemed happy about something, nodding at Jude as he went.

Jude hurried to tell Moorley, who nodded.

'I'll be quick,' Moorley said. 'In and out.' She ate some invisibility magic and slipped inside Grandleader's quarters without any hesitation.

One minute passed. Two. Grandleader's quarters were huge. It would take a while for Moorley to go around all the corridors.

The front door opened and Jude's father stumbled inside. Wind blew through the entrance hall and Jude caught a whiff of the sour smell of alcohol. He swayed as he stared at her and she tensed, worried he would ask her what she was doing. Then his unfocused eyes slid away and he stumbled down a side corridor.

The clock continued to tick, and Moorley still didn't return. Maybe she'd found something and got distracted? Jude bit her lip. She shouldn't be taking this long – they didn't know how much time they had before Grandleader returned. His meeting might be cancelled. He could decide to cut it short.

Twenty minutes had gone now. What could she be doing? Moorley wouldn't lose track of time – she knew Jude would be waiting.

Jude bounced on the balls of her feet. Something was wrong.

The family motto etched above Grandleader's door was lit with a soft light, shining above her head like a faraway star. A reminder that Ripons should never betray Ripons. A warning to stay out.

Squaring her shoulders, she opened the door and stepped inside.

She gasped. She had expected to walk into a sitting room. Instead she was standing in a long corridor lit by fires in the brackets on the green velvet walls. High above her was a ceiling decorated with gold swirls. The floorboards were dark, polished wood, so clean they were almost shining. Motes of dust swirled in the air but they didn't appear to settle on anything, and there was a faint smell of roses, welcoming her in. Unlike the rest of Ripon Headquarters, it was warm, and she was reminded of stepping into a hot bath after a long day. It felt as though she was finally *home*.

Slowly, of its own accord, the door to the rest of the house closed behind her and a tiny click of the lock focused her mind. She became aware of the silence pressing down, the only sound her hammering heart.

Was this still Ripon Headquarters? What had happened to the dingy corridors covered in layers of grime? What had happened to only lighting areas that were in use to save money?

'Moorley?' she whispered, taking a few uncertain steps forward.

The corridor stretched on – there were no doors leading off it, though from outside it seemed as though there was space for many rooms. Jude crept onwards, glancing over her shoulder every so often to check the exit door was still there.

The dust motes continued to swirl in the air, sparkling ever so slightly . . .

Dust doesn't sparkle. An alarm bell clanged in Jude's head. There was only one thing that sparkled in the way the particles in the air did.

Raw magic.

Floating in the air, as if it didn't have a care in the

world. She was breathing it in, inhaling it into her lungs. Suddenly, she could feel it clawing its way inside, digging into her heart—

She shook her head. That was just her imagination. She hadn't drunk the raw magic; she was safe.

The rest of Ripon Headquarters had been built with magic – but *tamed magic*, which caused the house to throw tantrums when it got bored.

Grandleader's part of the house had been built with raw magic.

The smell of roses was almost cloying now. Jude's head began to buzz with the beginnings of a headache – it was *too* warm.

A shiver went down her back. She continued to creep along the silent corridor until she finally saw doors set into the walls, slightly ajar.

'Moorley?' she hissed at each one, not daring to go inside. Then she came across a door standing open, revealing a brightly lit study. There were dark panelled walls and cubbyholes filled with books. A large chair sat behind a desk of polished wood. Silk curtains were drawn over the windows; the light came from more flames flickering in torches on the walls. The rug was thick, her boots sinking in.

Jude went up to the desk, where there was a stack of papers of calculations she didn't understand. She flicked through, pausing when she found a list of random names crossed out – except for one: Harrimore

Hardman. This name was circled, and scribbled next to it were the words: 'He can work it out'.

She frowned, trying to figure out what that meant. A cool breeze blew at her neck and she glanced around. In the far corner of the study was a door standing slightly open. There was an odd golden glow seeping through.

Jude edged forwards, peering inside. She gasped. The room was long and narrow, and gold was stacked in circular piles reaching the high ceiling. There was a small path through the treasure, along which she could walk.

At the end of the room was an enormous portrait of Grandleader and Grandma. It must have been drawn years ago, but Grandleader had hardly aged since then. He was looking at Jude's grandmother with something in his eyes she had never seen – deep, solid love. It was as if the woman beside him was the only person in the world.

A prickling feeling crept over her neck. The painter had drawn something almost fierce in Grandleader's expression: a fire that could burn away everything, leaving ruin in its wake. She'd never seen him look at anyone else in the family like that.

Jude turned her back on the unsettling painting. There was another linked room, and this one also had piles of gold inside. Jude thought she had discovered where all the money from the family business was going – but why was Grandleader hoarding it? What for? And where was Moorley?

There was one final door made from a dark warped wood in the corner of the second room filled with gold. Jude pushed it open to find herself looking into a windowless space. Blue flames flickered in the brackets, their dull light shining over—

A person.

Motionless and staring straight at her—

Jude stepped forward, sense overtaking her panic. She was looking at a life-sized stone *statue*.

She peered at its face. It looked familiar ...

The big eyes, the smile on the lips ...

'Grandma?' she muttered. As she looked closer, she noticed the statue was missing a chunk of shoulder. Scattered around the floor were remnants of other statues – a hand, another hand, another hand, the stone scorched as if it had been held in fire. Parts of Grandma's face, caved in as if it had been smashed. Legs and arms with sections missing, as though something had taken a bite ...

Jude shivered.

She didn't understand – and all she wanted was to leave. But she needed to find Moorley.

She went back through the study and into the main corridor, heading towards the door at the end. The walls around her flickered, briefly revealing darkness in all directions.

The raw magic in the air swirled more thickly and the walls returned, the dark panels seemingly solid once more. She reached out and her hand passed straight through, as though she had eaten ghost magic. She yanked her arm back as the door at the end of the corridor creaked open.

'Moorley?' she whispered. Beyond the door was darkness. Taking a deep breath, she stepped through.

Chapter Seventeen

Raw Magic

Jude found herself standing in a space so large the walls disappeared into darkness. Columns ringed in circles around what looked like a central pit, but Jude couldn't work out their purpose; the room was open to the night sky. Hundreds of stars twinkled above and a cold breeze lifted strands of hair around her face.

There was a smell of freshly baked bread in the air – of perfumed flowers ...

She took a few uncertain steps along the stone floor. This wasn't possible. The space was big – too big to fit inside Grandleader's quarters.

And yet, here it was.

Curiosity bubbled inside her. It couldn't hurt to take a closer look at the pit.

Her footsteps made no sound, and she felt exposed under the stars, as if each twinkling light was a beady eye.

The hole in the ground was about the size of the entrance hall of Ripon Headquarters. She went as close to the edge as she dared, to see it was a quarter filled with soft silver light, or liquid – she couldn't really tell. Even as she stood, a flash of light floated down from the stars above, adding to the contents of the hole.

A lovely smell, trying to lure her in . . .

Light, falling from the stars . . .

No – it couldn't be . . .

She blinked as she realised she was looking down on a pit of raw magic – probably the most raw magic anyone had ever seen in one place.

But raw magic did not fall in Farrowfell, and it did not gather like this.

The surface of the magic in the pit bubbled and popped as if it was boiling. A blob formed, rolling along the ground. To Jude's horror the shape lengthened, claws forming, the surface fizzing as it changed into a creature of shining silver. It was human-like, though longer and narrower, as if someone had taken a person and stretched their body too far. As the silver grew into legs and feet the creature slowly stood up, shaking as if with effort. Its face grew blurred features.

Jude's breath stopped in her chest. She was watching the birth of a raw-mMagic monster, a Lilthrum.

Her brain jammed, but she had enough wits about her to register that she needed to hide. She fumbled in her pocket, pulling out the little bit of invisibility magic. Her tamed magic might not be able to trick something of raw magic – but it was all she had. She nibbled at the edges, shuddering as a trickling cold washed over her and her body disappeared.

The Lilthrum stretched, its joints popping and cracking. Something brushed past Jude and she saw a Ripon helpling sidle up to the Lilthrum. The helpling took the Lilthrum's hand and silently led it away. They disappeared behind the columns.

Mr and Mrs Weston had been looking for a reason why there were more Lilthrum in Farrowfell – was this pit the answer? Had they discovered it – and been attacked by the raw-magic monsters? They would have been lucky to survive – but surely they *had* to be alive, otherwise the curse would have been broken the moment she apologised to Fin and Eri. So where had they gone?

Suddenly Jude wanted to get as far away from the raw magic and the Lilthrum as she could.

She tried to move but something about the pit's presence had locked her legs in place. The smell floating out of it was now of damp grass after heavy rainfall, a fresh breeze – she remembered fleeing across

Farrowfell with her mother while being chased by guard helplings. There had been so much joy in her chest it was almost painful, the feel of her mother's hand around hers, pulling her along.

What she wouldn't give to go back.

The surface of the raw magic in the pit seemed to whisper a promise – *Just a sip, and you could have everything you've ever wanted—*

She was stuck.

The light from the stars continued to fall like snow, drifting into the pit. Magic blew in from behind her as well, as if something inside the pit was calling to it.

A shiver ran down her spine. Why would anyone need so much raw magic? Surely, just a tiny bit of it would be enough to cast any spell you wanted.

And could there ever be *too* much raw magic in one place? The air crackled with heat, and the ground trembled slightly. She felt as though she was standing on the edge of a volcano about to erupt.

Raw magic has plans of its own.

She squeezed her eyes shut – maybe if she held her breath and tried really, really hard, she could get herself moving.

Nothing happened. She wouldn't be able to move by sheer willpower. Her mouth was parched, her tongue bumpy and rough. What she wouldn't do for just a little water to quench her thirst.

Hardly knowing what she was doing, she cupped her hands, willing the raw magic to fall down to her instead of the pit. Maybe her thoughts called to the raw magic. Maybe it would have fallen into her cupped hands anyway. Either way raw magic pooled in her palms so quickly she couldn't understand how the pit hadn't already filled.

It had to be the Lilthrum, she realised, being created in the pit and walking away with huge amounts of the magic which had fallen. The pit was like a glass collecting rainwater, but with hundreds of tiny leaks pouring out as fast as it was filling up.

She licked her lips, holding her hands to her mouth. The liquid frothed back and forth in her palms. Slowly, she stuck her tongue out – she only needed a little bit. One small sip and she would be strong enough to do anything – she could lift the curse in a second, she could reunite Fin and Eri with their parents, she could finally help the family business.

She would be a true Ripon.

Jude gasped. She didn't want to be like them, not any more. Family was meant to make you feel safe; they weren't meant to keep you on edge in case they lost their temper. They weren't supposed to forget your birthday. They weren't supposed to ignore you, or make you wonder what you'd done to make them stop loving you.

'I won't become like them,' she whispered, letting the raw magic fall to the ground. She wiped the silvery liquid on her trousers and took a deep breath. She needed to figure a way out of this room.

But the raw magic still called to her.

What harm could a tiny gulp do? It would help her get away—

No. She focused on digging into the contents of her pockets. There was her emergency chocolate bar. There was her yo-yo. She slipped it out, running it back and forth on her palms.

She remembered the way her mother had looked at her the day she'd given it to her. There had been warmth in her eyes, a smile as she watched Jude unwrap the present.

She hadn't looked at Jude that way since. Moorley had received eleventh, twelfth, thirteenth birthday presents – even a small fourteenth one, in the form of a special dinner. Moorley's fifteenth birthday was forgotten, but Jude hated that her sister had had more years of love in total.

Now Jude understood that it wasn't her fault. The change in her mother had been her mother's doing, no one else's.

The raw magic fell thick and fast, coating her arms and glittering in her hair like snowflakes.

Her invisibility magic flickered out and she reappeared, but the newly formed Lilthrum took no notice of her. She was covered in raw magic now. She was just like it.

Her thoughts were woolly and slow as she clutched her yo-yo. If Moorley was somewhere nearby, the yo-yo's noise would almost certainly get her attention.

Jude started swinging the yo-yo in circles. It let off the squeal, which echoed on and on, and Jude was heartened by the noise, calling to Moorley.

Then she felt a tug. A newly formed Lilthrum had grabbed the end of the yo-yo, tugging it out of Jude's hand. The creature swallowed it in one gulp, its throat bobbing as its black eyes fixed on her. It bared two rows of razor-sharp teeth, before a helpling led it away.

Jude stared at her empty hand in shock. That had been her last hope. She was all alone—

And suddenly she was moving. There was someone clutching her hand. She was being half pulled, half dragged out of the room.

Moorley was here.

Chapter Eighteen

A New Guard

Moorley yanked Jude hard, forcing her into a run. 'Faster!' she screamed. Jude made herself sprint. Her legs still felt sluggish and her mind foggy. She was dragging on Moorley, slowing her down. Behind them came a howl, too high-pitched to have come from the throat of anything human.

Jude sped up. She couldn't seem to make her limbs move like they usually did. Moorley should go ahead, escape. She tried to untangle her hand from her sister's but Moorley gripped tighter.

'Don't let go!' said Moorley, hair whipping around her face.

Ahead was the ghostly outline of the rest of the house – but when they tried running inside, the walls remained like a mist around them.

Moorley cursed. 'Think of home,' she said. 'We need to make it solid in our heads.'

But Jude couldn't think of Ripon Headquarters as home any more, not when the most important things appeared to be fear and power: every time she tried, her mind came up against a smooth blank wall. A home was somewhere like the Weston mansion, where everyone loved each other, where life wasn't a constant competition.

'Come *on*, Jude,' said Moorley. Sweat dripped down her face.

Jude concentrated with all her might, thinking of the dark corridors, the sullen rooms, the large spaces, the shadows, the gloom. Nothing happened. She tried again, this time focusing on her sister's scared face. On getting out of here, together. Ghostly walls formed around them, hardening into a corridor with green velvet walls lit with torches. Grandleader's quarters.

Moorley doubled over, panting. Relief swept through Jude. They had made it out.

'Where was that room?' said Jude. 'How did we travel there? We didn't use a port.'

'That was still part of Headquarters,' said Moorley. 'It was a where-and-when room ...'

Jude had learned about where-and-when rooms from the tutor obsessed with buildings. The rooms could be huge but still take up hardly any space and existed in two places: a location of the owner's choosing, and wherever they were anchored.

There had been raw magic falling inside – but raw magic didn't fall in Farrowfell ... Only in the Wild Lands.

'Grandleader's anchored the where-and-when room in Headquarters ... and chosen the Wild Lands as the second location,' whispered Jude. The corridor stretched in front and behind. Flakes of raw magic swirled around them, settling on her shoulders.

'But no one's ever managed to get a where-and-when room to stay in the Wild Lands ...' said Moorley.

Grandleader had worked out a way, though. Because Grandleader used raw magic.

'There were Lilthrum being made from that pit – the helplings were taking them somewhere.' Jude's voice came out a croak, her knees still feeling wobbly. She knew if she had stayed much longer by the pit, she would have given in to the urge to drink raw magic.

'I know,' said Moorley, her voice grim. 'I tried to follow one – I kept walking and walking but the room kept going. And then a Lilthrum saw me – almost clawed me. Come on, we need to get out of here.'

Moorley seized a torch from one of the wall brackets, holding the flickering flame above her head and sweeping over the shadows in the corridor. Jude grabbed another torch, glad of the light.

Together they crept down the corridor, their footsteps muffled on the thick carpet, which was red like old blood. The corridor took a sharp turn and she collided with Moorley, who had stopped.

'What—' She didn't finish the sentence. In the middle of the corridor something glistened. It looked like a thick, globby mess of silver slime, miniature bubbles popping every few seconds. Already the surface of the blob was boiling a little, expanding ever so slightly.

The raw magic fluttering around them drifted towards the slime. It was clumping together to form a Lilthrum. Right in the middle of Grandleader's quarters.

'What do we do?' said Moorley. 'Do you have any magic?'

Jude shook her head. She didn't even have her yo-yo any more. By the pit she had been coated in raw magic – but that had come off as she was running, and the raw magic in the air had no interest in falling on her shoulders and protecting her now, not when it could form a Lilthrum.

'How do you fight against raw magic?' she asked.

'I don't know,' said Moorley, her eyes locked on the blobby slime. 'The research into it is limited . . .'

They needed to act. And fast. Jude swished her torch, the flames crackling with glee. 'Let's try and burn it,' she said.

Even as she took a step forward, a hole in the blob widened to reveal two sets of sharp teeth. Spindly arms formed, scraping across the floor, allowing it to drag itself forward. Its mouth grew broader as it lurched towards them.

Jude moved at the same time as Moorley, thrusting her torch at the creature. The flames licked along the creature's body. It shivered, throwing its head back. With a pop, two eyes opened on its face, empty black orbs which reflected the flames flickering across its body, slowly fizzling out.

'You cannot burn me,' it hissed, voice scratchy. A fleshy purple tongue unrolled from its mouth.

Jude flinched back in horror. She didn't know Lilthrum could talk. That nugget of information wasn't in any of the stories about them – although she guessed that the people unlucky enough to hear them speak probably didn't have much of a chance to tell anyone afterwards.

'Run,' said Moorley. And they did. Moorley quickly outpaced Jude, whose body hadn't yet recovered from the after-effects of standing beside the pit. Her calf muscles cramped, her heartbeat was irregular. A door appeared ahead and Moorley wrenched it open.

Jude followed her and the moment she did, Moorley tried to slam it shut. But she was stopped by an impossibly long arm thrusting through, its spindly fingers ending in sharp points, scrambling for flesh—

Moorley crashed against the door, throwing her weight in to it. Jude joined her even as the Lilthrum's hand swiped at her face. She turned her head as the door budged a centimetre. Jude used the motion to force the door further and the creature howled, pulling its arm back. It wasn't fully formed – it didn't yet have the power to simply walk through the door.

The door closed with a thud and Moorley slid the bolt home. On the other side, the Lilthrum bayed again. The wood splintered, the hinges squealing in protest.

Jude spun around. A corridor stretched before them, disappearing into darkness.

'The house won't let us out,' she said. 'There's some sort of protection to stop us from leaving.'

Moorley swore.

The Lilthrum slammed into the door again and the whole corridor shook, dust falling from the ceiling.

'Let's move,' Moorley said.

They hurried along the corridor, up a set of stairs, and yet another corridor. None of the doors led to an exit. All the corridors ended in blank walls. It was as if Grandleader's quarters were completely sealed off from the rest of the house.

'The Lilthrum's going to catch us if we keep running around,' said Jude, as still another door revealed not an exit but a reading room lined with bookshelves. 'Let's hide in here.' They pressed inside and Moorley closed the door, pulling the bolt across.

Jude collapsed into a soft chair covered in a silk throw. Her whole body shook as she flicked hair out of her eyes.

Moorley frowned at a pair of small swords hanging on the wall, more like long knives than proper weapons. 'If that thing finds us, we need to be prepared to fight it.' She stood on a chair and lifted the swords down. Despite being just for show, the edges looked sharp enough.

'Fire didn't work – how's stabbing it going to help?' asked Jude. 'Does it even have any flesh?'

'The Farrowfell Guards always have swords,' said Moorley, giving one to Jude and keeping the longer, heavier of the two. She seemed jittery, moving around the room and slashing her sword through the air. 'There has to be a reason for that.'

Jude didn't point out that the Farrowfell Guards didn't seem to be very good at fighting off the Lilthrum. She didn't have any better suggestions.

'I guess we just wait – the Lilthrum's going to keep developing its power. It'll be able to walk through walls and doors and appear wherever it wants to soon enough.' Moorley eyed the door. Then she turned to Jude. 'What were you doing? I told you to stay outside and keep guard.' Her voice was snappy, disapproving.

The tone irritated Jude, but she bit back a sharp retort. There was no point arguing. She was here now. 'I came to rescue you,' she said. 'I was waiting and waiting and you didn't come.'

Moorley's nostrils flared. 'That was *incredibly* stupid—'

'How were you able to move in the where-and-when room?' cut in Jude. 'The moment I got near the pit, I was stuck.'

Moorley flushed. 'I didn't actually go near it – I followed the Lilthrum straight away.'

'And ... you didn't see any sign of Mr and Mrs Weston?' asked Jude.

Moorley shook her head.

Jude's head started to throb. 'Grandleader must have made that pit somehow. Why?'

'Well, we know some of our family drink raw magic.' Moorley closed her eyes and massaged her temples. 'They wouldn't need that much, though, not enough to need to fill an entire pit – but what if they sell it as well?' Her eyes snapped open. 'At the meeting at the Consortium, that man mentioned us being cheaper than gatherers.' Her eyes were wide. 'It all makes sense – our family has made this giant pit somehow to collect raw magic and sell it cheap. That's obviously illegal because the side effects of having too much raw magic in one place are more Lilthrum.'

Jude bit her lip. The Ripons had unleashed beasts who had killed innocent people. And for what – *money?* Grandleader must have spent a bit of it kitting out his quarters all fancy, but the rest he was hoarding for no apparent reason. 'What do we do?' she whispered, running a hand over the blade of her sword.

'We fight the Lilthrum when it finds us,' said Moorley, her voice full of determination. 'We stop them from filling up that pit. And then maybe we just ... get out? Leave Ripon Headquarters ... for good.' Her eyes flashed, her mouth set into a grim line.

'Run away?' The words felt wrong in Jude's mouth. They couldn't run away – Grandleader would find them. If they betrayed him, he would certainly come after them for revenge. He would never let them out from under his thumb – even people who worked for the family signed up for life.

'Yes.' Moorley swallowed, her throat bobbing.

'Where would we go?' asked Jude.

They could continue stealing – apples here, bread there – enough to keep them going when times got tough ... But that wouldn't be enough. They'd have to steal bigger things – they'd have to start their own business. And Grandleader would never let that happen.

'I can't stay here,' said Moorley. 'I won't let Grandleader control me like this. And I'm not leaving you behind.' She straightened, as if trying to look more grown up. In reality she looked as lost as Jude felt.

A tight bubble of guilt exploded in Jude's stomach. 'I've always been jealous of you,' she said, the words tumbling out. 'And after you told Grandleader I wasn't a true Ripon I didn't want anything to do with you . . .' She'd been wrong. She'd misjudged Moorley and now she needed to steel herself to apologise. 'I'm sorry.'

Moorley side-eyed her. 'You heard me say that to Grandleader?'

Jude nodded. 'I was eavesdropping. But it doesn't matter – I don't need to know why . . .'

Moorley was shaking her head. 'It was after my first heist – we broke into this huge house . . . the owners were home. I heard them pleading with Grandleader not to hurt them and I heard a crashing sound and . . . he was laughing . . .' She rubbed her forehead. 'It was the first time I ever thought we . . . we might be the bad guys, that being a true Ripon might be a curse. I knew Grandleader wanted to ask you on the next heist. I wanted to protect you – and Grandleader went along with it.'

'Because he wanted to keep us apart,' Jude realised. She thought of the way her mother had called her relationship with Aunts Morgol and Victi *constant competition*. Competing for Grandleader's attention – just like her and Moorley. Now she saw it, she couldn't believe she hadn't seen it sooner.

'What do you mean?' said Moorley, scrunching up her nose.

'Grandleader wouldn't let himself be listened in on if he didn't want to be heard,' said Jude. 'I bet he *knew*

I was outside. That's what he wants – if everyone's divided from each other it means they're all just focused on him.'

'I'm sorry,' said Moorley, rubbing the bridge of her nose. She looked ashamed. 'I didn't even realise he was manipulating me ...'

Jude felt like the light had been turned on in a dark room. Moorley had been looking out for her. She had *always* looked out for her. When they were younger, she'd been the one telling Jude to eat her vegetables and go to sleep – something their mother should have been doing but had never bothered with. And Moorley had never resented the fact that Jude disliked her, or didn't listen to her. In fact, she realised, Moorley might be the only member of her family who had ever really cared about her.

Jude crossed the room and gripped Moorley's free hand, squeezing it briefly before letting it go. 'Thank you,' she said, her eyes prickling with tears. 'For ... for everything you've tried to do for me. I'm sorry I never realised. From now on, we need to be a *proper* team. We need to look out for each other.'

Moorley nodded and Jude found her eyes prickling with tears. She glanced away, her eyes drawn to the corner of the room where a dark shape was forming in the air.

The Lilthrum had found them.

Chapter Nineteen

Ripons Are for Life

Moorley burst into action, her sword whistling straight through the Lilthrum, which roared as it vomited flames of silver. The raw magic which made up its body separated around the blade, re-forming moments later.

Moorley rolled to the side and the flames raced across the rug, burning through the material and the floorboards to reveal the room below. An acrid smell hung in the air.

Jude sprinted at the Lilthrum, swinging her sword wildly. It was heavier than she'd expected and her movements were clumsy. She sliced the blade through the raw magic, and a glob flew away from the Lilthrum's body, towards Jude. She caught it without thinking and lobbed it as far away from her as she could.

There was now a hole in the Lilthrum's form, above its stomach. Its body was made of raw magic – and raw magic hated itself. So if they split up its raw magic form, maybe they could kill it.

Moorley caught Jude's eye. She nodded at the creature. It was clear she had arrived at the same conclusion.

The Lilthrum staggered as it spun around, silver flames jetting at Jude, narrowly missing and licking at the wall instead. The flames left a hole through which pale moonlight shone.

Jude charged, Moorley bursting into action beside her. The Lilthrum whipped its arms around, howling as Jude hacked at the raw magic with her sword until it sunk into what might have been the Lilthrum's stomach, and stayed put.

She ducked, barely avoiding the silver flames that tore another hole in the wall. She picked up one of the heavy books on the shelf, flinging the volume at the creature's legs. Moorley swung low at the same time and together they lifted the creature so it crashed to the ground on its back. Flames poured from its open mouth, bursting through the ceiling, and the creature was up again.

Dust billowed everywhere. Jude covered her mouth with her arm, trying not to breathe in.

Moorley had been backed into a corner, and though she continued to swing her sword it didn't seem to make much of a difference. Was the creature slowing? Jude couldn't tell.

Her sword was still sticking *through* the Lilthrum, the tip appearing out of its back. Without thinking, she took a running leap at the creature, pouncing on its back and grabbing the sword. The creature howled, staggering as it tried to shake her off.

The distraction gave Moorley enough time to roll out of the corner, and she took a swipe at the creature's legs as she did, hacking another glob of raw magic away. Jude used the motion to wrench her sword from where it had embedded itself in the Lilthrum, falling backwards.

She jumped down, holding the sword above her head.

'You cannot defeat me,' hissed the Lilthrum. Flames crackled from its lips. 'You will tire eventually.'

'Don't worry about us,' said Moorley. Blood dripped from her nose and her voice was thick. There was a bruise already forming on her cheek. She ran at the creature and they clashed in a mixture of fire and blurred movements.

Moorley blocked another blow from the Lilthrum. It was flailing around, off-balance, and Jude lunged forward, swiping her sword at its head. She sliced at what might have been its skull, and it collapsed to the ground.

'Quick!' said Jude, dropping her sword and tearing at

the remaining raw magic. She and Moorley didn't stop until all that was left was a small silver puddle, innocently glimmering with a light it seemed to be emitting.

Jude didn't have time to feel relieved. The floor shuddered and more of the ceiling crashed down. The whole room was unstable. They needed to get out of here – and fast.

'Maybe we missed a door somewhere,' said Moorley. 'Grandleader walks in and out all the time.'

'Maybe only he can leave?' said Jude, gripping her sword.

'We came *in* just fine,' said Moorley, as a large crack formed in the ground.

Jude's mind fought a fog of dizziness. A Ripon could enter, which meant they should have been able to leave. Perhaps there was some sort of password, or code.

What code could Grandleader have? Jude cast her mind back to every family dinner, every encounter with Grandleader, trying to think of clues. But nothing he had said came to mind – but perhaps it wasn't anything he had said. The Ripon motto, etched into many walls of the house, was also hung above the entrance to Grandleader's quarters.

'If you're born a Ripon, you're a Ripon for life,' she whispered, and a door appeared in the far wall where there hadn't been a door before.

It swung open and Jude recognised the corridor that led to the dining room.

'Jude, you solved it,' said Moorley.

As they raced to the exit there was a splintering sound and a scream.

Jude spun around. The unstable floor had given way and Moorley was clinging to the jagged edges of the hole.

'Moorley!' Jude yelled, about to race across to save her sister.

'Don't do that,' said a quiet voice from behind. 'You'll go through the floor with her.'

Grandleader stood in the doorway, his arms crossed.

'Oh – Grandleader ... I ...' Jude's mind raced as she tried to come up with a reason why they had broken one of the unspoken rules of Headquarters, never to enter his quarters.

Grandleader stared at Moorley, who was struggling to hold herself up. 'What were you two doing?'

Moorley gritted her teeth. 'Grandleader – please, help me!' she gasped.

'What were you doing in my quarters?' repeated Grandleader, tapping his long fingers together. His calmness sent a chill through Jude's blood.

'I decided—' began Moorley.

'Spry dared me,' lied Jude, speaking over Moorley. It was her turn to protect her sister. 'I was supposed to bring something back to prove I'd come in – Moorley tried to stop me.' It was a risk involving Spry in her lie, but if Grandleader questioned him and he denied it, Jude could say he was simply trying to protect himself.

'Tell the truth,' said Grandleader coldly.

His icy gaze demanded explanations. Jude's best course of action was probably changing the subject. 'Why are you storing all that gold in your quarters?'

'Because I'm saving it for *later*,' said Grandleader silkily. Moorley grunted, her face tight with strain. Grandleader smirked and snapped his fingers.

It was as if an invisible hand had grasped Moorley, pulling her up and thrusting her at Grandleader's feet. Wood conjured out of thin air repaired the hole in the floor; bricks slid into place in the walls, along with a fresh coat of paint; the ceiling was once more a stretch of white; the dust vanished, and the rug was freshly swept; Jude's sword was tugged out of her hands and flew back to its place on display, along with Moorley's sword.

Once, Jude might have been amazed that Grandleader had restored the room without eating any tamed magic. But with the power of raw magic, this spell was probably as easy as breathing to him.

'I don't like being lied to,' said Grandleader softly. 'I don't like my generosity in trusting my family being taken advantage of. For example, yesterday a tiny piece of tracking magic was taken from the basement – by a Ripon. I did not authorise the sale of any tracking magic or the use of it by anyone in the family. There was only one Ripon unaccounted for last night ...' He raised his eyebrows. 'I didn't think this Ripon could be using it for any ... sinister purposes, being so young. But maybe I should have taken the break-in more seriously.'

Of course Grandleader knew about her stealing the tamed magic. Jude couldn't believe she'd ever thought she could take it without him knowing.

'I wanted to help the family,' she whispered. It wasn't a lie – just not the entire truth.

'You've both disappointed me,' said Grandleader after a pause, as Moorley struggled to her feet. 'Clearly, you are not good influences on each other. Come with me.' Grandleader turned on his heel and Jude and Moorley hurried after him to the main part of the house. Moorley was limping, blinking sluggishly.

Jude shot her sister anxious looks as they went. Clearly she couldn't trick Grandleader. They'd have to accept whatever punishment he gave them. She shuddered. Grandleader's punishments were always creative in how terrible they were – and always fitting for the crime.

Grandleader marched past the evening room, up a set of stairs at the back of the house. He stopped outside Aunt Victi's study, rapped once and opened the door.

They were greeted by an argument. 'How many times have I told you I do *not* want you cleaning in here?' Aunt Victi was roaring at a helpling, hands on her hips. The helpling stood still, clutching a duster. 'I will rip that duster out of your hands and jam it down your—'

'Victi,' said Grandleader. 'I need you. Moorley and Jude broke into my quarters.'

Why had he gone to Aunt Victi and not Jude's mother and father?

The answer came a second later, from the cruel smile lighting up Aunt Victi's face. 'Is that right? I can string them up by their ankles if you like – maybe the blood rushing to their heads will help them think about what stupid children they are. Or I can go the old-fashioned way and beat some sense into them ...'

Jude's mother and father wouldn't show any mercy in punishing them, but at least they wouldn't *delight* in the act like Aunt Victi.

'No need for any of that,' said Grandleader lightly. 'Come with me.' He led them out of Aunt Victi's study, continuing along the corridor. Jude's stomach had twisted into knots. Grandleader pointed at a plain wooden door.

'In you go, Moorley,' he said. The door swung open to reveal a room Jude had never seen before. There were bars on the narrow window, and apart from the single bed with a filthy mattress and no sheets, it was bare.

'W-what?' mumbled Moorley, her eyes out of focus.

'Well, you're injured,' said Grandleader pleasantly. 'So you need to rest.'

Moorley looked at him, confusion on her face. She glanced at Jude then wobbled inside. Jude went to follow but Grandleader held out a hand, blocking her.

'Where are you going?' said Grandleader. 'You and Moorley will not be allowed near each other any more.'

'But—' said Jude, panic clawing inside her. She tried to shove past Grandleader but Aunt Victi grabbed her. She struggled against her aunt's iron grip.

The door slammed shut and Aunt Victi let Jude go.

'Keep watch, Victi,' said Grandleader. 'Moorley is sick. She needs time to recover.'

'Moorley's not sick!' said Jude. 'She got hurt in your quarters – Moorley and I—'

'There is no Moorley and you,' interrupted Grandleader. He stared down at her. 'She's a bad influence. You've always cared so much about the family, Jude. Don't think I haven't noticed.'

'But . . .' Jude didn't know what to say. She was used to being ignored.

'Come – you need a rest. You look exhausted.' Grandleader laid a hand on her shoulder, steering her towards her room. He was right – she *was* tired. 'You are a *true* Ripon,' he whispered as they went. 'I know you'll get back on the right track now you're away from Moorley.'

A *true* Ripon. The warm tone in his voice, his steady hand on her shoulder. It was all Jude had ever wanted.

She was the golden child and Moorley was the disgrace.

'Goodnight,' Grandleader said, and his voice was the softest she had ever heard it.

Chapter Twenty

Visitors

Jude paced her bedroom.

You're a true Ripon.

The words she'd spent her whole life waiting for whispered again and again in her ears. She moved towards the door, to find Grandleader and tell him she would do whatever she could to make him proud. She would tell him about the tracking magic which had said Mr and Mrs Weston were trapped inside Ripon Headquarters. Which was obviously *wrong* because they were nowhere to be found.

And she would tell him about the curse, and

he would use raw magic to lift it because he was all powerful—

There was a loud thump behind her.

She spun around. Eri and Fin were lying in a heap on a pile of discarded books on her rug.

'Ow,' said Fin as he got to his feet. 'You know these things called *shelves* exist.'

Eri had picked up one of the books. 'Interesting choice of reading,' she said as she flicked through *A Beginner's Guide to Overthrowing the Consortium*, which had been a gift from Aunt Victi.

Jude stared at them. 'What are you doing here?' As far as they were aware, she was no longer of any use to them. They thought the tracking magic hadn't worked.

She didn't have time for them. She needed to speak to Grandleader—

Eri put the book neatly on Jude's desk, straightening her clothes. 'We came to see you. We wanted to check on you – make sure you didn't get caught after you stole the tracking magic from the basement.'

'You were . . . worried about me?' asked Jude, letting go of the doorknob. The words felt foreign. But she had to *go and see Grandleader*. Fin and Eri were nothing to her after all.

She froze. Where were these thoughts coming from? She *did* care about Fin and Eri. They were her friends.

Fin shrugged. 'It's been, like . . . two days since we saw you. With no one trying to break into our house . . . we were, you know. Concerned.'

'We have a little bit of transportation magic at home,' said Eri with a smile. 'Tastes disgusting but nowhere near as bad as that invisibility magic.'

'You shouldn't have come,' said Jude. If they were caught, Grandleader would take them away, just as he had taken Moorley after she and Jude snuck into his quarters to find Mr and Mrs Weston . . .

. . . whom Jude had found no trace of, despite having possibly discovered the answer to why there were more Lilthrum in Farrowfell . . . The pit . . .

A clump of guilt settled in her stomach. She had to tell Fin and Eri the truth.

'Jude, what's wrong?' said Eri, her eyebrows furrowing together.

'I – I . . .' Jude had never been lost for words before, and she didn't like it. They were going to hate her when they found out what her family had done.

But Fin and Eri had *worried* about her. Even when they'd thought she had no chance of finding their parents. They had shown up.

You are a true Ripon.

The words were a faint hiss in her mind, the pull of them weaker now that Fin and Eri were here. It dawned on her that the thoughts telling her she had to go to speak to Grandleader *weren't hers at all.* Grandleader had used raw magic on her, but Fin and Eri's presence helped her fight its influence.

Grandleader was trying to manipulate her – just as he manipulated everyone else.

Fin and Eri hadn't abandoned her – and she couldn't abandon Moorley.

'The tracking magic worked after you left,' Jude said, speaking quickly. 'It showed me your parents are, um, here. In Ripon Headquarters.'

Her cheeks burned as she looked up, expecting to see hatred in their eyes. Eri sat in a heap on the floor, her face pale with shock. 'They're ... here?' she repeated.

Fin had tensed. 'Why didn't you tell us?' he said. He turned away, staring out of the window.

Jude bit her lip, crossing the room so she stood behind him. She hesitated, then placed a hand on his shoulder. 'I'm sorry. I thought you might blame me or something – I wanted to be sure ...' All her excuses sounded hollow.

Fin didn't move, and Jude let her hand fall to her side.

Tears ran down Eri's face. 'Our parents have been *here*, in your home, for a year?'

'I'm sorry,' repeated Jude, balling her hands into fists as she looked at Eri's devastated face. *This* was what it meant to be a true Ripon – hurting people who didn't deserve it.

'How can we believe you?' said Fin, turning around. 'How do we know this isn't just some giant *game*—'

Jude opened her mouth but Eri spoke up first.

'Fin – don't say that,' said Eri, her voice wobbling as she bunched her knees under her chin. 'She told us, didn't she? She didn't have to. Mum and Dad are *here* – and we can save them. Nothing else matters but getting them back.'

Fin took a few deep breaths, his face red and his entire body trembling. When he eventually spoke, his voice was weirdly calm. 'Why'd your family kidnap our parents?'

'I don't know,' said Jude, rubbing her forehead. 'I . . . I think your parents found out we're – I mean, *they're* – collecting raw magic in a giant pit. That's what's making the Lilthrum. Moorley and I . . . we tried to find your parents . . .'

'What do you mean *tried*?' said Fin, each question a spear stabbing at Jude. 'How could you not know they were in your house? So many prisoners in your dungeons you lost track?'

'Because,' said Jude, beginning to feel annoyed – it wasn't like *she'd* kidnapped his parents – 'in Grandleader's quarters there's a where-and-when room. That's where we found the pit of raw magic . . . so much in one place. There were Lilthrum forming from it.' She bit her bottom lip as she remembered.

Fin ran his fingers through his hair. 'So our parents found out that Grandleader's the reason for all the Lilthrum attacks in Farrowfell ...'

Eri's bottom lip was trembling. 'But *where are they*? They're not ... they can't be ... Not dead ...'

'My curse would have been lifted if they were,' said Jude. She tried to speak as gently as she could to reassure Eri that things weren't as bleak as they seemed.

'The tracking magic wouldn't have worked if they were dead, Eri,' said Fin, his voice firm. 'You know what they would want us to do if they were here? They'd want us to stop more Lilthrum from forming.'

Jude thought hard. Surely that wasn't possible without destroying the pit – or making the where-and-when room move so it wasn't anchored in Farrowfell any more. Either way, they would have to risk going back through Grandleader's quarters. And then they would face the Lilthrum – and the raw magic.

There had to be another way, a loophole. Jude had spent her whole life looking for the easy way out. Now it was time to put her skills to the test. 'I could go to the library and ask the Hall of Knowledge if there's any way of ... I don't know ... making the pit disappear or something while we watch from a great, great distance? The Hall can tell us anything if the information is in one of the books in the library ...' It was far-fetched and slightly desperate, but Jude didn't have any better ideas.

She wanted to cling to the hope that she wouldn't have to go back and face the pit.

'That could work,' said Eri, perking up. 'The Hall is great – sometimes it tells you other stuff as well if you're lucky. We should definitely give it a try.'

It didn't feel strange to hear Eri say *we*. Now that the truth was out, they were a proper team. The thought made Jude feel warm.

'There's just one more problem,' said Jude. 'Grandleader's locked up my sister, Moorley. I don't know if I ever mentioned her to you? I need to get her out.'

'OK,' said Fin at once. 'Where is she?'

'On the second floor,' said Jude. 'My aunt is guarding the door and there's bars on the window. I think maybe I could distract Aunt Victi with a stink bomb or something, but the moment we get Moorley out, Grandleader's going to be alerted to what we're doing.'

'Then we should wait until after we've been to the library,' said Fin. 'Unless you think Moorley might be in danger?'

Jude shook her head. Grandleader just wanted to keep her and Moorley apart. He didn't want to harm either of them – yet.

'OK,' said Eri. 'We'll go to the library, figure out how to send the pit of raw magic far away, then we'll come back and stage a rescue mission.' She sounded confident now they had a plan in place, as vague as it was.

'Cool. What are we waiting for?' said Jude, grabbing a jacket.

'The library to open,' said Eri. 'It's the middle of the night.'

'We can break in,' said Jude as she began to root through her drawers in the hope of finding a scrap of spare magic lying around. All she had was the decision-making magic and a fat lot of use that was, since the curse meant she couldn't use it.

'The Hall won't answer,' said Eri. 'We need to wait until morning.'

Jude stopped scrambling in her drawers, frustration building inside her. She wanted to do *something*. Now she knew about the pit, it felt as though every second she spent waiting was a second wasted.

'Fine,' she said. 'We'll go first thing.'

Eri and Fin nodded.

'In the meantime,' said Eri, looking around. 'Why don't I tidy up a bit?'

Jude rolled her eyes, but she couldn't help smiling.

Chapter Twenty-One

The Broken Hall

Jude had arranged to meet Eri and Fin the moment the library opened the next day and was nearly out of the house when she almost collided with Grandleader.

Stupid bad luck, she thought at once. She plastered a smile on her face and tried to figure out how to act – he still believed whatever raw magic he had used on her yesterday had worked. Except he hadn't factored in that she would have Fin and Eri's support to help her fight its effects – and had also probably underestimated her and used less power than he should have.

'Where are you going?' he said, his eyebrows raised. He loomed over her, his hands tucked behind his back. Her heart thudded – she'd never appeciated how dangerous it was to have all his attention directed on her.

'Just for a walk,' she said, keeping her voice steady. 'It's such a nice day . . . I wanted to have a think about new business opportunities – like maybe we get friendly with someone who could make any illegal tamed magic we wanted.' The idea was rubbish. Even if the person could track down the relevant recipe for the magic, a challenge in itself, they would still have to source all the rare ingredients, which could take ages. And probably be ridiculously expensive anyway. It was a thousand times easier to steal magic which already existed.

For a stomach-churning moment Grandleader's eyes flicked over her. Then he smiled slightly. 'Excellent. Keep that focus on the business, Jude.'

She'd done it – she'd convinced him she was on his side. He was too arrogant to think she wasn't completely in his power.

'I'm actually planning a family lunch today,' he continued. 'Your mother is off on business, and of course Moorley and Aunt Victi won't be there, but everyone else will.'

'Great,' she said, trying to sound eager. Grandleader smiled and she heaved a sigh of relief as she left the house.

Had Moorley put on a show like this for two years?

No wonder she was so grumpy all the time. Jude had been on edge for the whole two-minute conversation.

Right, she needed to be back at Headquarters for lunch, but as the Ripons ate quite late she had plenty of time.

When she arrived at the library, she found Eri and Fin waiting by the empty front desk. The sulky boy she'd met the other day was obviously off doing another task.

The librarians and helplings had been hard at work to remove signs of the Lilthrum attack: the books were back on their shelves, the furniture upright, the rubble swept away. She thought back to the Lilthrum in Grandleader's quarters – she and Moorley had fought together and they still barely managed to escape. If they were going to attempt to get rid of the pit, they couldn't risk getting into a fight with multiple Lilthrum at once. They would be easily overpowered.

Eri, of course, knew the way through the maze of corridors to the Hall of Knowledge. She probably knew the layout better than any of the librarians.

'I thought the Hall of Knowledge was at the other end of the library?' said Jude, as Eri stopped outside a set of plain stone doors.

'Nope – right in the centre. Oldest part of the library. First thing built, I think.' Eri shot Jude a look out of the corner of her eye. 'Erm ... in case anyone's unfamiliar with the rules of the Hall, only one of us can ask questions at a time. Otherwise the Hall might get confused.'

'I'll do the talking,' said Jude, rolling up her sleeves. She needed to do something to push away her nervousness that there might not be any way to get rid of the pit – no loopholes, no tricks, no way out of the mess Grandleader had created.

They stepped inside and the door closed behind them. For a moment they stood in darkness. Then, as if sensing someone in the room, the Hall lit up slowly with a golden glow.

They were in a vast, empty space with a sunken circle in the centre. A bright beam of light shone on to the middle of the circle, and Jude stood right in the centre, Eri and Fin on either side of her.

Jude cleared her throat. She didn't have a question so much as a desperate need to know as much as she possibly could.

'If too much raw magic collects in one place ... how do you get rid of it?' She waited for the Hall to answer. The Hall remained silent. 'Er – hello? Are you there?'

'Be more polite,' hissed Eri. Fin elbowed his sister.

The light beaming down on Jude did not get any brighter. The soft glow gently pulsed.

'Maybe the Hall needs to warm up or something,' whispered Eri.

Jude rolled her eyes, but tried to think of an easy question to ask. 'How many magic-keepers are there in Farrowfell?'

'There are currently twenty-three magic-keepers in Farrowfell. All are bound to only work for the Consortium.' A soft male voice spoke. She flinched at the warmth on her shoulders, as if someone stood behind her, their hot breath brushing down her back. She twisted around, but there was no one there. The man's voice was simply the Hall responding to her question.

'OK, so you *are* there,' said Jude. 'Right. Hall of Knowledge, is there a way to transport a giant pit of raw magic far away from Farrowfell ... without going anywhere near it?' She tried to speak with authority. 'Answer me.' Eri coughed. 'Please.'

There was a long pause and Jude thought it was going to ignore her question. But then the man's voice came again, even quieter than before. 'You ask a question with an impossible answer.'

Maybe it had been a long shot. The next best thing would be sending the where-and-when room far away, where the Lilthrum forming from it couldn't hurt anyone. 'How do you unanchor a where-and-when room so that it leaves Farrowfell – and takes the giant pit of raw magic inside it away too?' Jude tried again. The question was probably too specific but there might be something in it the Hall could respond to.

'Where-and-when rooms are anchored in place by tamed magic that responds to darkness. To find the anchor of a where-and-when room you will need to search for a dark, damp space. More information can be found in section seven thousand and two of the library.'

Jude nodded as she looked at Fin and Eri. This was good information. Before she could ask another question, however, the Hall started speaking again.

'There should *not* be a pit of raw magic in the first place. Humans are all the same – repeating the same mistakes.' The Hall of Knowledge spoke louder this time, and Eri and Fin flinched. 'But any visitor to the Hall of Knowledge is given the knowledge they seek if it is knowledge I keep. That is the rule of the Hall.'

Jude waited for the voice to go on. 'Er – do you want me to say something?'

'Raw magic hates humans who twist it, *tame* it,' said the Hall. 'Raw magic will do whatever it can to destroy humans – that is why it births Lilthrum.'

A shiver went down Jude's spine. *Raw magic has plans of its own.*

'You are not asking the right questions,' said the voice. It was muttering quietly to itself now, almost hissing, and Jude only caught flashes of what it was saying. 'Humans do not deserve … the same … all the same …'

Jude shared a concerned look with Fin. The Hall was supposed to be a simple source of knowledge – she hadn't heard of it ever offering opinions on people's questions, or going off track in its answers. Had the Lilthrum attack last week damaged it?

'How could anyone ever collect that much raw magic in one place?' she asked. She might as well keep trying to get answers. It would be good to know as much about the pit as possible if they were going to try and search the where-and-when room for its anchor. 'Humans attract raw magic,' said the Hall, speaking loudly and clearly.

'Yeah, I know,' said Jude. 'Why's that important ...' She trailed off. Did that mean ... the Weston parents. No. Could they really be ... in the bottom of the pit ... alive? The tracking magic had *said* they were somewhere in Ripon Headquarters, and it would explain why she and Moorley had found no trace of them in Grandleader's quarters.

'Humans?' said Fin, shaking free of Eri and clearly forgetting only one person was supposed to ask questions at a time. 'Could they even survive that much raw magic?'

The Hall fell silent again.

'How do we get them out?' said Jude, looking at Fin and miming a zip over her mouth. Fin scowled.

'Finally, you have asked the right question,' said the voice. 'I shall show you the answer.'

The ground rumbled and a great crack formed beneath their feet. Jude barely had time to react before the sunken circle where they stood split in two, forming a gap out of which blinding white light poured.

Suddenly they were falling through the white light, hurtling towards grass and a large pit. Everything inside Jude screamed because she recognised the pit as the one in the where-and-when room. Her stomach lurched into her mouth as she fell, falling, falling, falling, *still falling*—

And then she reached the bottom, stopped from crashing by some invisible force, which lowered her to the ground. She got to her feet, blinking rapidly. How were they *here*? Everything around her seemed blurred. In front of her, distorted by the magical mist, were two shadowy figures.

'What happened?' said Eri, getting to her feet and brushing herself down. 'Where are we? Hall of Knowledge, are you still there?'

'Yes,' came the reply. 'This is a vision. You are still inside the Hall.'

Fin was walking towards the shadowy figures, as if in some sort of trance. Jude followed him. For a moment she couldn't register what she was seeing. But, no, it was real. There were two people, a man and a woman. They were lying on the ground, their hair fanning around their faces, their arms splayed. Their eyes were open, staring up at the children before them.

Jude *recognised* these people. She had seen their pictures many times. She had tried to find them with her tracking magic.

They had found the Weston parents.

With a sob, Eri ran to her mother. But her hand passed straight through. Mrs Weston disappeared into smoke. Eri reached for her father but he vanished too.

'What's going on?' said Eri.

'These humans are attracting the raw magic so it gathers in one place – otherwise it would float away naturally,' said the Hall of Knowledge, its voice floating eerily around them. 'There is a hidden stair starting at the bottom of the pit that leads out.'

Jude's gut was telling her something was wrong – she had a sense the Hall of Knowledge was telling the truth about Mr and Mrs Weston ... But *how* did it have this information? There was a mysterious force at play here, something she didn't understand. 'You should only know what's in the library books,' she said. 'Who told you about Mr and Mrs Weston?'

'This Hall was built with tamed magic – and a little raw magic,' whispered the Hall. 'Over time my consciousness has grown beyond the walls of the library ... I grow stronger – I find out information beyond library books ...'

'You're lying,' said Fin. 'Using raw magic is illegal – the Consortium would never—'

The ground started to rumble.

'What's going on?' said Jude, backing away.

'You should go,' said the Hall of Knowledge, its voice bored. 'You might get hurt – if too much raw magic gathers in one place ... the world becomes unstable.'

Jude whipped her head left and right. 'But we're not really in the pit! This is a vision!' She started to run, but her movements were sluggish and, with a thrill of horror, she saw that the ground was turning soft and her feet were sinking.

Shadows raced down the sides of the pit and the rumbling began to sound less like an earthquake and more like deep laughter.

The shadows swept towards them and Jude held her hands over her face. She squeezed her eyes shut and waited for pain to come.

Nothing happened. She opened her eyes – the shadows were circling her, passing over. A cold wind blew her hair and the laughter continued.

And then she was lying on the cold stone floor of the Hall of Knowledge beside Eri and Fin. The crack in the ground was gone and the lights were dimmed.

She got to her feet, her heart still racing. Silver liquid dripped down the walls, and she looked at Fin and Eri, nodding towards the exit. They needed to leave.

They slipped up the staircase, and it took everything Jude had within not to break into a run. She could hear the Hall of Knowledge muttering again.

'Humans responsible . . . made this prison . . . their fault – *their fault* . . .'

Jude swallowed. *Whose fault?*

What had her family done?

Chapter Twenty-Two

Farlow Higgins and the Truth

The bright beam of light that lit up the sunken circle in the centre of the room blinked off; the Hall was done speaking.

Jude hurried to the exit.

'Mum and Dad are in that pit,' Eri was saying behind her. 'You heard the Hall, Fin. They're there – we can get them back! We can rescue them – and then find the where-and-when room's anchor and pull it, and that will send it somewhere into the Wild Lands.

'What if the Hall was lying?' whispered Fin. 'No

one could survive in there. What if we find them and they're not . . . them any more?' Jude caught a glimpse of him wiping his eyes. She nibbled her lip. Surely there could be no way Mr and Mrs Weston had survived a whole *year* in the pit, surrounded by raw magic, and not been tempted to touch it. Maybe it had corrupted them too. Maybe they were under Grandleader's sway just like the rest of her family.

Eri turned to Jude. 'It all fits – it does,' she said, her eyes shining with hope. 'We'll find our parents and everything will be OK.'

But Jude couldn't share Eri's confidence. Even if Mr and Mrs Weston *were* in the pit, rescuing them would be almost impossible. She, Fin and Eri would have to go back through Grandleader's quarters . . . and *enter* the pit. They would have to face Lilthrum – and possibly even Grandleader.

They didn't have a hope of succeeding.

And yet . . . they had to try. Even if it seemed impossible, and scary, and she wanted to run as fast as she could as far as she could.

They walked through the library and Jude glanced at a clock. It felt like for ever, but they'd only been in the Hall for thirty minutes.

She turned over all the Hall's answers in her mind, and something about its very first one tripped her up: its response to her question about magic-keepers. If all twenty-three in Farrowfell worked for the Consortium, why had one cursed the Westons' decision-making magic?

There had been a few odd things about the magic-keeper, she remembered – in fact, about Jude's whole experience with the Westons. Now she thought of it, it was a huge coincidence that the people she had been cursed by just happened to be the ones her family had trapped at the bottom of the pit.

Plus, Farlow Higgins had avoided explaining exactly how he'd heard about the decision-making magic. Had someone put him up to telling her because they wanted her to know the truth about her family? A spark of hope ignited in her chest. The magic-keeper had shown more of an interest in her than was necessary. Was there a long-lost Ripon on her side, helping her work out that her family weren't the heroes she thought? A *good* Ripon? Someone who could perhaps help them rescue Mr and Mrs Weston?

'Eri,' she tried to say as casually as possible, 'your magic-keeper . . . how much do you know about her?'

'What do you mean?' said Eri, her stride faltering as she went to follow Fin, who had sped up ahead of them, walking so fast he was almost jogging.

'Like, how long has she worked for your family?'

'A year, maybe?' said Eri, her eyebrows knotting together. 'I'm going to catch up with Fin, make sure he's OK. We need to come to Ripon Headquarters and rescue Moorley now, right?'

Jude rubbed her forehead. 'I want things to die down a little bit before I attempt a rescue. I'm supposed to go to a special lunch with Grandleader – but after that, let's meet up again at your house. Figure out our next move.'

Which definitely involved a visit to Farlow Higgins.

***

At lunch, Moorley was missing, along with Jude's mother and Aunt Victi – but the rest of the Ripons were present.

Grandleader ran through business and Jude forced a smile, trying not to rush her food, but at the same time wishing it would hurry up and be over.

At the end of the meal, instead of dismissing everyone as he normally did, Grandleader stood and raised his glass of orange juice.

'I'd like to take a moment to say there is one person in particular who has impressed me with their commitment to the family,' he said. Aunt Morgol straightened her back. 'Jude! It is time for you to take your place as a *true* Ripon. Tonight, you will join us in a *special* meeting, when we drink a *special* drink.'

Jude's father was staring at her, his mouth open. Spry and Trudie looked equally shocked, and Uncle Runie's eyes were wide. Aunt Morgol was shooting her venomous looks.

Jude's smile was fixed on her face as she tried to hide her panic. This moment would once have been everything she had ever wanted. But now she knew it meant drinking raw magic – tonight. She'd thought she had more time to rescue Moorley and Mr and Mrs Weston. She had to act.

She realised they were all waiting for her to say something.

'Thank you,' she managed, the words hanging limply in the air. 'I'm ... so overwhelmed. With gratitude.'

'She can't find the words,' said Trudie, clutching her chest. 'It's a common phenomenon you know, when someone gets something they've always wanted. They find it difficult to speak ...'

For once, Jude was grateful for Trudie's droning. She nodded along while all her family came up to her and patted her on the back.

When it was over, she hurried up the stairs. But instead of going to her bedroom, she slipped into Moorley's, grabbing some ghost magic from her drawer. She had to rescue Moorley *now*. Her plan wasn't well thought out – she would give Moorley some ghost and invisibility magic, and they would simply walk to freedom.

In her own room, she leapt on to her bed so she could be comfortable while she ate the magic and waited for the side effect of gagging to pass.

'Oof,' said a quiet voice.

At once Jude leapt up. Moorley was scrambling out from underneath her bed.

'Finally,' she grumbled.

'You're supposed to be locked up!' said Jude. To her own surprise (and Moorley's too, most likely), Jude found herself lunging at her sister and gripping her in a tight hug.

Moorley grinned. 'I have my ways . . . It's a great story – involves me finally making friends with the house.'

'You need to give me *all* the details later,' said Jude. 'But we don't have time right now. Grandleader wants me to drink raw magic *tonight*.' She told Moorley all that had happened in the Hall of Knowledge and her suspicion about the magic-keeper. 'When I don't drink it, Grandleader will know I've betrayed him as well. We'll lose any chance to get away.' It felt good to pour out all her worries. 'So now . . . we need to go and find Farlow Higgins. For once in his miserable life, he's going to tell us the truth.'

***

Jude and Moorley ate the invisibility magic and climbed out of a back window of Ripon Headquarters, sprinting to the port. They didn't slow down until they were safely in Mergio Market, where they made themselves visible, startling an old lady carrying bags of shopping.

They found Farlow Higgins hanging about outside the clothes shop next to his, peering through the window.

'Weren't stealing nothing!' he said when Jude tapped him on the shoulder. 'Oh, it's you,' he grumbled, pulling his jacket tighter around himself. 'Did you steal that magic from your family? You get caught? No, of course you didn't – you're still alive.'

'About that . . .' said Jude, not really sure how she should dive into the current situation.

'Hang on,' said Farlow, holding his hands in front of his body as if to protect himself. 'You ain't dead, are you? I can't be dealing with ghosts again.'

'What? No. When did you deal with ghosts—?'

'Jude,' warned Moorley.

'Right, sorry,' said Jude. They didn't have time to get sidetracked. 'We need your help.'

Farlow considered her. 'What sort of price we talking?'

Moorley's nostrils flared. She shoved Farlow against the wall. 'Listen here, you maggot—'

'All right, all right,' said Farlow. 'Just thought I'd give it a shot. Gots to make money, don't I? First priority for anyone.'

'Let's go inside your shop,' said Jude, aware now that the baker was hanging out of his door to watch them. Farlow wriggled out of Moorley's grip and wiped his coat down.

He led them inside, which seemed to have got even dingier since the last time Jude was there.

'What do you want, kid?' said Farlow, drumming his fingers on the counter. 'You got something for me to sell?'

'Remember that magic you told me about? Where did you say you heard about it?'

Farlow shrugged, though his eyes flicked left and right as though he was looking for some sort of escape. 'I don't remember, do I? I hear a lot of things from a lot of places.'

Jude narrowed her eyes. He'd told her previously he'd heard it from someone at the pub. He couldn't keep his story straight.

'Who put you up to telling Jude where to find that magic?' said Moorley, arching an eyebrow.

Farlow bit his lip. 'You know what, I don't want nothing to do with this.' He made to move past them, but Moorley blocked his way.

'Tell us what you know, you little toad.'

'I don't want to get involved,' Farlow tried again, and this time he dropped a pellet and shoved past them. A stink bomb of some kind exploded, dousing Moorley in a foul yellow pus.

'Blegh!' she yelled, retching. Jude, who had been standing far enough out of the way to avoid the splash zone, chased after Farlow. He dodged down another alleyway, huffing and puffing, and it didn't take long for her to reach him. She didn't even need to grab him – he came to a halt himself, clutching his side.

The pause gave Moorley the chance to catch up. She blocked his way, still dripping in the yellow pus and looking decidedly unimpressed. Jude fought the urge to laugh. She'd only just started getting along with her sister – she didn't need to ruin that already.

'Fine, you got me,' grumbled Farlow. He licked his lips and suddenly looked a whole lot sweatier. 'Look, the woman who told me about that decision-making magic has connections high up. If she finds out this information came from me—'

'Don't worry, we won't say anything,' said Jude impatiently.

'Look, I don't know too much, all right? This woman asked if I knew the Ripons. I said, sure, thinking she was a new customer. Asked a lot of questions. Wanted to know if the Ripons had kids – I said, yeah, they've got an . . . eight-year-old – you're eight, right? Nine?'

'I'm *twelve*!'

'Anyway, I said they got one kid who needs a good wash—'

'You're one to talk,' muttered Jude. Moorley elbowed her.

'—and the woman said she'd get the Consortium to forgive a few of my crimes,' Farlow ploughed on. 'You know how they're always on my back for no good reason. All she wanted was for me to tell you about a special kind of magic in the Weston Mansion and give you a map to help you out.'

'What did she look like?' said Jude. Moorley leaned in.

Farlow shrugged. 'Little blonde woman.' He perked up. 'I can draw her if you want. Good at that, I am.' He led them back to his shop and picked up paper and a pencil. Jude racked her brains for any Ripons with blonde hair. From Moorley's intense expression, she was doing the same.

Farlow drew on the paper with broad strokes, his tongue sticking out of the corner of his mouth as he concentrated. 'Ta dah!' Farlow leaned back. He'd drawn a rough sketch of a woman's face, with hair swirling around her shoulders.

Jude was about to point out that the drawing could be anyone until Farlow blew a little magic on to the paper and the sketch coloured itself in, filling in the details, until she was looking down on an incredibly lifelike drawing of a blonde woman. Jude had seen that face before – but where? The long nose, the blue eyes . . .

Ice crept over Jude's heart as she stared down at the paper. She had seen a portrait of this woman, painted by Fin.

Eri's voice came back to her . . .

That's Aunt Annelia.

But that made no sense. Eri had told her Annelia Weston was dead . . .

Except she wasn't because she'd been making deals with Farlow Higgins.

Jude's mind raced. Annelia had wanted Jude to break into her niece and nephew's home, to steal magic she knew was cursed—

The magic-keeper had blonde hair too. And she had always kept her face hidden.

The Hall of Knowledge had said there were twenty-three magic-keepers in Farrowfell, all working for the Consortium.

There had never been a rogue magic-keeper who had cursed the Westons' magic – only a woman pretending to be one. And if there had never been a magic-keeper—

There had never been a curse.

She had been tricked.

Chapter Twenty-Three

The Plan

Jude knocked on the front door of the Weston mansion.

Spikes of betrayal cut through her. Fin and Eri were supposed to be her friends.

Plus, she couldn't *believe* they had tricked her – *she* was supposed to be the one good at lying, the criminal. Although they had been shifty when she'd asked about the family friend looking after them, and Eri had flamed red when Jude asked her about her aunt. Maybe Jude just hadn't been paying enough attention – she'd been so wrapped up in her own family problems.

Fin had been outraged when he found out she

hadn't told him Mr and Mrs Weston were at Ripon Headquarters – and yet he hadn't bothered to come clean himself, even though it was the perfect opportunity to put all their lies behind them.

A helpling opened the door and she walked inside as Eri came down the stairs.

'Oh – Jude,' she said. 'Hi, and … you must be Moorley? That's great, how did you—'

'Where's your aunt?' said Jude, looking around and tapping her foot. She hadn't figured out how she was going to play this. Should she act like she had known all along? Maybe she could still save face, show them no one got the better of Jude Ripon.

This was the sort of scheme *she* would have come up with. She didn't like being on the other end of it. She felt stupid, as though Eri and Fin hadn't really been her friends at all. As if they'd been using her.

'Jude, maybe she doesn't know her aunt isn't dead,' hissed Moorley. But judging from the way all the colour had drained from Eri's face, she knew exactly what Jude was talking about.

'Well, aren't you going to say something?' asked Jude, raising an eyebrow.

'I … er …' Eri trembled, clutching the banister of the stairs. 'Aunt Annelia's at work – at the Consortium. She isn't dead. There was no family friend. She's been looking after us and …' Thick tears dripped down her face. 'Jude, I'm sorry – I'm sorry …'

'I know I'm a thief, but at least I never made anyone think they had cursed their own family,' said Jude. It felt odd to have the moral high ground for once in her life, but she couldn't enjoy it – Eri looked too upset. The anger swilling inside her dripped away. 'Where's Fin?' she said, after a long pause in which Eri kept sobbing. At least he might be able to explain properly.

'Upstairs,' hiccuped Eri. 'I'll . . . sh-show you the way.'

She led them through corridors, up another set of stairs.

'Nice place,' Moorley muttered behind her.

At last, Eri stopped by a door. Jude didn't bother to knock. Inside was a spacious, airy room with sun pouring through the windows. A large four-poster bed stood against one of the walls. Against another was a long wooden desk covered in drawings. Beside the bed sat Fin in an armchair, his legs propped on a footstool as he sketched in a notebook.

Fin looked up, surprise flashing across his face. He thrust the notebook aside, getting to his feet as he looked from Jude to his sister. 'Eri – what—'

'Hello, Finibert,' said Jude with a fake smile. 'Care to explain?'

Fin bit his bottom lip and went to his desk. He rifled through the stacks of papers and slid one out, handing it to Jude. It was a picture of a woman identical to the one in Farlow's painting. 'This is our aunt, Annelia Weston. She's an adviser to the

Consortium but she pretended to be a magic-keeper.'

'Why?' said Jude with a frown.

'It was my idea,' burst out Eri. 'We were desperate.'

'The magic-keeper—' Jude had to shake herself – there had never been a magic-keeper. 'Your Aunt Annelia was using transportation magic – the same stuff you used when you came to visit me.'

Fin nodded. 'We've got access to a lot of expensive and rare magic. Aunt Annelia works for the Consortium – she's got connections with loads of important people.'

Jude looked from one guilty face to another as a sad truth hit her. There was no long-lost Ripon on her side. No one in her family cared about her at all. Moorley, as though she knew what Jude was thinking, placed a hand on her shoulder, the weight comforting.

'You know, making me think I was cursing my own family was *not* a nice thing to do,' said Jude.

'Well, you *were* stealing from us,' muttered Fin.

'When we got to know you, we wanted to tell you,' said Eri, twisting her hands together. 'Fin never wanted to go along with this.'

'Because he didn't trust me,' said Jude. 'He thought I was a thief—'

'You *are* a thief,' Moorley pointed out, her hand remaining curled on Jude's shoulder. 'But that's not important – I'm still not hearing an explanation from you two.' She hadn't been angry when she'd heard how

Eri and Fin had tricked Jude, but she also hadn't been very impressed.

'Everything we told you is true,' said Fin. 'Our parents were looking for an explanation about why there have been so many more Lilthrum in Farrowfell. We thought they discovered something bad – which we now know they did – and they went missing. We really *did* do everything we possibly could to find them. But as a last resort we . . . we asked the Hall of Knowledge.'

'We weren't really expecting an answer,' said Eri with a shuddering breath. Her face was stained with tears. 'Then out of nowhere, it said, "You need a Ripon's help." Kept saying it didn't have any answers after that.'

'We'd never heard of the Ripons – you're not like the Sillians and Fordimores,' added Fin. 'We tried searching all over and eventually Aunt Annelia figured your family might be so shadowy because they had something to hide. She asked her connections in the Consortium if they knew of any criminals who might have had dealings with the Ripons. They suggested someone called Farlow Higgins.'

Jude opened her mouth to say that both Eri and Fin had *met* Farlow Higgins – they had even gone to his shop. Then she stopped, confused, because if her memory served, she'd never properly introduced him. Neither of them had known who they were speaking to.

'We'd just been told we needed a Ripon's help – it didn't seem like it mattered which one. So, Aunt

Annelia went to ask Farlow Higgins whether the Ripons had any children – she thought a kid might be easier to trick,' said Fin. 'He told us about you. Said you seemed like you had a lot to prove. He didn't want to help but Aunt Annelia can be ... persuasive.'

'All he had to do was tell you about some magic in this house,' hiccuped Eri. 'Then Aunt Annelia would pretend to be a magic-keeper and tell you about the curse, which could only be lifted if you helped find our parents.'

Jude scratched her head, trying to think. 'But there actually *was* a curse. That's why we lost the shipment of magic and Grandleader blamed Dad. And why the meeting at the Consortium was interrupted, and a Lilthrum attacked Mum, and the grefers got into Ripon Headquarters and ...' She trailed off. '*What*?' Eri was shaking her head. Frustration bubbled because she didn't understand.

'It was us. Well, not the Lilthrum or the grefers,' said Eri, picking at a loose thread on her sleeve. 'But we disrupted a few shipments of magic rumoured to belong to the Ripons until we struck gold and found one that actually belonged to your family. Aunt Annelia planted listening magic in the rooms of a few of the more ... rule-breaking members of the Consortium so we could interrupt a Ripon meeting. And we figured once you'd bought into the idea of the curse, you'd start seeing bad luck everywhere,' added Fin.

Jude tried to hide her embarrassment – the more they explained, the stupider she felt for being taken in so easily. But, also, she was . . . relieved. For the first time probably ever, her decisions were completely her own to make.

There was one last thing that still wasn't clear. 'The library said you needed a Ripon's help. Why couldn't you have just *asked*, instead of tricking me?' Her voice came out as a croak.

Fin's mouth twisted. 'All we knew was that the Ripons were very dangerous.'

'Please, Jude,' whispered Eri. 'You wouldn't have helped us otherwise.' She picked up Fin's discarded sketchbook, smoothing the pages as she placed it neatly on the bedside table. 'We just wanted to find our parents. That was all we could think about. And, well, now we know it was your family who stole them away.'

Jude didn't want to admit it, but they were right: if they had suddenly appeared in front of her and asked her to find their parents, she would have told them she was too busy trying to become a proper Ripon to help them.

Jude nibbled her bottom lip. Everything was out in the open but nothing had really changed. The pit was still filling up, the Lilthrum were still bad, and Mr and Mrs Weston had to be saved.

'Let's finish this,' she said.

Chapter Twenty-Four

Transport

E ri told the helplings to bring more armchairs and they sat in a circle. 'We'll need to tell Aunt Annelia everything,' she said, looking at Fin. 'I wanted to, but—'

'After we decided to steal that illegal tracking magic, I told her we'd tried but you wouldn't be able to help us,' Fin cut in. 'Aunt Annelia would never have let you steal and use illegal magic that could ... make you explode.'

'Well, she doesn't sound like someone who needs to be brought into the loop right now,' said Jude, and Moorley nodded vigorously.

Jude might have forgiven Fin and Eri – they just

wanted to find their parents and she could understand that. Annelia Weston was different. She was an adult who had figured Jude would be easier to take advantage of because of her age. Jude had spent her whole life being ignored because she was the youngest and she didn't want to work alongside someone who might be another version of the adults in her family.

'But Aunt Annelia could bring guards with her,' said Eri, biting her bottom lip. 'Protection. It'd be stupid of us to try and deal with this on our own.'

'No way,' said Jude. 'Our family has had meetings with the Consortium. It could get back to Grandleader. This is our one chance – and your Aunt Annelia might mess it up.'

'Agreed. If we want to fix this, we need to do it ourselves,' said Moorley. Jude nodded. She had never felt more in tune with Moorley in her life.

'Fine,' said Eri with a sigh. 'No guards.'

Moorley and Jude looked at each other and grinned.

***

The Westons did not have fighting magic helpfully tucked away.

'What's fighting magic?' said Eri.

'I don't know,' said Jude, frustrated. 'Magic that makes you shoot lasers out of your eyes or gives your superstrength or something. Have an *imagination*.'

'Why on earth would we have that sort of thing in the house?'

'In case you ever need to fight your way through a bunch of Lilthrum to rescue your missing parents at the bottom of a pit of raw magic,' replied Jude. 'Really, Eri, you should be more prepared. Wait ...' A wonderful thought occurred to her. 'The decision-making magic! There was never a curse – which means we can use it to help us figure out a plan ...' After finding out it was useless because of the 'curse', she had put it into a drawer in her bedroom for safe keeping until she could give it back to Mr and Mrs Weston. But she could eat it now!

Eri grimaced. 'Well ... the thing is ... Er ...'

'Spit it out,' said Jude impatiently.

'It's fake,' said Eri quickly. 'That was why we told you it had a curse on it. So, if you decided to use it and nothing happened, you would have an explanation.'

Jude tried not to groan at how well she had been tricked. 'So, you *never* owned decision-making magic?'

'Well, it *is* really rare magic,' said Fin. 'Almost impossible to come across.'

'I know,' said Jude through gritted teeth. 'That's why I wanted to steal it.'

'We don't need magic to fight and we don't need a fancy plan,' said Moorley. 'We've got invisibility magic at home. Once we're in the where-and-when room we'll be able to sneak past any Lilthrum.'

256

'Our invisibility magic is rubbish!' pointed out Jude. 'It's so cheap that when I went to the pit before, it didn't last long before it stopped working. All the raw magic interfered with it.'

'We just need it to work well enough to give us enough time to get into the pit,' said Moorley, her voice calm.

'And how do we get to the bottom of the pit without breaking our necks?' said Jude. 'We don't have any flying magic, and we might not have time to find the hidden stair the Hall of Knowledge mentioned.'

'If this pit is full of raw magic, we can just jump in. The raw magic will slow our fall,' cut in Moorley. 'It's one of the properties of raw magic – really interesting. When I first learned our family drank raw magic, I did a bit of research into it. I guess the hidden stair is to help you get *out*.'

Jude rolled her eyes at Moorley's thoroughness. Looking into the properties of raw magic hadn't occurred to her when *she'd* discovered what their family was doing.

'Great,' said Eri in her chirpy voice. 'So, when we jump into the pit we'll float right down to Mum and Dad.'

'But what if it's not that simple?' said Jude. 'What if something goes wrong?' No one answered and she sighed. She had to do everything. 'Look, Eri, you don't have magic to fight with – fine. But even if you never had decision-making magic, you've still got loads of rare magic in this place, right? Your parents have all those connections at the Consortium, plus you're really rich.'

'Er … well, we've got quick magic that makes you run super-fast?' said Eri, sucking in her cheeks. 'But it's very expensive – we're not allowed to play with it.'

'We're not *playing*,' said Jude. 'We're saving your parents. And get Moorley a knife as well – what?' she added to Moorley, who had rolled her eyes. 'You fight well with a knife.'

'My plan will work,' was all Moorley said. 'Once we've got Mr and Mrs Weston out of the pit, we can search the where-and-when room for the anchor. If we try to move the anchor *before* we find them, we'll all be transported to the Wild Lands and we'll be in much more danger.'

'Or we could even just save Mum and Dad and then come back with the proper authorities,' said Eri. Jude rolled her eyes again, not bothering to reply.

Fin went and found the quick magic and finally they were ready to go. Eri gave them each a few grains of the transportation magic. 'It's nowhere near as bad as invisibility magic but doesn't leave you feeling great.'

'Got any orange juice?' Jude said, catching Fin's eye. His mouth twitched.

'This magic shouldn't be mixed with anything,' said Eri firmly. 'Otherwise, you might get sent somewhere you really don't want to be. I heard one man ended up in another kingdom where there are these enormous animals that eat children.'

'I was *joking*,' said Jude. 'But good to know.' She cleared her throat as she held up the magic. 'Let's jump right into Grandleader's quarters.'

Moorley batted her hand. 'This transportation magic might not be strong enough to get us inside his quarters,' she said while Jude glared at her and rubbed her smarting hand. 'They're protected by raw magic. The rest of Ripon Headquarters is just protected by tamed magic.'

'Fine,' said Jude. 'Let's transport to my bedroom. At least we won't suddenly appear in front of Aunt Morgol or someone.'

She popped the magic into her mouth. It had a foul, acidic taste, which stayed in her mouth even after she had swallowed.

At once the surface of her skin bubbled, as if she was boiling. A dizzying feeling swept over her, and the furniture of the family room of the Weston mansion seemed to get larger, as if she was shrinking. Rainbow swirls surrounded her, spinning faster, and even when she closed her eyes, the rainbows continued to spin. Her skin seared with heat, as though the magic was burning away her flesh, her bones, leaving nothing behind.

Then there was a *pop* and she crashed to the floor of her bedroom. At once she lurched to her window, fumbling with the latch. She heaved but nothing came up. Moorley was gasping on all fours. Fin and Eri seemed to have fared better. They both shuddered, though neither had turned the delicate shade of green Moorley had.

Once everyone had got over the taste, they ate the invisibility magic Moorley had stashed away.

'You know what,' said Jude as she turned invisible, 'I think I'd rather eat invisibility magic than that horrible transportation stuff. Who'd have thought I'd see the day?'

Moorley grabbed her hand. 'Come on – hold on to me or we'll lose each other while we're invisible.'

Jude grabbed Eri's hand as she disappeared, and Eri grabbed Fin.

Moorley pulled at Jude. It was slightly disturbing to be led by an invisible force, and Jude concentrated on not falling over as they headed to the entrance hall.

The door to Grandleader's wing still didn't have a lock. Clearly Grandleader did not expect them to disobey him again.

As they got closer, Jude's heart beat faster. Grandleader would know they had entered his quarters. She and Moorley hadn't discussed that issue – there was no point. They would have to hope they could rescue Mr and Mrs Weston and maybe unanchor the where-and-when room before he arrived to stop them.

'I'm opening the door,' said Moorley softly and Jude felt her come to a halt.

The door creaked open, apparently by itself. Jude was ready to start moving again – but something heavy landed on her foot. She hissed. What was Moorley doing?

'Hello?' said Aunt Morgol, peering out of the door, eyes narrowed. Grandleader had posted her as a guard – he didn't trust Jude after all.

Jude held her breath as Aunt Morgol's eyes scanned over her. *Don't let the invisibility magic fail.* 'Is someone there?' asked Aunt Morgol. She was so close that Jude could see the blue-green of the bulging vein on her forehead. If she took one more step she would walk into Jude.

Eri gripped Jude's hand so tightly Jude worried her bones would be crushed. Jude felt a tug on her left hand – Moorley was pulling her towards the open door.

Jude inched around Aunt Morgol, hoping Fin and Eri had got the message to move. Eri's hand remained tight in her own as they entered Grandleader's quarters.

'If you're invisible, I will find you,' came Aunt Morgol's voice from behind them. Jude looked back to see her walking around the entrance hall swatting her hands like she was hoping to hit someone.

They shuffled down the corridor in silence until they reached the end, where the walls became ghostly and there was a single door. Jude pushed it open to find herself in the where-and-when room, in front of the pit.

Chapter Twenty-Five

The Pit

The raw magic in the pit smelled like a meadow of flowers, reminding Jude of summer and freedom and long, lazy days . . . She pushed the thoughts away. It smelled like whatever it thought would manipulate her into drinking it.

A huge blob of silver liquid rose out of the pit, rolled along the ground, and a Lilthrum formed, with arms that ended in knives and teeth that resembled the points of a saw. Her heart fluttered with horror and she took a step back before she remembered it couldn't see her. To her right, she heard two sharp intakes of breath and she silently willed Fin and Eri not to scream.

A helpling shuffled up to take its hand, leading the Lilthrum away.

Unlike the last time she had visited, Jude wasn't trapped on the path. She wondered why, until Moorley squeezed her hand.

She wasn't alone, that was the difference. Something about being with her friends – her sister – lessened the power the pit had over her.

Jude let go of Moorley, ducking around the Lilthrum and helpling to stand on the edge of the pit. The raw magic swirled beneath her. She hoped Moorley was right about raw magic being able to slow their fall because she saw no sign of the staircase the Hall of Knowledge had mentioned.

'So, we just jump?' said Fin, somewhere to Jude's right.

'Yup,' replied Jude, her stomach lurching as she thought about tumbling into the unknown. 'Why don't you go first? Just to, er ... make sure it's safe.'

'Coward,' said Fin.

'Rather be a coward than dead,' muttered Jude. The pit did something to her – it seemed to suck her confidence away, leaving her small and afraid.

'We jump together,' said Moorley from Jude's left. 'Right ... On the count of three ...'

In places the raw magic was transparent and Jude could make out the jagged sides of the pit. She didn't want to think about how much it would hurt if she didn't get clear of them.

Moorley yelled, 'Three!'

There was a flash of light and, in horror, Jude watched Moorley, Fin and Eri suddenly reappear, their invisibility magic gone as they flew backwards away from the pit.

'What happened?' she said.

'The raw magic must repel tamed magic,' said Moorley, getting to her feet. 'Wait – where are you? Why are you still invisible?'

Jude squeezed her eyes shut, letting her invisibility wash away. She decided to ignore the question – Moorley didn't need to know she'd been too scared to jump. 'You think if we don't have our invisibility magic, we'll be able to get into the pit?' She remembered the Weston mansion and how the cabinet with the fake decision-making magic had forced her back when she was using her ghost magic.

'Yeah.' Moorley's eyes went wide. 'But we've got another problem now.'

The Lilthrum being led away by the helpling had spun its head towards them. Another Lilthrum dragged itself out of the pit and was quickly followed by two more.

'Why are they forming so fast?' said Eri, stumbling backwards.

'Start eating the magic we brought,' ordered Moorley.

'But then we won't be able to get into the pit,' said Jude.

'Worry about that later!' said Moorley. 'Otherwise we're going to be dead before we get anywhere *near* the pit.'

The three Lilthrum were slowly dragging themselves forward, and although it was annoying that Moorley was right, Jude decided she'd rather be alive than argue the point. Fin chucked her the quick magic, which she chomped down, hardly tasting it. Her legs shook, her whole body jittery as she pocketed the rest. Nausea threatened to swallow her whole – she needed to *move*.

Moorley clutched her knife, her face grim. She hadn't eaten the magic Fin gave her, pocketing it instead.

The Lilthrum in front of Jude let out a roar of blue flames and she dodged it, her body reacting before she had time to think. She dodged another blow. Now the Lilthrum was blocking her path to the pit.

Moorley appeared suddenly on her right, sliding at the Lilthrum's legs and slashing. The Lilthrum tumbled to the ground and Moorley rolled to her feet and dived head first into the pit.

This time Jude didn't hesitate – this was her chance. She focused on the magic inside her, imagining it all leaving her body and floating into the air – turning it off.

Her movements felt sluggish after the effects of the quick magic. She ran at the pit and jumped, arms windmilling as she sailed through the air towards the raw magic, which she would slip through as gracefully as a majestic dolphin cutting through water—

Bright white light surrounded her and she was flung backwards, crashing to the floor of the where-and-when room with such force she lost all the air in her lungs.

Before she had time to get her breath, a Lilthrum's razor-sharp fingers zipped down, aiming for her throat. A knife sliced through the air and the Lilthrum's arm was cut from its body.

She grabbed the arm, flinging it as far away as she could.

Moorley was fighting the rest of the one-armed Lilthrum, her knife glinting in the glow of its body. The Lilthrum seemed to be off-balance and confused, and Moorley used that to swing at its feet. Jude charged, shoving it backwards as it stumbled from Moorley's blow. It fell into the pit and vanished beneath the surface of raw magic.

'Why's the pit not letting us in?' panted Jude. Fin and Eri were a blur of colour on the other side of the pit, dodging the attacks of a Lilthrum stalking them.

'I don't know,' replied Moorley.

Jude paused for a moment. Four Lilthrum had formed from the pit, she recalled. Two had returned to the pit and the third was fighting Fin and Eri – where was the fourth?

She got her answer a second later as a Lilthrum

lunged for her from the sky, grabbing her arm and dragging her upwards. Its claws dug into her skin and she yelped in pain.

Lilthrum could *fly* as well as everything else? Since when?

'Let me go,' she yelled, her stomach flipping with nausea as the got further and further from the ground. She scrambled to get away from it, panic taking over as its claws dug in tighter.

The Lilthrum, unsurprisingly, ignored her, until even the pit was nothing more than a dot far below.

Jude struggled, trying to wriggle out of the Lilthrum's grasp – but as its grip briefly loosened, she had a moment of clarity. If it let her go, she would crash down.

The creature's wings flapped a little slower, as if it was getting tired. Its grip on her loosened further.

'Oh, no, you don't,' grunted Jude. 'You brought me here, you can take me back down!' She used her other arm to hoist herself on to the creature's back. Its flesh, if she could even call it that, was wet, sticking to her palms. 'You're disgusting,' she groaned as the Lilthrum took a sudden turn. Without thinking, she wrapped her hands around its head, covering its eyes. The wings stopped flapping, and then she and the Lilthrum were hurtling towards the pit.

Jude shrieked, pulling her hands away from its eyes. The creature's wings started flapping once more.

She couldn't believe it – she'd figured out a way to control it!

A thought occurred to her as the Lilthrum bucked, trying to get rid of its passenger. The pit had allowed the Lilthrum to enter but thrown her and Moorley back. Maybe she could trick the pit into letting her inside. Gritting her teeth, she covered the Lilthrum's eyes.

Wind slapped at her face and she dug her nails into the creature, gripping even more tightly as tiny bits of silver rose around her. The speed was enough to break the creature apart; it was losing bits of itself.

And then they were in the pit, the creature disintegrating beneath her as they raced through the raw magic.

Her breath came in short, sharp gasps. She had done it. She was at the bottom of the pit. Everything was as the Hall of Knowledge had shown them; the ground was a deep purple with scorch marks across it. Swirling fog hid everything else.

The Weston parents were nowhere to be seen.

The fog stretched away in all directions.

OK, she had to think. In the vision from the Hall of Knowledge, the Weston parents had been by the pit wall, so if she walked around the edges of the pit she'd eventually bump into them, wouldn't she?

Picking a direction at random, Jude stepped forward. The fog disoriented her, and she walked for long enough that she began to wonder if she was turning in circles. But finally, she reached a craggy, stone wall, and she began her trek around, keeping the wall to her right.

She was alone. Or, at least, the fog made her *feel* alone. She wished Moorley, Fin and Eri were with her.

She comforted herself with the idea that the Lilthrum seemed to form *out* of the pit, so there shouldn't be any of them at the bottom.

Her footfalls were the only sound in the silence.

She gasped. A dark shape loomed in the fog ahead of her. She edged forward, to find herself staring at a middle-aged woman with dark red hair sleeping curled in a ball on the ground.

'Er . . . Hello?' said Jude. She bent down and tapped the woman's shoulder, but though the woman's eyelids fluttered she continued to sleep. 'Ma'am?'

The woman didn't move. Jude stood, frowning. The fog parted slightly, enough for her to see another body a few metres away – this time an old man, also asleep.

What were these people doing down here? How many people had Grandleader kidnapped? This was worse than she'd thought.

Jude stumbled onward, passing several sleeping people until she reached a statue of a woman made of stone. *Grandma.* Exactly like the one she had seen in Grandleader's quarters, only this version had no missing chunks.

But she couldn't dwell on the strangeness of the

statue. Because huddled beneath it, their cheeks pressed against the ground, were a man and a woman fast asleep. The Weston parents.

Mr Weston's face was pale, almost grey. Mrs Weston's lips were pressed together in a pout, her eyebrows furrowed, as if she was angry in her dreams.

'Mrs Weston? Mr Weston?' Jude muttered, shaking first one then the other. 'I'm a friend of Fin and Eri's – we're here to rescue you ...' She looked around at the other sleeping bodies. 'All of you.' She didn't know how that would be possible – she couldn't leave the pit the way she'd entered, and if she managed to find the hidden stairs she could hardly drag an adult to safety up them. But she'd worry about that part later.

'If you could just wake up, that would be really helpful ...'

'They won't wake up,' said a soft voice to her left. Jude's heart lurched and she spun around. A man with snow-white hair hobbled forward, bent over a walking stick. He was wearing a three-piece pinstripe suit and a sunshine-yellow bowtie, and he had little round glasses that were halfway down his crooked nose. If it wasn't for the smears of grime on his cheeks and the faint whiff of body odour, he would have been very presentable. 'They're in an enchanted sleep.'

'Who are you?' gasped Jude. Her voice sounded too loud, breaking through the thick silence.

'Forgive my poor manners,' said the man, as though

they were exchanging pleasantries in the street, not under a churning pit of raw magic. 'I'm Harrimore Hardman. I've been trapped down here for … oh, a few weeks now.'

She recognised that name. This was the man Grandleader had been looking for. The list in Grandleader's study. The words – *He can work it out.*

'Grandleader was searching for you,' said Jude, her heart beating fast as she stared at the mysterious Harrimore Hardman.

Harrimore nodded. 'Yes. I was in the middle of a lovely piece of carrot cake when several Lilthrum showed up at my door – not the sort of visitors I like. The Lilthrum have been … ah, running errands for your family, so to speak. In between their usual killing.' His voice was disapproving and Jude couldn't help feeling as though she was being told off even though she didn't have anything to do with his kidnap.

'Errands?' squeaked Jude. 'For my *family*? How's that possible—'

'Your family uses raw magic to control them,' said Harrimore, as though the answer was obvious.

'What *sort* of errands?' asked Jude urgently. 'Why did Grandleader bring you here?'

'I was part of a top-secret research group run by the Consortium. We looked into the properties of raw magic – how exactly it works for different spells and that sort of thing.' Harrimore pushed the glasses up his nose, his face becoming more animated as he spoke. 'Oh, I *have* missed talking to people – this is a treat. The research was intriguing – we rely on raw magic so much and yet our understanding of its properties is very limited, so there was a great deal to figure out. It was the most marvellous time, although all good things come to an end... Just being around raw magic started to affect us. It's most powerful when drunk, of course, but it's possible to breathe in droplets in the air – it's part liquid, part gas. We wanted to use it for *other* purposes... Little things, you know – removing a few wrinkles, giving ourselves a bit of extra power at work... Making gold. It whispered to us.'

Jude found herself nodding along. She knew about the allure of raw magic.

'We each drank a small sip, just once. For research.' Harrimore shook his head. 'I had never felt so powerful. But we got into an argument about what to do next. Some wanted to keep drinking. Others were strong enough to say we had to stop. A fight broke out – in the confusion, someone was killed.' He cleared his throat. 'The research group was disbanded. We all moved on with our lives. I retired. My close friend became a toymaker...'

'Yes, but *why are you here*?' said Jude impatiently.

Harrimore's smile wavered. 'Ah,' he said. 'That's the tricky part. I confess I was always the best out of anyone in the research group at the calculations involved

272

in using raw magic ... But I've been helping with something terrible – calculations of how much raw magic might be required for a ... a spell. An unnatural spell. Lord Ripon said he would kill me if I didn't help.'

Jude swallowed. The threat sounded like Grandleader. She eyed Harrimore suspiciously. Was he telling the truth?

'What spell?' she asked.

Harrimore looked up as a low rumble of displeasure suddenly filled the air. The raw magic, instead of floating around their heads, started to fall towards them like flurries of snow.

'What's happening?' said Jude.

Harrimore went pale. 'I don't know ...'

Chapter Twenty-Six

A Falling Star

Jude looked up. Barrelling through the air on the back of a Lilthrum was Moorley, followed by Eri and Fin on their own twisted monsters. They dropped towards Jude, Moorley pulling out of the dive with a grace Jude never could have managed. The Lilthrum dissolved as the three jumped off.

Jude's feeling of relief was cut short as she spotted a patch of blood blossoming on the side of Moorley's shirt. Moorley didn't seem to have noticed it. Eri and Fin stumbled towards where their parents lay limp, their bodies like dolls.

'What's happened? What's wrong with them?'

said Eri, shaking her mother. 'Wake up. Mum. Mum. Mummy?' She looked small and lost.

But what if no one at the Consortium believed them? Or the Consortium came to the pit and then couldn't defeat Grandleader? This was far beyond anything Jude had thought Grandleader capable of.

'Who are you?' said Moorley, staring at Harrimore.

Jude hardly listened to Harrimore's reply. Maybe they shouldn't be trying to rescue Mr and Mrs Weston at all – maybe they should simply attempt to unanchor the where-and-when room and risk the Wild Lands. At least it would be much more difficult for Grandleader to follow them.

Fin's bottom lip trembled as he grabbed his father's arm. 'They need to wake up,' he said. 'They need to ... They ... I need to tell them I'm sorry!'

His shaking voice cut through Jude's racing thoughts. 'Sorry for what?' she asked him.

'The last time I spoke to them I ... I said horrible things. About how they cared more about saving the world than us,' Fin said.

'Well ...' Jude shifted from foot to foot. 'You say mean stuff all the time and none of us take it seriously. Your parents would've known.'

Fin looked at her oddly before turning back to his parents.

'So what do we do now?' Moorley's hands shook as she gripped her knife. The patch of blood on her side had got bigger. She squinted at the swirling fog. 'Are there . . . other people down here?'

'What happened?' said Jude, distracted by the blood.

'A Lilthrum cut me,' said Moorley, waving away Jude's concern. 'There's something weird in its claws – some poison or something . . . it doesn't matter—'

The ground trembled and above them there was a glowing light. A cold wind blew across Jude's neck like fingers along her skin.

'What's that?' said Moorley, nodding upwards. Jude was already looking around for an exit. Whatever it was, it couldn't be good.

Harrimore was counting on his fingers, his mouth moving wordlessly. 'Oh no,' he said, looking up. 'I think I've made a mistake in my maths.'

The fog swirled faster, the deep rumbling around the pit getting louder as the earth tremored. A crack appeared beneath Jude's feet.

'Jude,' hissed Eri, tugging at her sleeve. 'There's someone coming.'

There was a dark figure in the fog striding towards them. In the shadowy light it was hulking, impossibly tall, a monster—

But then the figure stepped out of the fog to reveal Grandleader. Normal size, smartly dressed and a calm expression on his familiar face.

Fear flooded through her, worse than any terror she had felt at seeing the Lilthrum or the pit.

'My dear granddaughters,' Grandleader said, his voice mild. 'Nice to see you together again.'

'Hello,' said Jude, trying to sound casual. But she couldn't stop her voice quivering. The ground vibrated slightly, and she wondered if her legs would buckle beneath her.

His lip curled as he looked at Mr and Mrs Weston, at Eri and Fin. 'So, you have chosen to help these ... people ... above your own family? Your own flesh and blood?' He took a step forward but before Jude could respond, Eri had stood in front of her.

'You leave Jude alone,' said Eri. She was shaking but held up her fists. Fin stepped forward as well and Jude's cheeks grew warm. Here Fin and Eri were, doing what no one in her own family had ever been brave enough to do: stand up to Grandleader. They were real friends.

Grandleader raised his eyebrows. 'Moorley,' he sighed, his eyes sliding to her as if Jude, Fin and Eri no longer existed. 'Never have I seen such a fall from grace. You were the grandchild I was the proudest of.'

Moorley stared at him, her nostrils flaring. Jude knew Grandleader was trying to remind her and Moorley that they were supposed to be in competition. She wanted Moorley to argue with Grandleader, to be defiant and brave. But Moorley was trembling, clutching the point where the Lilthrum had cut her. She was just as scared as Jude.

Jude forced back her own fear and looked Grandleader dead in the eye. 'What you're doing with raw magic is wrong. You don't have the right to keep these people here.'

'Yes, Jude!' said Eri.

Irritation flashed across Grandleader's face. 'You two wouldn't even be involved in this if your parents hadn't been so nosy – finding their way here, poking around. I didn't *want* to keep them but they left me no choice. So now you may leave, your parents too, while I speak to my granddaughters.' He was lying – he would never let them go so easily. But Fin and Eri looked at each other, their faces unreadable, and for a horrible moment Jude thought they would abandon her.

'Not without Jude,' said Fin.

'That's sweet,' said Grandleader, pretending to dab his eyes. 'But I think this is a family problem, don't you?' He waved his hand and Fin slumped to the ground. Eri lay down, resting her head on her arm as she closed her eyes, breathing steadily.

Family. He said that word, but he didn't know what it meant. He didn't care about anyone but himself. 'What have you done?' croaked Jude. The crack beneath her feet got larger. A few stones clattered to the ground nearby and Jude glanced behind her, wondering where they had come from.

'I've put them to sleep,' said Grandleader with a shrug.

'Er ... Sir?' squeaked Harrimore as a flash of light burst above them. It was followed by what sounded like a roar of thunder. 'There's something I must warn you about ...'

'Not now, Harrimore,' said Grandleader, holding a hand up to silence him. Harrimore shut his mouth immediately but his agitation made Jude wonder if Grandleader should let him speak. 'Go on, Jude, I'm sure you have plenty more questions.'

The temperature was dropping. Goosebumps rose on Jude's skin. She wanted to run but didn't know where to go. And Grandleader was waiting for her to ask more questions, a single eyebrow raised.

'How did you collect all this raw magic?' she asked.

'Using raw magic gives you power,' said Grandleader, as he waved his fingers at her and Moorley. The tips glowed silver and for a moment, so did his eyes. 'More power than you can imagine. I used raw magic to create this pit. And raw magic is attracted to humans. So, I've been, ah – collecting volunteers. People who've ... become less useful to me.'

Jude widened her eyes. All those unconscious people in the fog – Grandleader had trapped them here to bring more raw magic into the pit? 'You're doing all this so you can sell raw magic to the Consortium?'

Grandleader raised his eyebrows. 'You think I did all this for money? Come on, try harder.'

'It doesn't matter why,' said Moorley, finding her voice at last. 'It's wrong. Raw magic destroys your soul – it turns you into a monster...'

'No, it doesn't,' said Grandleader dismissively. He stared down at the Westons. 'And, well, even if it does... it's your own soul. You should have the choice about whether you destroy it. You don't hurt anyone *else* by drinking raw magic.'

Jude laughed in disbelief. Had Grandleader forgotten about all the people he was keeping down here, taken from their families, suspended in a charmed sleep?

'But—' began Moorley.

Grandleader raised a hand and she gurgled, clasping her throat. He seemed to have grown tired of their questions. 'Listen to me, my *dear* granddaughters. Raw magic gives you the power to *stop death*. No more pain, no more suffering... I could help so many people in Farrowfell. I could help *you*, Moorley. I know how a Lilthrum cut can hurt – it rips into your soul so the Lilthrum can suck the humanity from you...' His eyes flicked to her cut and Moorley fell to the ground, her teeth bared in a grimace of pain.

'You're making it worse,' she hissed, staring up at Grandleader. He smiled, showing his bright white teeth.

'I could fix it,' he said. 'With just the tiniest amount of raw magic, all your pain would go away...'

Jude wavered slightly as she stared at her sister, who

was clearly in agony. Then she shook her head. 'You don't care about anyone,' she said. 'What would be in it for you?'

Moorley slumped forwards in a faint. Jude darted towards her but an invisible force pushed her back. Grandleader gave a small smile. 'Don't be rude, Jude. We're having a conversation.'

'Er ... Sir!' Harrimore tried again, as another rumble from above sent a shower of stones into the pit. He cleared his throat. 'The calculations . . . I didn't factor—'

'Be *quiet*, Harrimore,' snapped Grandleader. He turned back to Jude. 'I must confess, Jude, you're smarter than I thought. You're right – I don't care about healing Moorley, and I don't care about helping people in Farrowfell. I have worked for years to learn how to use raw magic, but there is one power that still escapes me – bringing someone back from the dead.'

His eyes flicked to the statue of Grandma. Jude remembered the broken statues she'd seen in his quarters, the portrait of them together, the expression on Grandleader's face as he looked at her. 'You want to bring Grandma back to life,' she breathed. Grandleader nodded.

'I used to have friends in the Consortium, high up. After dear Jessamine died, I asked them to help me and they refused. They said it wasn't possible.' Grandleader's throat bobbed as he spoke, his voice almost cracking at the use of Grandma's first name. 'I was furious. I thought that *someone* must have made illegal tamed magic that could do it. But I began to realise … there are always limitations with tamed magic. It doesn't go far enough. I began to wonder about the raw magic being used to make it …'

The air turned even chillier, the fog swirled faster. Jude's eyes were fixed on Grandleader. She didn't want to hear what he was going to say but she couldn't look away.

'My connections in the Consortium told me about research that was done into raw magic,' continued Grandleader. 'It was all very secretive, the team had disbanded long ago, the members scattered around Farrowfell – and beyond. I tracked them down one by one over the years – slowly, painstakingly, they were each able to give me a tiny bit of information. They told me drinking raw magic wouldn't kill me like so many thought – so I tried it. And … wow.' His smile was full of a warmth Jude had never seen on his face. 'I grew stronger than I ever could have imagined. I initially stole it from gatherers but I could only source a little at a time. It's the one limitation of raw magic, you see. It can do anything you want, but if the task is something big and complex, you need *more* of it. Which is why I made this pit. That's where I started to struggle.'

He paused to shoot a look at the sleeping bodies behind him.

'Most of the group was useless – they kept getting the calculations for how much raw magic I needed wrong. And every time that happened, I had to start gathering raw magic again from scratch.'

'All the people sleeping in this pit are the researchers?' said Jude as the truth dawned on her. 'But ... some of them must have been down here for *years*.'

Grandleader shrugged. 'When I was done questioning them, I decided to keep them here as a way to attract more magic.' He smiled. 'It was the perfect crime – the Consortium had made the research project so secret it was like the researchers themselves didn't exist. No one was looking for them.'

Jude's hands trembled as she looked at the unconscious forms of the Weston parents. Eri and Finn had spent a year searching for them – she was sure the other researchers had people who cared about them too. For Grandleader to suggest they weren't *missed* was awful. It was cruel. It was evil. This was the man Jude would have once done *anything* for.

Grandleader continued, 'Whilst I waited for the information I needed, I realised our little business of selling illegal tamed magic was doing fine – but there was a way to make more money, by selling raw magic to crooked members of the Consortium who needed a cheaper alternative to the gatherers. It's all for Jessamine, of course. When she returns, she will live a life of luxury.'

'But why did everyone else start drinking raw magic too?' said Jude. 'My parents, Aunt Morgol, Aunt Victi...'

'This had to be a family effort,' Grandleader said simply. 'I needed them to do their bit – using raw magic to control Lilthrum so they could kidnap members of the research group, for example. And there is always the risk that the pit might become unstable – that it might collapse and send out a ripple of destruction that destroys Farrowfell. I needed the rest of the Ripons to be strong enough to deal with any issues while I focused on leading Jessamine back to life.'

He sighed heavily and turned to the statue of Grandma, placing a loving hand on its shoulder. 'This shall be her new body; it will turn to flesh and blood upon her return. It took a few attempts to prepare it – I kept getting the spell wrong... Felix Snuggleton helped me solve that problem.' Grandleader nodded at a sleeping figure lying a few paces to his right.

Grandleader's failed attempts explained the broken pieces of the other statues of Grandma in his quarters. 'So, the statue will ... become Grandma?' whispered Jude. There was a small part of her, the part that had yearned for his approval all her life, that felt sad for him. That he had lost the one person who he might ever really have loved, and would do all this just to get her back.

But she pushed that part of her away. Because his

love was destructive. And the worst part was, he didn't see that. Nothing else mattered but *him*. *His* twisted love. How *he* felt.

Love wasn't supposed to be selfish.

As Jude tried to understand the implications of what Grandleader was saying, Harrimore twitched and tentatively raised his hand.

Grandleader frowned at him. 'What *is* it, for goodness' sake?'

'Sorry to interrupt, sir, I truly am.' His whole body trembled. 'It's just . . . I've been trying to tell you . . . The number I gave you – the number of people it would take to draw enough raw magic into the pit to safely carry out your plan. Well . . . it's been far exceeded in the last thirty minutes.'

'Get to the point,' said Grandleader.

'With your granddaughters here, and the two Weston children, and you . . . the raw magic is *pouring* in – in a highly unsustainable way. If it keeps going at this rate, I'm afraid the pit will become volatile and . . . well, I don't know what will happen. But I can't think that it will be good.' He flinched as the floor vibrated and a large shower of stones rained down on them. 'I suspect that if you're going to attempt to bring your wife back to life, it needs to be *right now*.'

Grandleader swallowed and for the first time in Jude's life, she saw what looked like genuine emotion on his face. 'Then it will be now,' he rasped.

'Grandma wouldn't have wanted this,' cried Jude. She had no idea if it was true – all she knew of her grandmother was the smiling portrait with kind eyes in the entrance hall of Ripon Headquarters. But it was a last, desperate attempt to make Grandleader see sense.

'You don't know what she would have wanted,' barked Grandleader, his pupils pinpricks.

The raw magic around them was floating upwards, forming a hazy cloud. Jude squinted at the shining light getting brighter above them. It was an enormous ball of raw magic . . .

Like a star.

Horror rooted her to the spot. The fog parted, pressing against the walls like it was trying to escape – only there was no way out.

Jude's face burned. She had to look away from the light. But she couldn't bring herself to close her eyes. She needed to know what was happening. The temperature was rising rapidly. Heat blistered at her skin. The star burned away the air and her lungs screamed for oxygen.

'There's too much of it!' yelled Harrimore. 'We've missed the window – it will kill us all if you don't shut down the spell—'

Grandleader held out his hands and the raw magic in the air floated into his palms, pooling together into a liquid. He gulped it down and for a moment he shuddered with pleasure, his throat bobbing as he emptied his hands.

He clicked his fingers and Harrimore slumped forward at once, unconscious.

Grandleader laughed, his face turned towards the rapidly forming star. 'I shall use this magic to draw her down into the statue! Get ready to welcome your grandmother home!'

Moorley stirred, her eyes unfocused as she blinked. Grandleader was too fixated on the star to notice Jude crouch by Moorley's side, grasping her hand. Relief swept through her as Moorley squeezed back.

The raw magic in the air flowed directly into Grandleader's mouth, and silver light danced at his hands as he turned them upwards to face the star . . .

From which there was a shape forming – the blurry outline of a person.

'What's going on?' said Jude. She gripped Moorley tighter. 'Is that . . . Grandma?' Could Grandleader's plan really be working?

Silver droplets flowed from the shape into the statue of Grandma.

Moorley's attention wasn't in front of them, but all around. 'The pit's collapsing!' she said.

Jude dragged her eyes away from the statue. Large rocks were crumbling and choking the air with waves of dust. The crack beneath her feet was spreading. The ground was splitting apart.

'We need to get out,' said Jude as a column from the where-and-when room crashed into the pit, sending up a wave of dust. Its tip narrowly missed a sleeping person.

'The whole room's collapsing,' whispered Moorley. The blood staining her clothes was now an enormous patch. Her face was colourless. 'Everyone in this pit is going to die if we don't do something...' But it didn't look like she was capable of doing *anything*. Her face was a sheet of sweat as she took gulps of the dust-filled air.

It was down to Jude. She looked around desperately – maybe if she could make Grandleader *listen* to her. 'You need to stop!' she called to him. 'We're *all* going to die if you don't end this. Make the raw magic go away—'

'I will never stop!' roared Grandleader without looking at her. His eyes were still fixed upon the star, the shape of the person high above them. Silver droplets flowed in an arc over him to the statue, which was glowing deep silver. 'She is coming BACK!'

He'd never listened to her – never noticed her—

A good thief wasn't supposed to be seen.

And she was a good thief. She was the best.

Grandleader couldn't bring Grandma back without the statue. Jude could steal it, take it out of the pit. Then he would be forced to stop the spell.

He was too transfixed on the star to notice what she was doing.

But the statue would be heavy – and there was no way out of the pit, anyway.

Except . . . She was surrounded by magic that could help her . . .

Raw magic.

No, she couldn't. If she drank raw magic she would become like the rest of them – like Grandleader and her mother and father, power-hungry and cold, and thinking of no one but herself . . .

Jude looked back at the unconscious Westons, at her sister bleeding on the ground – and made her choice.

She would drink raw magic to save them. And if the raw magic tried to change her into a monster, she would find the strength to fight it. She would make her own path. She would *not* be like her family.

She wasn't a true Ripon and she was proud of that.

Jude held out her cupped hands and raw magic settled into her palms. It was neither hot nor cold, its cloudy surface sparkling as if it was catching the last of the sunlight. For a moment she remained still, spellbound. The sound of Moorley's breath coming in ragged gasps brought her back to the present.

She drank.

The magic slipped down her throat like honey. A warmth like she had never known spread through her. She flexed her muscles and the weariness washed away, replaced by a dizzying feeling of power. Along with the warmth came a sense of peace, of belonging—

And the feeling that she could do anything, be anyone, that nothing could stop her. She was Jude Ripon and the world had better watch out—

Anger shot through her as she stared at Grandleader. Every moment she'd ever felt unloved, unwanted, roared within her. Every time her mother had ignored her. Every time her father had yelled for no reason.

The raw magic flowing through her whispered that it was Grandleader she needed to fight, that she should hit him, *hurt* him—

'*No*,' she told herself. She controlled the raw magic, not the other way around. All she needed was to steal the statue.

But first she needed to make sure Moorley, her friends and the researchers were safe from the collapsing pit. Almost as soon as she had thought it, a shield bubbled as it appeared, a thin layer spreading over them.

She gasped – she had done it! She had controlled the raw magic.

Now she needed to use it to help her steal. But there were only really two tools a good thief needed: invisibility magic and ghost magic. She thought of all the times she'd eaten those magics, the way her body had disappeared and she'd been able to walk through walls. The raw magic responded to her memory, and when she looked down her body was gone and she was floating a few inches off the ground.

With a grin she glided forwards to grab the statue,

willing it to become smaller and turn invisible like she was. It shrunk to half its size.

'Make a decoy,' she whispered to the raw magic inside her. It seemed to respond to her thoughts. With raw magic she could do *anything*. She imagined a fake version of the Grandma statue that hadn't been properly prepared, that wouldn't be able to host Grandma when she came back from the dead.

In front of her a fake version of the statue popped up. It looked just like the one she had stolen, except that the droplets from the star arching over Grandleader bounced off the surface instead of soaking into the stone.

She rose away with the real statue – she needed to get it away from Grandleader. Her mind started to wander as she imagined what else she could do with this power—

Focus. She gritted her teeth. This was the raw magic trying to influence her.

As she floated out of the pit there was a roar beneath her.

'JUDE!' bellowed Grandleader. 'Where have you gone? Bring her *back*!'

She glanced down to see Grandleader looking around wildly. His skin was glowing silver and the silver droplets which should have been going into the statue were going into *him*.

He'd prepared the statue with raw magic. Coated it with raw magic. And now that the statue was gone, the silver droplets of Grandma were mistaking *him* for the host.

Jude's heart thudded as she landed on the ground above the pit. She remained invisible and the Lilthrum trotting around the edges ignored her. She broke at once into a run – she had to get the statue away.

Her legs pounded beneath her. This was just like every other steal she had ever done – Grandleader was a dangerous version of a guard helpling—

'You're invisible, are you?' came Grandleader's voice. She glanced behind her. He was rising out of the pit even as more of the droplets from the star were pouring into him. 'I can make that magic disappear!'

She sped up as an icy cold wind blew over her. Terror filled her as she realised her invisibility and ghost spell were slipping away. He'd drunk so much more raw magic than her – for so many years – that he was much more powerful.

'There you are!' roared Grandleader. She spun around, expecting an attack.

Instead she screamed. 'What's happening?'

Grandleader's eyes were black orbs, his skin entirely silver – he looked like a monster. Nothing like the man who had sat at the head of every family dinner Jude had ever attended, who encouraged her to learn how to swim, who had smiled with pride when she acted as a lookout on a heist and raised the alarm because the owners of the house came home early.

Except he'd always been both – her grandfather and a monster.

A monster who was disintegrating, dissolving into particles of silver that were getting sucked back up to the star. Grandleader roared. 'Bring me the statue and I can fix it—'

The columns of the where-and-when room were collapsing one by one, the crashes echoing around.

'Stop the ritual!' screamed Jude. 'Shut it *off*!'

But he couldn't because his legs had disappeared, his arms, his torso, crumbling into millions of particles and being pulled towards the star. Jude took one final look at the black orbs of eyes before the last of her grandfather disappeared into the blinding bright star. Jude had to close her eyes, and when she opened them again Grandleader was gone.

Chapter Twenty-Seven

The Where-And-When Room

The star spun in circles as it drifted upwards, away. Exhaustion flooded Jude's body. Grandleader was gone.

But it wasn't over, not yet. She nose-dived into the pit, landing beside the others with a thud. Everyone apart from Moorley was unconscious, and it was eerily quiet. Moorley was sitting, staring into space as she clutched her side, like she hadn't noticed Jude's return. The star was still rising far above them, a speck in the distance.

Raw magic has plans of its own.

It hadn't wanted to help Grandleader, that much was clear.

Jude closed her eyes, directing all her concentration on the magic swirling inside her, telling it to help her *get out* with everyone. Nothing happened. She had to think of a specific task for the raw magic – that was why it had worked before. She'd wanted to become invisible, so it had let her. She had wanted to create a statue, so it had done that for her.

Transportation magic. She needed to transport them all.

The raw magic responded as she directed its power over the sleeping bodies around her. The dust was so thick she could barely see anything – she hardly knew how much of the pit was left, if there even *was* any of it left.

Nothing was happening. The magic wasn't working, it wasn't working, *it wasn't working* . . .

She gritted her teeth. *Focus.*

And slowly she began to dissolve, though she could feel the magic fighting against her. It didn't *want* to save her. This was its last revenge, its final way of making sure that she would still lose.

She wouldn't let that happen.

With a final scream she forced the magic to *transport them out of the pit*—

The world melted into blackness and there was a band around her lungs, squeezing tightly, as if she was being forced through a gap that was much too small.

The pressure in her ears built and she bit her lip, the pain keeping her mind on task—

She landed with a thud and rolled over, her entire body shaking. Dust billowed upwards like a reverse snowstorm and she closed her eyes as she waited for it to clear.

Carefully she opened one eye, then the other. She was sitting on a cliff overlooking Mergio Market. Above her were thousands of stars, innocently twinkling. From a distance it was impossible to tell that they were the source of raw magic.

She wondered if one of them was the one that had sucked Grandleader into its burning core. He'd *had* to be stopped, but ... could she have saved him?

The Westons were next to her, unconscious, but she could see their chests rising and falling. Further away Harrimore and the other researchers were also lying in a row. Moorley was sitting up nearby, her face pale as she pressed her hand to her side.

Jude could feel a tiny buzzing inside her, like a caffeine boost. The last of the raw magic was waiting to be used. A part of her wanted to use it for something wild – she could go down to Mergio Market and turn Farlow Higgins into a sipling, so he could join all the other teddy-bear-like creatures toddling around his shop. But she forced the thought away; that was raw magic trying to control her. Her sister needed help.

Jude leaned forward, lightly brushing against Moorley's wound. 'Heal,' she whispered. And with that, the energy was gone. Suddenly she was exhausted, every limb aching.

Moorley's eyes widened as she pulled her hand back, lifting up her shirt slightly to reveal smooth skin. 'You drank raw magic.' For a moment there was a flicker of fear in her eyes.

'I just used up the last of it, I think,' said Jude. She felt as if she hadn't slept in days.

'But the side effects . . .' Moorley swallowed.

Jude shrugged, pushing the worry away. Every drink of raw magic was supposed to twist a human soul – just look what had happened to the researchers. They'd only taken a sip and someone had died. 'Let's focus on the important thing – I got us out.' A bubble of laughter escaped her as she stood and looked down at the market.

The Westons were starting to stir.

'It'd be really helpful if you all could wake up,' Jude told them. But even as she watched, Eri mumbled something and Fin frowned as he turned over. Harrimore and the other researchers continued to sleep. One had his thumb in his mouth.

'Jude ... where's Grandleader?' said Moorley suddenly. 'Is he ... gone?'

Jude swallowed, then nodded. She could see her own emotions reflected on her sister's face. He wasn't the man they had thought he was. But no matter what, he was still their grandfather and always would be.

'It's my fault,' whispered Jude. 'I . . . took the statue of Grandma out of the pit. The magic had nowhere to go, so it went into him . . . It was too much . . .'

'It's Grandleader's fault,' said Moorley firmly. 'He messed with something he shouldn't have – he would have killed all of us. He would have killed half of Farrowfell.' She paused. 'The family is never going to forgive us, you know.' She got to her feet. 'If nothing else, that pit was making them a lot of money.'

'Well, I'm never going to forgive *them*,' said Jude, trying to sound braver than she felt.

For a moment a wave of sadness about everything that had happened threatened to drown her. She wanted to rest somewhere safe, but that place wasn't her bedroom with the scarlet rug and her collection of books on overthrowing governments. It wasn't with her mother, having her hair stroked while they laughed about being chased by guard helplings. Where on earth would they go now?

Then Moorley smiled, staring at the hundreds of lights twinkling below as people did their evening shop. 'What do you reckon it's like to be . . . normal?'

Jude shrugged as she turned the question over in her mind. It wasn't something she'd ever properly considered.

They sat, side-by-side, gazing out at the view, the stars glowing above them.

Chapter Twenty-Eight

The Weston
Mansion Again

Within ten seconds of waking up, Mrs Weston, encouraged by Eri and Fin, had invited Jude and Moorley to live with them. The next few days at the Weston mansion slipped by in a blur. Jude's favourite moment was on the first night when Moorley, waking up completely confused with no idea where she was, tackled three helplings, then escaped through a window. She was halfway across the grounds before Jude caught up with her.

The Ripons were now the most wanted family in

Farrowfell. Ripon Headquarters' protections meant it was hidden from the Consortium, so they needed a Ripon to tell them where to go to make the arrests, and despite everything her family had done, Jude couldn't bring herself to reveal Headquarters' location. She needed to speak to them first.

But not just yet. She wasn't ready.

Jude finally met Annelia Weston properly. She apologised for tricking Jude, and then told her, Fin and Eri off for all the dangerous risks they had taken. Jude was surprised that she owned up to what she had done and said sorry, which meant she already ranked higher in Jude's estimation than Aunts Morgol and Victi.

As the days went by, Jude tried to keep an eye on herself. Drinking raw magic was supposed to bring out her worst traits – and she knew she was reckless. But she couldn't tell whether her wishes to do things like slip more quick magic from the Westons' stash and use it to steal from Farlow Higgins were because of the after-effects of drinking raw magic or because it was *fun*.

Worse still was the small part of her that had liked the power that came with raw magic – she could do *whatever* she wanted with it. She could do good things too – she could cure sick people, or magically make millions of kira and hand it out to random people at Mergio Market. Using raw magic didn't have to be a bad thing...

It was Mrs Weston who sat Jude down in the sunlit family room and gently explained that, no, she hadn't been permanently damaged by using raw magic.

'You used raw magic for a selfless reason,' said Mrs Weston with a smile. 'You displayed all the best qualities of humans down in that pit, and because of that it cannot take your humanity. You've not been damaged, though I wouldn't make a habit of drinking it.' She grimaced. 'My husband and I – being exposed to it for so long in the pit – it will take us longer to recover. But we will, in the end.'

Jude paused, wondering whether she should tell Mrs Weston that she wanted to drink a little bit more. Then Mrs Weston spoke.

'Raw magic does not want to help humans,' said Mrs Weston gently. 'Even if you thought you could change the world, it would find a way to make your good deeds evil.'

'Out there, in the pit ...' Jude didn't know how to put into words how she felt about Grandleader vanishing into the star. She kept reliving the moment he had disappeared and wondering if she could have done anything differently. 'My grandfather ... He's gone because of me.'

Mrs Weston shook her head. 'Your grandfather knew the consequences of using raw magic. He brought many Lilthrum into the world and didn't care about who suffered.' There was something haunted in her eyes. Then she smiled. 'You saved many people with your bravery. Including me and my husband. And we'll always be grateful.'

And yet despite their kindness, Jude felt awkward around Mr and Mrs Weston, and she knew Moorley did too. She kept waiting for them to change their minds, to tell her and Moorley it was time for them to leave.

She knew part of the reason she felt so on edge was because they still had unfinished business at Ripon Headquarters.

On the fifth day of their stay at the Weston mansion, she knocked on Moorley's bedroom door. 'We need to go and see them,' she said.

Moorley nodded.

They made the journey in silence. The gloomy manor was a blot of grey against the pale blue sky. The pointed gates swung open and together they walked up the path to the front door.

Jude pushed it open.

Her mother was standing at the top of the stairs.

'I saw you get to the port,' her mother said. 'We've been expecting you.' She turned on her heel and walked away. Jude knew where she was going: to the dining room.

It was time for a Ripon family meeting.

Her mother was sitting to the left of Grandleader's old seat at the head of the table. Jude's heart gave a twang at the empty seat. They were waiting for Grandleader to come back. They didn't know.

Aunts Victi and Morgol were sitting opposite each other, and Jude's father was at the other end of the table, as red-faced as ever. Trudie was sitting alone in the centre.

Uncle Runie and Spry weren't present.

'Grandleader's gone,' said Jude. She wasn't used to the attention of the entire family. 'He tried to bring Grandma back, down in the pit, and the raw-magic spell went wrong and he . . . vanished.'

Her words were met with silence, until Aunt Victi spoke.

'Where did he vanish?' she asked. She didn't sound surprised.

'Er . . . into a star,' said Jude, looking over at Moorley. She wished they had rehearsed what they were going to say. Moorley had her arms folded, eyes fixed on their mother.

'Well, there you go,' said Aunt Morgol. 'Mystery solved.'

'You . . . knew?' asked Jude, looking from one face to the next. She couldn't read their expressions.

'Five days ago there was a terrible earthquake that completely shut down Ripon Headquarters – and Grandleader's quarters sealed themselves off,' said Aunt Morgol. 'When we finally got inside, we discovered the where-and-when room was gone. Rosalittia managed to interrogate a helpling that was at the scene—'

'I don't know how, since it couldn't *talk*,' muttered Aunt Victi, shooting Jude's mother a look of suspicion.

'I have my ways,' said Jude's mother. 'Of course it couldn't tell us everything. But we knew the raw-magic ritual Grandleader was performing … went wrong.' Jude's mother tilted her head as she looked at Jude, who got the feeling she knew exactly *how* it had gone wrong. Jude stared back.

Her mother did not continue. She looked indifferent. It occurred to Jude that her mother had only drunk raw magic in the first place to help Grandleader – and now even he didn't matter to her any more.

'Where have you two been?' said Aunt Victi suddenly as she looked at Jude and Moorley. 'I assumed you had gone off with Runie and Spry.'

Jude scratched her head in confusion. 'Er … no. Where have they gone?'

Aunt Morgol rolled her eyes. 'Turns out that the flying carriage Spry was building was some sort of mobile home. Now they're off living a *quieter life*.' She spat the words as if they were something disgusting.

Jude and Moorley exchanged a glance. There were other Ripons out there, then, who had turned their back on the family. Even if those Ripons *were* just Uncle Runie and Spry. Jude didn't know how she felt about that – it wasn't like they'd been close. They'd run off and happily left her and Moorley behind.

But, more than that, everything really had

changed. There was no going back to their old life in which Spry made up stories about the basement and Uncle Runie got injured surfing mattresses down the stairs, where helplings never did their jobs, and invisibility magic was put in a safe that everyone knew the passcode to.

'There's something I don't understand,' said Aunt Morgol, slowly rising to her feet. 'Why were you two with Grandleader in the pit?'

'We went to rescue the Westons,' said Moorley, speaking up at last. 'And all the other people you were keeping prisoner down there—'

'The Westons shouldn't have been snooping into something that was none of their business,' said Aunt Morgol. 'Besides, we only found the people Grandleader wanted. We thought he would question them and let them go – we didn't know he was *keeping* them.'

'I mean, we could have asked,' pointed out Aunt Victi. 'I'm sure all of us suspected—'

'I didn't suspect anything unpleasant at all,' said Aunt Morgol with a sniff.

'And you thought the Lilthrum were pets—'

'I thought we were training them and releasing them into the Wild Lands,' said Aunt Morgol. 'It's not our fault the helplings sometimes released them in Farrowfell instead. Should have trained *them* better ...'

They'd gone off track.

'We're living with the Westons now,' interrupted

Jude, wanting to see their reactions. 'And all of you are wanted criminals.'

'Have you told them where we are?' said Jude's father, his voice getting louder.

'No,' said Jude. An idea occurred to her. 'And we won't – not if you promise to stop drinking raw magic. And never make another pit, or try to control more Lilthrum.' There were tiny sparks of hope inside her, that maybe with Grandleader gone this could be a proper change for her family. Maybe there was still a chance for them . . .

Her parents' eyebrows twitched in surprise.

'We're not giving up the power of raw magic,' said her mother, and the hope inside Jude fizzled out. 'But we will agree not to make another pit, and we're done using Lilthrum. They're too unpredictable.'

'OK – so use some of that raw magic power for *good*,' Jude pressed on. 'Get rid of any Lilthrum remaining in Farrowfell. The Farrowfell Guards are mostly useless at killing them.'

'Surely the Westons won't simply let you get away with not telling them where we are,' said Aunt Victi.

'We can make something up,' said Jude, looking at Moorley, who nodded. 'We can say there's magic over Ripon Headquarters so we can't tell them its location – or you've gone on the run . . .' She felt bad at the thought of lying to the Westons, but deep down she knew it was the right thing to do.

Jude's mother looked at the other Ripons. Aunt Victi gave a small nod.

'Fine,' said her mother. 'We agree to these terms. And when you're done with your foolishness, you can come home.' She folded her arms. 'We'll forgive you.'

'Whether we can ever *trust* you again is another question,' muttered Aunt Morgol.

'This isn't home any more,' said Jude, amazed at how steady her voice was. The Weston mansion was hardly perfect. There were loads of pointless rules, like using a coaster before she set her glass down, and no night-time journeys into other people's homes to steal stuff, but it was better than Headquarters. People spoke to her as though she mattered. No one ignored her. And there was no secret pit of raw magic. Well, not as far as she knew anyway.

'Right,' said her mother, her voice brisk as if she'd marked them off her to-do list. 'Plenty to do.'

She swept from the room without looking back. Everyone but Aunt Victi left. She eyed them both.

'Do come for a visit sometime,' she said.

***

When they arrived back at the Weston mansion, it was nearly time for lunch.

'What do you reckon we should do?' Moorley asked as they went inside.

'Well, I am actually quite hungry—'

'Not about the food.' Moorley flapped her into the sitting room. 'We don't belong here – not living like this.'

Jude knew at once what she meant. They had been safe the past few days. She had been stealing a new treasure: stolen seconds of an ordinary life. But there had been something . . . off.

She thought back to when she had stolen the decision-making magic from the Westons, when she had been flying through the house, an excitement nothing else could rival, and it hit her: she missed the thrill of the chase.

The Westons had already talked about enrolling them at the same school as Fin and Eri – they'd want her to do chores and homework. But she couldn't imagine that making her happy – not when she lived for adventure.

'Want to start our own criminal empire?' Jude was only half joking. In an instant she was imagining sourcing new, exciting magic, stealing from the rich, doing the business deals.

Moorley shook her head. 'We can't repay the Westons' kindness by starting a criminal empire.'

Jude deflated at once. Moorley was right, of course. The Westons were upstanding, moral citizens. It would be a poor way to say thank you for letting them stay.

'The Westons are good people . . .' Moorley bit her

bottom lip. 'To be honest, I don't really know how we wouldn't be betraying them by being *us*.'

A wonderful idea sparked in Jude's mind. 'Well, maybe the Westons are *too* good. Maybe to make a change they need to be willing to break the law just a little bit . . .'

Moorley tilted her head.

'We know for a fact that some of the Consortium are crooked,' continued Jude, excited now. 'Remember that man, Everiste, who Grandleader did that deal with? Well, why don't we use our . . . skills to help weed out the bad guys?'

'I like that idea,' said Moorley, a devious smile spreading across her face. 'I like it a lot.'

And just like that, things settled into their proper place. Jude grinned. 'Looks like the Ripon sisters are in business.'

Then, arms linked, they headed for lunch – ready for their next adventure.

Acknowledgements

This story began with a single question – what if you could steal magic? Jude came shortly afterwards – stubborn, determined and in many ways the opposite of a classic hero . . . But ultimately just as brave. There have been so many people involved with this story since that initial spark of inspiration.

First, thank you my editor, Alice Swan. All your editorial insights have always been so spot on. Thank you as well to the rest of the Faber team, for your incredible hard work – Natasha Brown, Ama Badu, Emma Eldridge, Bethany Carter, Sarah Connell, Simi Toor, Paul Bougourd, Maurice Lyon and Sarah Barlow. And thank you to everyone involved in the FAB Prize.

A big thank you to Alessia Trunfio for your gorgeous illustrations, that capture both the joy and darkness of the world of Farrowfell so brilliantly.

Thank you to my agent, Alice Sutherland-Hawes, for seeing the potential in this story and taking a chance on me.

I'm one of many authors to thank the WriteMentor community. It led me to great friendships – and helped me find my voice. Thank you, Lindsay Galvin, for your mentorship. And thank you, Stuart White, for creating WriteMentor in the first place.

Writing is sometimes billed as lonely – but my critique partners have been with me from the beginning, brainstorming with me, reading rough drafts, chatting about all things books. M. K. Painter and Tess James-Mackey, I don't know where I would be without you.

Thank you to my friends. Rachel, you've always been there to send me cute dog pictures and encourage me. Alice, I remember sending you an early draft and being completely shocked when you actually read it and told me you loved it. Matt, you've been determined to read everything I write – even the bad first drafts.

As ever, as always, thank you to my family. My brother, who shares the same love of reading. And my mum, who is my biggest supporter.